THE LONELY MILE

ALLAN LEVERONE

WITHDRAWN

Thanks to StoneHouse Ink for accepting and publishing the First Edition
of THE LONELY MILE in 2011. This Second Edition has been revised
slightly with the goal of making the narrative leaner and tighter, and some of
the dialogue more realistic and harder-edged.

Thanks also to Kealan Patrick Burke and Elderlemon Design
for the outstanding cover art adorning THE LONELY MILE,
and to Jane Dixon-Smith for the print edition formatting.

1

Three Weeks Ago

Amanda Lawton sagged sideways, groggy and disoriented, her blonde hair hanging in sweaty strings in front of her eyes. She was prevented from falling to the cold cement floor only by strips of duct tape securing her arms and legs to a heavy wooden chair.

She shot a pleading look at her captor, trying her hardest to focus on him but unable to do so thanks to the disorienting effect of the drugs. She wondered what she'd been given. In a different time under different circumstances she might actually have enjoyed the surreal sensation, a twist of irony not lost on the pretty college girl even in her present state. The man swam in and out of focus, moving around in her field of vision like some jittery Casper, although he was not a ghost and he certainly wasn't friendly.

The room—she thought it might be one of those aluminum-sided storage places with the different sized units you could rent by the month or the year but she wasn't sure—yawed and buckled in her watery eyesight and Amanda knew she would have fallen out of the chair were it not for her bonds. She imagined this was what it would feel like to be adrift on a small boat in heavy seas. Her stomach lurched and she thought she might puke and hoped a gag wasn't part of the man's plan for her immediate future.

Her captor wrapped a final strip of the reinforced tape around each of her legs until they were immobile, finishing with a flourish of which a concert pianist would have been proud. He stepped back to admire his handiwork and Amanda knew this was her chance, probably her last chance, to beg for her life and her freedom, to play on his sympathies, if he had any; his humanity, if he was actually human, and to plead with him to release her.

She sat silently though, trying to focus her gaze on him and failing, attempting to sit up in her chair and failing at *that*, too. What could she possibly say that she hadn't already said? What pleas could she try? What promises could she make? Over the past week, the nightmarish seven days that had at once seemed like an eternity and an instant, Amanda had begged and reasoned, threatened (that was a good one, threatening this monster. He'd taken it in stride, though, laughing at her feeble attempt to intimidate him like he was untouchable, which, she supposed, he was) and cried.

Nothing had worked. Nothing had made a damned bit of difference. He handcuffed her to a filthy little bed in the damp, nasty basement of his crumbling house, taking her when he wanted her—and in all sorts of disgusting ways—feeding her when he felt like it, letting her go to the bathroom only occasionally, and in general treating her like an animal—or worse, a piece of garbage—while lovingly whispering words in her ear that were totally inconsistent with his treatment of her.

One thing he had told her, though, was that his home was only a waypoint, his stewardship a weeklong interlude that would end with her being moved somewhere—to this makeshift prison, as it turned out—and turned over to another group of strangers. These strangers would then take her to her new, permanent home.

A home that was not in the United States.

A home that was not even on the North American continent.

In fact, the man told her, he wasn't exactly sure *where* she would be taken, and he didn't seem to much care, either. He said she would wind up in the freezing cold of Russia or the blast-furnace heat of the Middle East, depending on how her appearance matched up with what his contacts were currently in the market for.

She would never again see her home. She would never again see her boyfriend or her parents or her college roommates. She would never hang out at the pizzeria in her tiny hometown, listening to music on the old-fashioned jukebox and teasing the local boys by wearing tight jeans and tank tops.

She would simply disappear. She supposed she already had.

Amanda Lawton began to cry. She hadn't thought it possible, thought she'd exhausted her tears at least three days ago and didn't have the capability of manufacturing more, but there they were.

She had no words left with which to plead, but the tears came of their own accord. She cherished the tears. The tears meant that somewhere deep inside the terrified shell of her former self was a sliver of hope, a dream that she might still escape the fate that had been laid out for her by this awful man.

She was wrong. She knew she was wrong.

Her captor stood and watched her cry, impassive and unmoved. He raised his arm slowly and pointed to one side of the tiny enclosure and Amanda tried to follow his gesture, a reaction that normally would be automatic on her part but one that required intense concentration now, thanks to the cocktail of drugs she had been forced to take to ensure compliance.

Finally he spoke. "See the tiles on these walls?"

Amanda shook her head, trying to clear it, not sure she had heard him correctly. Why would he think she cared about the walls?

"Do you see them?" he repeated, annoyance clear in his tone.

Amanda nodded, stifling a sob, still confused. "Yes, I see the tiles on the wall."

"Good. These are professional grade acoustical tiles, very expensive and very effective at accomplishing their purpose. And do you know what that purpose might be?"

Amanda shook her head again, confused and disoriented but not so confused she couldn't tell he was playing with her. Taunting her.

Somehow this meaningless little humiliation hurt worse than the physical pain he had inflicted on her over the past week with the rapes and the various other indignities. It was the last straw.

She closed her eyes and sniffled as the tears came harder. She knew the man well enough by now to know this would only infuriate him but she couldn't help it.

And of course she was right.

"Answer me!" he shouted. *"What is the purpose of these incredibly expensive tiles?"*

"I don't know," Amanda cried, not wanting to die but wishing that if his plan was to kill her he would just hurry up and do it already.

"Thank you," the man said with exaggerated politeness. "Now, was that so difficult?"

The swiftness of his mood changes was impressive and horrifying.

"Since you're now showing an interest, I'll tell you. These professional grade acoustical tiles are so expensive because they are extremely effective at muffling sound and preventing it from leaving this room. Radio stations and music studios use it to preserve the integrity of the recording and broadcasting process, and the people I deal with use it to preserve the integrity of *their* operation, which in this case means not allowing anyone outside of this room know that you are here.

"Now, in case you're wondering—and undoubtedly you are—this little 'office,' as I like to call it, is located in an out-of-the-way area surprisingly free of traffic. Not many people come here at all, either by car or on foot. But in the event someone does pass by while you're here, you can scream all you want at the loudest volume you can manage, and all you will achieve for your effort will be a set of strained vocal cords.

"My point, sweetheart, in case you are so addled by my drugs you need me to explain it further to you, is that even though I will be leaving soon and I'm not certain how long it will be before my contacts arrive to start you on the journey to your new life, it will do you no good to call for help. It would be a pointless waste of effort and would only serve to tire you out for no good reason. Do you understand me?"

Amanda nodded. She understood. She wished she didn't, but she did. She tried again to raise her sagging body and sit upright in the chair. It was difficult to accomplish with all four limbs duct-taped to a big wooden monstrosity that looked like an electric chair, and some bizarre combination of psychotropic drugs coursing through her body, but she strained and worked and eventually managed it and felt marginally better about herself for doing so.

Then her stomach lurched again and her vision jumped and blurred and the man she had come to know intimately over the last seven days began walking toward the door. The tiny enclosure felt like an oven. Sweat streamed down Amanda's forehead and into her eyes, stinging them and mixing with her tears.

At least it looked as though there would be no gag stuffed into her mouth. If what the man said about the acoustical tiles was true—and why would he lie?—then there was no reason to gag her, which was a good thing, because as he reached the door and swung it open, taking one last long look back at her, she finally gave in to the relentless demands of her body and threw up all over the floor.

Her captor shook his head in silent rebuke and walked out the door into the bright May sunshine. It slanted in through the open door like gold and Amanda wondered whether she would ever see the sun again. She waited to hear the sound of the engine in his rattletrap truck starting up, which would be followed presumably by the sound of him driving away, but of course she didn't hear a thing—the incredibly expensive acoustical soundproofing tiles, remember?

She counted to one hundred in her head, nice and slow, and when she was sure enough time had passed that he must have gone, she tested his theory about the tiles. Amanda Lawton screamed.

And screamed.

And screamed.

And he must have been right.

Because nobody came.

2

Present Day

Martin Krall was a ghost.

A wraith.

He was legendary.

He haunted Interstate 90, its ribbons of pavement winding through the mostly rural towns and thickly forested hills of western Massachusetts and eastern New York State.

He was invisible, ethereal, terrifying. On the mental movie playing non-stop inside Martin Krall's head he saw himself as an avenging angel, taking what he wanted when he wanted it, the mere mortals populating the surrounding areas powerless to stop him and afraid to try.

Today what Martin Krall wanted was a girl. A teenage girl, specifically, closer in age to twenty than ten. Someone with a little bit of a body. Someone developed. Martin was not into that nasty pedo stuff that so many of his contemporaries were hung up on, the guys who took young children and did disgusting things with them.

He never understood the urge to enjoy a child in that way and was thankful he was more advanced than that. More evolved, so to speak.

He pulled his aging white cargo truck—it was practically invisible, the vehicular equivalent of a raggedy street person in some large city, steadfastly ignored by the rest of the population—off

I-90 and onto the access ramp leading to the rest area's massive parking lot. He passed a sign on the right directing the eighteen wheel tractor-trailers to KEEP RIGHT HERE. Martin slowed and then eased into the second right turn, the one leading to the parking area for more normal-sized vehicles.

He cruised the access lane, scanning the rows of stationary vehicles. He finally selected a parking spot three rows from the entrance to the traveler's plaza and killed the engine. It knocked and bucked as if disagreeing with Martin's decision before finally giving up the ghost. Martin made a mental note to get the old piece of shit tuned up soon; he couldn't really afford the expense but on the other hand didn't want to risk getting stuck somewhere like this with a vehicle that wouldn't start.

That would be the sort of disaster that could land him on death row.

The authorities had been chasing Martin ever since the first kidnapping way back, oh, more than three years ago now. They had never come close to catching him and Martin was confident they never would, despite the fact that he always utilized the same five hundred mile stretch of highway as his hunting ground. He was smart and, much more importantly, he was careful.

So many of the men who shared his particular urges and tastes made the mistake of getting careless or resorting to boastful, showboating tactics that invariably led to their downfall. Things like taunting the police with cutesy notes or wiseass telephone calls, leaving behind little "calling cards" for the media, drawing unnecessary attention in an attempt to differentiate themselves from the misfits who had gone before, all in a vain attempt to make themselves unique in some way, like it was important to separate themselves from the pack.

Martin wondered what these fucking idiots were thinking when they did such patently self-destructive things. Sometimes he felt they must have some deep-seated desire to be caught. Why else would you intentionally implicate yourself and give the enemy a better chance to apprehend you, in the name of celebrity? Of cheap self-promotion?

Martin hated publicity. He would have preferred the public never learn of his existence, although of course by now that dream was nothing more than the most baseless sort of wishful thinking. Somewhere around the third kidnapping a clever television news reporter hung a nickname on Martin, a nickname that stuck to him like vacuum wrap and forever removed his cloak of anonymity. Martin Krall was the I-90 Killer.

He stepped down out of the cab, the searing midday heat softening the pavement and radiating off it, warming his legs beneath his jeans and causing a film of sweat to break out on his forehead.

Martin slammed the driver's side door closed but left the truck unlocked. It would be foolish to lock it. It was a work vehicle and it was old, and as such was not equipped with anything as exotic as remote control locks. Martin knew he might be leaving in a hurry, hopefully with a new playmate in tow.

Plus, he was a ghost and his truck was as invisible as he—who would pay the least bit of attention to a nondescript beat-up old box truck adrift in a sea of shiny, more interesting vehicles?

Things slowed as they always did when Martin was hunting. Everything seemed to move at half-speed as he strode purposefully toward the glass double doors marking the entrance to the travelers' plaza. Families with young children jostled Martin as he walked, some moving, as he was, toward the rest area and some away from it and back to their cars.

They all looked to Martin like they were walking underwater, their movements slow and exaggerated. He assumed this strange phenomenon was a function of his heightened sense of awareness, of his advanced predatory senses.

Not that he really cared. He only knew it was like this every time.

All of the travelers were potential victims, although they didn't know it, and none saw him or were even aware of his presence among them; he was a stalking lion among the oblivious sheep.

It made sense, though. Martin Krall was a ghost, invisible, ethereal and terrifying. The sheep instinctively seemed to shy away as he approached, the Red Sea parting for Moses, mothers holding their children's hands a little tighter without even realizing they were doing it or why.

Martin felt incredibly alive and hyper-aware. Today was a special day. Today Martin Krall would add another victim to his collection.

3

Bill Ferguson sat alone at his table, one arm resting along the back of the booth's bench seat, legs stretched comfortably across the red vinyl. Steam swirled through the plastic lid of his Styrofoam coffee cup. He loved the coffee they served at this anonymous traveler's plaza on this anonymous exit off Interstate 90 in extreme western Massachusetts. It wasn't the fancy upscale stuff the yuppies seemed to enjoy overpaying for—although Bill had no doubt that before long that too would be available here—but it was hot and it was rich and it was tasty, and that was good enough for Bill Ferguson.

As the owner of a pair of moderately successful independent hardware stores, one located in rural Massachusetts and one in rural upstate New York, Bill had occasion to travel I-90 often, ferrying inventory between stores and cash receipts to the bank. Whenever possible he tried to take a few minutes out of his day to sit back and enjoy the coffee while watching the world pass by. It took time he couldn't really afford to spare and added caffeine into his system he didn't really need, but it was something he enjoyed so he did it anyway.

The weather today was atypical for late spring: hot and humid, more like August than May. Sweaty travelers, most dressed in shorts and t-shirts, hurried inside to use the facilities and stock up on food and drinks before hurrying out again and barreling back onto the highway to mix it up with the rest of the early-season vacationers. Truckers gathered around long tables sipping coffee and shooting the breeze with their buddies as they falsified their drivers' logbooks in the event of a surprise inspection by the DOT somewhere down the road.

Bill sipped his coffee, enjoying the slightly acidic taste as it burned its way down his gullet. With his right hand, he absently traced the bulge of the Browning Hi-Power semi-automatic pistol secured in a well-worn leather shoulder holster. A loose-fitting blue windbreaker with FERGUSON HARDWARE stitched in off-white thread on the breast pocket concealed the handgun nicely. He carried the weapon whenever it was necessary to transport cash or valuable merchandise for his stores, and in sixteen years had never had occasion to remove it from its holster unless he was at the practice range.

Bill often found himself touching the weapon absently through his jacket like a security blanket, which he supposed in a way it was. Carrying large sums of money at all hours of the day and night on an interstate highway, often lonely and secluded over the forty mile stretch between stores, was no kind of avenue to a long and healthy life, and although Bill had never yet run into trouble, his theory was that you could never be too careful.

Better to have the gun and not need it than to need it and not have it.

He drained his coffee and stood, stretching his muscles, feeling the usual popping and cracking of bones and tendons. He couldn't remember experiencing any of that until his fortieth birthday last year. Now he couldn't recall *not* feeling it.

He tossed his coffee cup into a trash receptacle roughly the size of Rhode Island and turned toward the plaza's entrance. The coffee was good, but nothing lasted forever.

His failed marriage testified to the accuracy of that statement.

What the hell. It was time to hit the road and get back to work.

4

Martin pushed through the door and into the traveler's plaza, grateful to be out of the heavy summerish air. Already his shirt stuck to his back uncomfortably. He mopped his brow with the palm of his hand, scanning the interior of the crowded building for a likely prospect.

The plaza was set up in similar fashion to a shopping mall food court, with counters running in a long semicircle around the outside of the room, beginning immediately to the left of the glass double doors and ending to Martin's right at the entrances to the men's and women's rest rooms.

Spaced at intervals behind the counters were the usual fast-food suspects: the pizza place, the fried chicken place, the burger joint, the coffee shop, the combination yogurt/soft-serve ice cream franchise. Tables and booths filled the dining area, with carts and stands scattered throughout the room hawking t-shirts, knick-knacks and cheap collectibles.

The place was filled. Martin loved the bustling activity, the way all the people were so absorbed in themselves, in their own little worlds, that they took note of little else. Even now, after over a dozen kidnappings in plazas identical to this one all along the eastern portion of Interstate 90, most people remained blissfully ignorant, unaware of their surroundings, certain of their own safety and their apparent belief that random tragedy would always strike the other guy.

Martin walked slowly toward the pizza counter, not because

he was interested in eating any but because that vantage point offered the clearest view of the big open room and thus the best opportunity to scan for potentials. He was reasonably certain he had already made one "withdrawal" from this particular plaza, maybe even his very first, but there had been so many over the last three-and-a-half years that they all began to blend together, a satisfying mishmash of pretty young things forcibly abducted in broad daylight in front of dozens, sometimes hundreds, of potential witnesses.

He regretted losing that clarity in the memories of his earliest conquests, but it was inevitable, really. In a way those fuzzy remembrances served as testament to his methods: he was so good at what he did, and had taken so many girls, that the individual details of all but the most recent kidnappings had begun to merge together into a kind of delicious nostalgic stew. Perhaps he couldn't recall the specifics of all of them, but in total the memories served to warm his heart, to cause a little tingle in his belly whenever he thought about them.

You couldn't ask for much more than that in this world.

Besides, Martin thought, *it's not like I can ever truly forget any of them. I have my trophy case at home, stocked with precious souvenirs and all prepped and ready to display another.*

It was risky keeping the prizes. Martin knew that. If the authorities ever searched his house they would certainly prove to be his undoing, but he was far smarter than the people pursuing him, so as long as he continued to exercise caution in his hunting he had nothing to fear.

Besides, what exactly was the point in exercising his life's passion if he could not enjoy the fruits of his labor?

Martin scanned the plaza, his practiced eye immediately zeroing in on a few potential targets, girls in their late teens or early twenties who, at first glance, seemed to fit his requirements for age and appearance nicely.

This was where things could get a little dicey. He had to be careful to choose a target whose parent or guardian or boyfriend or traveling companion was not paying too much attention to her. That part was becomingg more and more difficult. With each passing success, the media coverage of the I-90 Killer became more and more sensational, causing nervous parents to pay more and more attention to their charges.

For a while.

Then time would go by and Martin would lie low and the coverage would die down as other stories moved into the news cycle, picking up again only when Martin plucked another victim out from under the not-so-watchful gaze of her parents or friends.

Martin strolled past the pizza counter, moving behind the lines of people herded by a series of tension barriers with retractable colored tape. He passed the line for the pizza and burger joints, taking his place in the crowd of people waiting to buy a cup of coffee. His heart hammered wildly in his chest and he practically quivered with anticipation—this was the hardest part, the knowledge that he was so close to his next plaything and would have to wait to enjoy her—but he forced himself to slow down and proceed with caution.

And this was exactly why he would never be caught. Others of his kind rushed in with little regard for the potential consequences of their rash actions. Or they were careful in the beginning but became sloppy after a few successes, leaving themselves open to committing the kind of mistake that resulted in capture and humiliation and eventually life in prison or even the death penalty.

Not Martin Krall.

Martin Krall was too smart for that kind of carelessness. He knew when to take bold, decisive action and when to hang back and observe, and this was the time to hang back and observe. Scan and plan before leaping into action.

The line at the coffee counter moved slowly. Its length surprised Martin because of the stifling heat outside. Of course, like most coffee franchises, this one offered all sorts of fancy iced drinks and frothy ten thousand calorie concoctions composed mostly of water and sugar, and Martin figured the majority of the sheep were probably purchasing those.

He waited patiently, eyes scanning the crowd behind his mirrored sunglasses, keeping tabs on the girls he had determined were the most promising targets.

Finally he reached the front of the line. A tall, skinny kid in his late teens with serious acne issues and greasy long blond hair looked down at him through lifeless blue eyes. Pinned at a careless angle onto his shirt was a nametag that read JAMIE. The shirt was wrinkled and partially un-tucked in the back.

"Help you?" Jamie asked.

Martin was immediately turned off. He was no neat freak, not by any stretch of the imagination, but this kid reeked of grime and germs. It was disgusting. Martin's first instinct was to turn away. He certainly didn't want to drink anything "Jamie" had put his dirty paws all over.

But then he stopped himself. Waiting all that time in line and then leaving without buying anything just as he got to the counter would be noteworthy. It would make him stick out. Make people remember him.

And that would be unacceptable, given what would soon take place here. He reluctantly forced a smile onto his face, wondering whether it looked as insincere as it felt. Figured it probably did.

He said, "Small coffee, please."

Jamie stared at him without moving, as if Martin had spoken in some foreign language. For a second Martin wondered if maybe the kid didn't speak English, but of course that was absurd. He had been serving a whole group of people, most of whom must have been speaking English, and no one else seemed to have had any trouble.

What was this moron's problem?

Finally the kid asked, "Hot?"

Now it was Martin's turn to stare uncomprehendingly. Of course it was hot; it was at least ninety degrees outside, for Christ's sake.

Suddenly he realized what the kid was asking. His earlier supposition that most of the people in line were buying those iced drinks was correct, and this idiot wanted to be sure he understood Martin's order correctly.

"Yes, hot," Martin said, trying and mostly succeeding in keeping the sneer he felt out of his voice. "I'd like hot coffee."

The kid drew the brew out of a huge stainless steel urn set up on a counter behind him, handing the cup to Martin and receiving payment without another word. Martin wanted nothing more than to stiff this loser out of a tip—his service was poor and his personal hygiene nonexistent—but of course that might draw the attention of some of the sheep, too, so he reluctantly dropped a buck into the plastic tip jar strategically placed next to the cash register.

Then he moved away, shaking his head slightly. He grabbed a table near the front of the room where he could maintain a decent view of the facility.

No sooner had he sat down than he spotted the one. There was no doubt about it. She was perhaps seventeen, tall and athletic, willowy, all coltish legs and youthful energy, her long blonde hair tied back in a ponytail.

She was perfect. She was just what Martin liked and just what the others would like as well. The girl was entering the plaza, traveling with a man and a woman, presumably her parents. She was not one of the likely targets he'd been monitoring, and he congratulated himself on his patience.

The family moved into the plaza and split up, the girl turning toward the rest rooms and Mommy and Daddy staking out a spot in line at the burger joint all the way across the room. There were so many people milling about that Martin figured there was no way they could even *see* the rest rooms from where they were standing.

This was ideal.

It was time for bold action. Martin left his coffee untouched on the table—*just as well,* he thought. *I really don't want the damned thing after that greaseball behind the counter put his grubby paws all over it*—and meandered slowly toward the rest rooms. The men's and women's rooms were located adjacent to each other and featured open doorways with interior walls preventing anyone outside the facilities from seeing in.

He took his time.

Moved slowly.

Determinedly.

The plaza was busy and there was a good chance the girl would have to wait for a stall inside the rest room. Even if she didn't, it would take at least a couple of minutes to do her business and then wash her hands.

Martin hoped she washed her hands. Hygiene was important.

Stopping at a t-shirt stand a few feet from the rest rooms, Martin pretended to check out the cheap wares while he waited for the girl. Shirts with silly puns on them were displayed next to other shirts featuring scenic views of the Adirondack Mountains, or one of the thousands of lakes dotting the region, or a depiction of the sun setting over the Atlantic Ocean. The only thing all the shirts had in common was that they were, without exception, poorly made and overpriced.

Martin watched the rest rooms closely, knowing he would get only one chance. Hopefully the girl would exit the ladies room alone, but even if she didn't, it would pose no more than a minor problem. The girl's parents were still cooling their heels in line at the hamburger joint and anyone who happened to walk out of the ladies room at the same time as the target would undoubtedly not be paying the slightest attention to her. That person would be no different than the rest of these people, anxious to get her food or coffee or whatever and get back on the road.

Martin Krall patted the Glock 9mm jammed into the waistband of his jeans and covered with a long t-shirt and waited. The girl would exit the ladies room any second now. He could feel it. He didn't know how he could tell but he could. He had done this many times before.

He stood at the display stand surrounded by the cheap t-shirts and the unsuspecting people and waited, unnoticed, a predator stalking its' prey.

5

Bill approached the entrance to the rest rooms, dodging left and right, avoiding masses of people, all seemingly oblivious to everyone and everything around them. A fat middle-aged woman with thinning brown hair waddled straight at him, staring through him as she careened toward the food counters like she had just wandered in out of the desert and hadn't eaten in weeks. He stepped aside and let her pass, shaking his head half in frustration and half in amusement when it became clear she had had absolutely no intention of altering her course.

Sidestepping the overweight woman caused him to bump into a thin, wiry man in a billowing t-shirt who was apparently headed toward the rest rooms as well. The man rocked back onto his heels and glared as Bill smiled and offered an apology.

"No problem," the stranger mumbled unconvincingly, and then turned away as if anxious to end the brief encounter.

Bill stared in surprise before shrugging and turning again toward the rest rooms. He advanced three steps and then had to dodge a young woman exiting the ladies room. She was a teenager, tall and blonde, with hair streaming behind her in a ponytail protruding from the back of a New York Yankees baseball cap. Her head was raised and her searching eyes bypassed Bill. It was clear she was looking for someone.

Two more steps brought Bill to the men's room entrance, a feeling of ill-defined unease nagging at him. He had served two tours on the ground in Iraq half a lifetime ago and learned very quickly that the fastest way to an early, sandy grave was to ignore what your senses were telling you, even if you couldn't quite decipher the message.

Something was wrong.

He stopped and turned. A man bumped into him from behind and muttered, "Asshole," then kept walking into the men's room.

Bill ignored him. The man he had nearly deposited on his ass over by the t-shirt rack a moment ago abruptly changed course, veering away from the restrooms and picking up his pace. Bill watched as the man approached the blonde teen girl from behind.

When the man reached a point immediately behind the girl he moved to her right and raised his left arm as if to drape it over her shoulder. Bill's first thought was that the man must be the girl's father, but that didn't make sense. There was no way she could have missed seeing him as she came out of the ladies room if they were acquainted; they had to have passed within a foot of each other. The man was obviously unknown to her.

Bill's internal alarm bells were jangling now; his sense of vague unease morphing quickly into alarm, and what happened next caused all the other people milling about in the traveler's plaza to melt away from his consciousness until only Bill and the blonde girl and the strange-acting wiry man existed.

The man continued to raise his arm, hooking it over her shoulder as if preparing to settle her neck into the crook of his elbow. With his right hand he pulled a handgun out from under the back of his shirt, displaying it before her startled eyes for a fraction of a second before pressing it to her ribs and clamping his left hand over her mouth.

The girl's eyes grew wide and instantly fearful, and the man steered her toward the double-doors and the intense heat of the parking lot.

And escape.

Bill did a double take, not sure his brain was correctly processing the information his eyes were sending it.

He glanced quickly around the plaza. Everyone was still milling about quietly, oblivious to the drama unfolding in their midst.

He shifted his attention back toward the man and the girl and decided he really was seeing what he thought he was seeing. The man was hustling the girl out of the traveler's plaza. They had by now nearly reached the exterior doors.

In precious few seconds they would be out of the building and safely away to an unknown but unimaginable fate. He made a snap decision, one he would later question and even in some ways come to regret.

Bill Ferguson drew his Browning, dropped into a shooter's crouch and took dead aim at the center of the man's back. Incredibly, almost unbelievably given the large number of people and the bustling activity inside the plaza, no one stood between Bill and the kidnapper. He had a clear, unobstructed shot.

Undoubtedly that wouldn't last long.

He held the Browning in two hands, making a conscious effort to keep his grip loose and relaxed, and screamed, *"Freeze!"* at the top of his lungs.

The man stopped instantly and stood motionless. His gun was still firmly planted into the girl's side, but at least he hadn't pulled the trigger. Yet.

One full second of utter monastic silence fell over the inside of the traveler's plaza.

No one spoke.

No one moved.

The clatter of plates and silverware stopped.

Cash registers fell silent.

Then everything went to shit.

6

Martin was instantly aware the shouted warning was meant for him. It had to be, unless another kidnapper happened to be stealing another girl out of this plaza at this exact moment, and what were the odds of that?

The relevant question, though, was simple: who had shouted the warning and what sort of hardware, if any, was backing it up?

It wasn't a cop who had yelled across the plaza, of that Martin was reasonably confident. First of all, a police officer would have announced his status as he was warning Martin to stop. They liked to make sure guys like Martin knew the full force of the law was behind them.

Plus, Martin knew from extensive personal experience that cops enjoyed throwing their weight around.

Besides, this wasn't the first rodeo for Martin Krall. The very first thing he had done upon entering the plaza—before getting in line for his coffee and even before scoping out likely victims—was to make good and goddamned certain there were no uniformed officers of the law sitting on their fat asses at a table or a booth drinking coffee and eating donuts and ripping off the taxpayers.

Of course, it was always possible a plainclothes officer or detective had picked exactly this moment to take a travel break, but Martin figured that was unlikely in the extreme. Even a pig in street clothes would not have been able to stop himself from impressing everyone by identifying himself as a police officer while yelling at Martin.

No, the most obvious possibility was that an ordinary citizen had seen the kidnapping go down, as unlikely as that seemed, and decided to play hero. Martin had been taking girls from travel plazas for years now utilizing this exact methodology and had never even come close to being detected, but he'd always known that it might eventually happen. Most people were utterly unaware of their surroundings, but there was always the occasional exception to even the most ironclad rule. He concluded that must be what had happened here.

The situation was still bad. He had no way of knowing what kind of weapon the pain-in-the-ass hero wannabe was toting, if any. But the situation was certainly much more manageable if it was just some joker trying to save the girl than if a real cop was drawing down on him.

He might be able to get out of this.

Martin turned slowly and carefully, avoiding any sudden or unusual movements that his attacker might interpret as threatening. He kept his handgun pressed firmly into the girl's side, shoving it hard against her ribs in an unspoken warning not to do anything stupid, like starting to run toward her misguided—and hopefully soon to be dead—savior.

He had completed roughly half his turn when the stunned silence inside the plaza came to an abrupt and chaotic end. Screams echoed through the building, the sound ricocheting madly off the ceramic tiles and bare walls as people took cover under tables and behind booths.

A teenage boy performed a beautifully executed swan dive over the top of the burger joint's counter, disappearing completely on the other side, the sound of his landing lost in the cacophony of noise.

Dishes crashed to the floor, glass and ceramic smashing.

Tables were overturned as quick-thinking citizens dumped them on their sides to use them as cover.

In front of Martin the girl whimpered softly, breathing hard, clearly terrified. Her weight was heavy on his arms as he pulled her body tightly against his own, using her as a human shield.

He completed the turn and found himself face-to-face with the same man who had bumped him just seconds ago. The man was crouched, and he held his weapon in a two-handed shooter's grip, training it steadily on the center of Martin's body, which of course meant it was now also trained on the girl.

He smiled, knowing that no matter how powerful the man's handgun was it was as good as useless unless he could shoot like Annie Oakley. The odds were that he would hit the innocent victim if he attempted to fire now, and unless the dude was totally off his rocker, he would not do something so rash. The man had had his chance to take down Martin but he'd blown it with his stupid fair-play warning.

Now Martin was back in control.

His smile widened into a cocky grin. The buttinsky was dressed in a blue windbreaker with FERGUSON HARDWARE stitched on the breast pocket. It should have been a dead giveaway to Martin that the dude was carrying. It had to be ninety-five degrees outside; there was no possible explanation why someone would don a jacket in this heat unless it was to cover a concealed weapon.

Martin mentally kicked himself, careful not to let the guy see the anger in his expression. He didn't want the wannabe hero to know he was anything other than supremely confident. But there was no way he should have overlooked such an obvious warning sign—it was one of those careless mistakes he had sworn he was too smart ever to make.

Oh well, he decided. *No point crying over spilt milk.*

He could still escape this disaster and when he did, he would chalk the episode up as a valuable lesson learned; one that was annoying and stupid and inexcusable, but one that ultimately turned out to be harmless and one he would never make again, that was for damned sure.

Martin smiled at the man pointing a gun in his direction, oblivious to the chaos around him as the sheep bleated pathetically, roused from their torpor and completely lost now, confronted with this frightening and confusing new reality.

The man still had not moved. He remained in a crouch, holding the gun on Martin and his new girlfriend. Martin wondered if it had occurred to the Good Samaritan yet that he had lost control of the situation.

He doubted so; this guy was just another idiot. He was brave,

Martin would grant him that, but ultimately he was just another lost sheep whether he knew it or not, unable to match Martin's intelligence or cunning.

But that was okay. He would find out soon enough.

7

Bill kept the Browning trained on the kidnapper.

The man held the girl tightly in front of him. The pair had turned as one at his shouted warning and now stood facing him, the kidnapper with a creepy grin plastered on his face, the girl wearing an expression of sheer terror. Bill was suddenly thankful for his untold hours spent at the practice range, firing the weapon and honing his technique until he had complete confidence in his ability with the gun. He'd been an expert marksman in the service and felt sure his ability now was just as good, if not better, than it had been back in Iraq.

The noise in the plaza was deafening, a rich mix of screaming, cursing, running feet, and glasses and dishes smashing on the floor.

Out of the confusion, plaintive and panicked, came the sound of a wailing woman's voice. "Oh my God, he has Allie! He has Allie!"

Bill ignored the tortured voice, tuning it out as he attempted to tune out all the other background noise. It served only to act as a distraction he did not need, and he knew he had to remain sharp and focused, because the next few moments would determine whether this clusterfuck ended well or disastrously.

The kidnapper continued to smile, his eyes sharp and predatory. Maybe it was a trick of perspective caused by the harsh fluorescent lighting, but his teeth appeared long and yellow, wolfish even.

He stared Bill down, the challenge in his eyes unmistakable. Bill knew the man had regained the advantage, and worse, he knew the man knew it. There was no way Bill could fire on him now without risking hitting the hostage, injuring and perhaps even killing her. For just a moment he was back in Iraq, the intense heat and dust and life-and-death pressure returning with a vengeance, so real he felt if he opened his mouth it would fill with burning desert sand.

He hesitated, his hand beginning to lower, and then he shook his head, clearing it of the cobwebs, and once again raised the weapon, training it on the kidnapper and his young victim.

It was a classic standoff. Bill knew he couldn't fire on the kidnapper because of the presence of the hostage, but the kidnapper couldn't shoot the girl because as soon as he did he would lose his shield and open himself up to a bullet. Likewise, the man couldn't turn to get away because doing so would expose his back.

The kidnapper reached the identical conclusion as Bill and at the same time. His grin widened. It was unnerving. He slid the gun smoothly away from the girl's body and pointed it at Bill, who arose from his crouch and began moving forward ever so slowly.

The two handguns were now pointed directly at each other, frightening mirror images locked in a deadly standoff. Bill had a sudden, absurd cartoonish vision of the two men firing their guns at the same time and the bullets striking each other halfway toward their respective targets and falling to the floor.

He didn't have a plan beyond a vague notion that if he could get close enough to the girl, perhaps he could grab her and pull her out of the scumbag's grasp, using his own body to shield her from harm. What he would do after that was unclear.

As plans went, Bill knew it was pretty goddamned thin. Nonexistent when you got right down to it. But he couldn't think of anything else to do and felt the situation slipping away, moving from bad to worse, sliding inexorably toward a disaster involving death and tragedy and a lifetime of regret.

He crept closer, neither man speaking, the girl sobbing quietly in the man's arms. Under the circumstances, Bill thought, she was doing an admirable job of keeping herself together.

The rest of the people in the crowded plaza watched the confrontation from behind overturned tables, peeking over counters and around booths and chairs. The noise hadn't subsided, but the chaos of a few seconds ago had resolved into a low murmur, a buzz of shocked excitement as observers began to realize they, at least, were probably not in any immediate danger.

Not like the people they were watching.

Bill was now eight feet from the hostage...now six...four. The gunman shuffled steadily backward as Bill moved forward, but at a slower pace, as he dragged his reluctant companion with him.

Still neither man spoke. The tension was palpable. Something was about to break, something had to happen soon, but no one had a clue what it was, least of all Bill Ferguson.

He continued to close the gap. He was now so close he could smell the rancid stench of the kidnapper's fear. Outwardly the man appeared calm and in control, an arrogant smirk pasted onto his face, but the sweat dripping out of every pore revealed his tension. The odor was sour and Bill nearly gagged.

He was within arm's reach now.

It was time to make a move.

He pulled his left hand off the Hi-Power. Reached forward to grab the girl's right shoulder and yank her toward him, to spin her behind him to relative safety, to shield her with his own body. He moved as quickly as he could, his hand shooting out toward the girl, but as he did—

8

Martin had known almost from the beginning what the hero's play was going to be. It was the only one he had, once he'd screwed the pooch by not shooting Martin in the back.

So when the idiot reached for the girl, Martin *shoved* her, hard, directly at him. The pair went down instantly in a tangle of arms and legs, crashing to the tile floor with a thud.

As soon as they did, Martin turned and sprinted for the entrance, barely slowing as he raced through the glass double doors, smashing into them and rocking them back on their hinges. He burst into the brutal May heat radiating off the acres of pavement.

He was going to make it.

This failure would rankle him for days, and of course he could expect a brutal dressing-down from his contact, a person who was never a model of patience even in the best of times.

But the important thing was Martin was going to escape. He pounded toward his truck and freedom.

9

Before they even hit the floor Bill knew he had fucked up. Not *majorly* fucked up, not dead teenager bleeding out on the floor fucked up—after all, the girl *was* safe and sound, protected by the two hundred pounds of his bulk—but still, there was no denying he had screwed the pooch by getting close enough to the kidnapper to allow the guy the opportunity to make such an obvious play.

Still, what else could he have done? Maybe the guy hitting the bricks was the best thing that could have happened, all things considered. The alternative was unthinkable—a desperate man loose inside the building with a lethal weapon in his hands and several dozen potential victims just waiting to be slaughtered. Not a pretty picture there.

The girl moaned and Bill realized he was probably crushing her. That would be ironic—save the kidnap victim only to suffocate her immediately afterward. He rolled to his right and pushed himself off the floor. A jagged flash of pain ran through his left elbow, and he could already feel an egg rising on his forehead from where it had impacted the floor. He supposed he was lucky he hadn't broken a nose or lost any teeth from the bone-jarring collision and resulting fall.

Hopefully the girl had been just as fortunate.

He shook his head to clear some of the cobwebs. "Are you all right?"

She shot him an incredulous look that would melt steel, the kind of look only a teen can pull off.

Then she giggled. It was probably a reaction to stress, but the sound was so unexpected, Bill had to laugh. She reminded him of his daughter, Carli. He guessed they were roughly the same age. The girl seemed okay, at least physically. And her mother was even now charging across the glass-littered floor toward the two of them, screaming something unintelligible. Her father was right behind, gamely attempting to keep pace.

"Oh, Christ almighty," the girl muttered when she looked up and saw them, and Bill laughed again, which started *her* laughing again. She was going to be fine.

He rose to his feet, staggered, and dropped to one knee, spitting out a curse. His head was swimming. He must have knocked it harder than he realized.

He picked his Browning off the floor where he had apparently dropped it in the violence of the collision—some hero, losing his gun at the critical moment—and began moving in an unsteady gait toward the plaza's entrance, the same one the failed kidnapper had exited just moments ago.

By the time Bill crossed the fifteen feet to the doors he felt a little more like himself. He was suffering the beginnings of what he suspected was going to be a whopper of a headache and his left elbow was sending constant angry admonitions to his brain, but he knew it could have been much worse.

He was still alive and so was the girl.

He picked up the pace, hitting the doors at a dead run. The unseasonable heat and humidity descended on him like a wet blanket as he leapt the four steps from the plaza to the concrete walkway. He staggered upon landing and continued into the parking lot.

An elderly couple glanced at him and did a double take. Bill wondered what he looked like to them and decided he was probably better off not knowing. He probably looked like the lunatic he was, chasing after a man rumored to have murdered at least ten people.

And Bill doubted the I-90 Killer would have any objection to adding one middle-aged goddamned fool to his tally.

He took three running steps onto the hot pavement and then realized it was hopeless. There must be over a hundred cars in the mammoth lot and while it wasn't even close to being full, the odds of picking the I-90 Killer's vehicle out of all of the ones glittering in the bright May sunshine when he had no idea what it even looked like were stacked overwhelmingly against him.

For all he knew, the guy had been parked in the first row and was already gone.

Bill slapped his hands together. "Goddammit!" he screamed in frustration, and his headache spiked and the I-90 Killer roared past him, not twenty feet away, tearing across the parking lot toward the highway on-ramp. He was driving a battered off-white piece of shit box truck, which trailed blue smoke as he made his escape. The vehicle had obviously been repainted, and not professionally. It was devoid of any markings, at least as far as Bill Ferguson could see.

He shuddered, thinking about what sort of horrible fate that young girl back inside the travelers' plaza had narrowly avoided.

Bill squinted, peering at the rear of the vehicle in an attempt to decipher the license plate, but the heavy blue smoke pouring out of the exhaust made an effective screen. He could see the tag but couldn't make out any numbers or letters.

He cursed again and wondered if the escaping kidnapper realized how lucky he was right now to be driving a vehicle that needed a ring job.

He turned and sprinted toward his vehicle to give chase. How hard could it be to catch that crappy truck?

10

Martin stomped on the accelerator and the truck responded like what it was: a twelve-year-old delivery vehicle that had spent most of its life ferrying vegetables and produce from one location to another. It bucked and hesitated before finally getting the message and picking up steam.

He roared past the building and saw the man he had grappled with staring at him in open-mouthed surprise. It would have been comical if Martin wasn't so goddamned pissed off.

He hit the highway doing almost seventy-five, pretty close to the old vehicle's max speed. As tempting as it was to continue hauling ass, Martin immediately eased off the gas and slowed to a sensible, non-confrontational sixty, immediately rendering himself invisible in the traffic. There was no reason to draw unnecessary attention by driving too fast. By the time the police arrived at the plaza and finished sorting out what exactly had happened, he would be home relaxing on his couch, drinking beer and watching porn.

Sweat poured off Martin's body. His hands were slick with it as he tried to grasp the steering wheel, and his t-shirt felt like a wet sponge.

He was rattled. He had been doing this for well over three years now, had taken more than a dozen girls utilizing this exact method, and in all that time had never even suffered a single close call.

Until now.

Plucking pretty young things from out of a crowd had always been simple and easily accomplished. Most people would assume that a large number of bystanders would complicate a kidnapping, but Martin knew the opposite was true.

It was simple human nature. Group psychology. Strangers would always make a concerted effort not to become involved in the activities of other strangers. It was no different than the way most people acted when stuck inside an elevator in a crowd. They would avert their eyes; keep conversation to a minimum. The situation was inevitably awkward and uncomfortable.

Martin had been successfully stealing girls for three-and-a-half years *because* of the crowds populating the plazas when he took his victims, rather than in spite of them. That knowledge made today's close call and ultimate failure much more difficult to stomach.

He supposed he had been overdue for a little bad luck, but that didn't make today's goat-rope any easier to accept.

Martin Krall had always lived his life by a few hard and fast rules, the first of which stated overestimating the stupidity of the average American traveler was damned near impossible. People were so convinced of their own invisibility and *invinc*ibility, and always in such a hurry, that Martin had long ago come to the conclusion he could practically announce his plans on a loudspeaker and still get away with them.

Finally he had run across a traveler who actually paid attention to his surroundings, and to top it off, *the guy was carrying a gun!*

Martin wanted to hurry, not just to escape the police but to outrun his humiliation, Still, he forced himself to maintain his sedate pace. Cars passed him in the left lane in a nearly continuous stream, but he paid them no attention. He focused on slowing his breathing, reducing his heart rate. He had begun shaking, the adrenaline flooding his body after the narrow escape back at the travelers' plaza, and the resulting crash was making him feel logy and slow.

He felt like shit. Smelled like it, too. Hopefully that fucker with the goddamned gun had gotten a good whiff of him. It was exactly what he deserved.

The thought made him smile.

Soon Martin would arrive at his exit. He was anxious to get

home where he could relax and begin deciphering what had gone wrong and more importantly, how he could ensure nothing like this ever happened again.

Thinking of home reminded him that for the first time ever he was returning from a hunting expedition empty-handed and alone and Martin felt a seething rage bubbling inside him. It lurked just below the surface, hidden beneath his carefully constructed veneer of quiet control. He was once again that helpless high school freshman, the geek with no friends, the skinny kid stuffed into a locker.

The helpless fury was almost overwhelming.

Just who the hell did that self-righteous busybody motherfucker think he was, anyway? Why couldn't he play by the same rules as everyone else and just mind his own goddamned business and walk around in a daze like all the other sheep? Why did he have to pick that exact moment to stop at the rest area for gas or coffee or a burger or to take a shit anyway? Life was so fucking unfair.

The blackness settled over Martin like a blanket. He now had no girl. No one to keep him company, no one with whom he could release his stress over the next seven days.

The worst part was the knowledge that after this monumental fuckup he would have to lie low for a long time. The media would be all over his spectacular failure; it would probably get even more coverage than it would have if he been successful today.

This of course meant people would be much more careful for a while until they eventually crawled back into their default modes of unseeing and uncaring bliss.

Martin would have to alter his routine if he wanted to find a playmate and satisfy his contact sometime before the fuss and furor died down. Doing so would take a couple of months and there was no fucking way his contact would be willing to wait that long.

It was a conundrum. Taking a girl from a highway rest stop was going to be damned near impossible for a while, but waiting two to three months because of that bastard back at the travelers' plaza was simply unacceptable.

This will not stand, he vowed to himself through teeth clenched so tightly shut it made his jaw ache. *It most certainly the fuck will not.*

Already the beginnings of an alternative plan began taking shape in Martin Krall's head. He smiled and nodded, all alone inside his box truck. He would have to spend more time fully developing the idea he was considering, fleshing it out and thinking it through until it was rock-solid.

But for the first time since hearing that guy yell "Freeze!" behind him, he thought things might work out okay after all.

11

Bill took a couple of wobbly running steps toward his vehicle, a dark blue Ford Econoline van with FERGUSON HARDWARE stenciled on each side. It was parked a couple hundred yards away in the ocean-sized lot.

He could chase down the kidnapper. It would be a race of turtles, sure, and the scumbag had gotten a pretty sizeable head start, but that piece of crap truck Bill had seen was certainly not built for speed. It might take a few miles, but he could catch the guy, assuming he was even still on the highway.

After just three steps, Bill slowed and then stopped in his tracks.

Sure, he could run the kidnapper down.

Maybe.

But there was another consideration. Leaving the scene of an attempted kidnapping where handguns had been brandished about like swords was not something that would sit well with the cops, who were undoubtedly just moments away. If he were to leap into his vehicle and careen down the highway in search of a little vigilante justice—Clint Eastwood in a hardware store van—there was a very strong possibility it would not end well. If he didn't end up dead at the hands of the I-90 Killer, the police might just put him down, not realizing he was one of the good guys.

"Goddammit," Bill muttered again, slapping his hands together as he had done just seconds before. The adrenaline was still coursing through his body and the thought of doing nothing but sitting and waiting for help was frustrating in the extreme.

A young couple strolling toward the plaza gave him a wary glance and a wide berth. He turned and followed them back into the plaza, smiling slightly at their reaction when they opened the doors and came face-to-face with the devastation inside the building. It looked like a twister had touched down in this one spot and then disappeared, leaving the exterior untouched. Overturned tables were everywhere and smashed glasses and dishes littered the floor.

People milled about, uncertain of exactly what to do until the authorities arrived and took control. The young girl Bill had saved was on her feet, still in the exact spot where she had become tangled up with Bill and fallen to the floor.

"I'm fine," the girl insisted to her mother, who fussed over her like she had returned from the dead while her father stood to the side, clearly uncomfortable with nothing to keep him busy.

When Bill really thought about it, maybe she *had* returned from the dead, especially if the kidnapper was the I-90 Killer.

She looked like she was fine, too, at least compared to her mother, whose face was flushed and who was shaking like a leaf. Bill could see it from where he stood at the door, at least fifteen feet away. He thought the mom might need the ambulance more than her daughter when it finally arrived.

He moved unnoticed across the floor toward the counter where he had purchased his coffee a few minutes ago, stepping around, over and through plastic serving trays and shattered glasses and dishes. He walked past the strained little family reunion and into the throngs of people, the majority of whom were still congregated on the northern end of the room away from the exterior doors, as if maybe the guy with the gun was going to come back and try again.

He approached the coffee counter and the crowd parted before him like the Red Sea before Moses. Bill wondered whether it was because they recognized him from the armed confrontation and were just as nervous and uncertain about him as they were about the guy he had driven away, or whether the people were simply in shock from what had just happened and were acting without any real conscious thought.

Not that it mattered. All he cared about at the moment was

getting another cup of coffee to sip while waiting for the arrival of the cavalry—he clearly wouldn't be going anywhere for a while—and the crowd was cooperating nicely. He stepped up to the counter, his shoes crunching on broken glass, and waited for the teenager who had served him before, the vacant-eyed one with the acne problem. The kid wasn't around. In fact, no one was around who seemed to be in any sort of official capacity, at least not at the coffee franchise.

Behind most of the other counters employees were taking the first tentative steps toward reestablishing service. Broken glass was being swept off the floor, tables and chairs were being righted, even some orders were being taken over at the pizza place.

That seemed monumentally unfair. Shouldn't it be easier to start pouring coffee than to cook and serve pizza? He wondered whether the kid behind the coffee counter had been working alone and had hauled ass out the back doors when the trouble started—there had to be an employee entrance somewhere—and was even now sprinting toward town.

Tired of waiting, Bill clambered over the counter. He dropped to the other side and grabbed a small Styrofoam cup. A small should do, because once the cops arrived he would be pretty busy for a while. No point being wasteful. He placed the cup under the spigot and enjoyed the rich aroma as the brew drained out of the urn. Employees behind the other counters looked at him curiously but no one challenged him.

He walked to the register and placed two one-dollar bills in front of the drawer. There was still no sign of the coffee kid.

He climbed back over the counter and ambled toward the plaza's entrance. This time as he moved through the crowd, he thought he could hear people whispering and muttering, "That's the guy," as he passed, but nobody spoke directly to him. He imagined people nudging each other and pointing.

Bill crunched through the mess and out the glass double doors, back into the oppressive late-May heat. Staying inside with the comfort of the air conditioning would have been nice but the prospect of all those people staring and pointing at him like he was some kind of circus freak or crazed lunatic was unappealing. His headache felt a little better as the adrenaline rush drained away, although the bump on his head didn't seem to be getting any smaller.

Sipping his coffee, Bill eased down into a sitting position on the four steps leading from the walkway into the building and waited for the arrival of the police. Judging from the sound of things, they were now only seconds away. He could hear the scream of multiple sirens getting noticeably closer and wondered how many cruisers the dispatcher had sent at the report of two men with guns scuffling inside the travelers' plaza.

Probably everyone available.

He would find out soon enough.

He took another sip of his coffee. It really was quite good.

12

The police cars slewed into the parking lot. They screeched to a halt in the travel lanes, blocking access for motorists attempting to enter and exit.

The cops didn't seem to care.

There were dozens of cruisers, including a blocky dark blue armored truck that Bill assumed must be some kind of tactical response vehicle. He rose from his sitting position and stood in the parking lot directly in front of the entrance to the travelers' plaza, hands held above his head for the benefit of the cops. He figured they were probably about as stoked as they could get and didn't want to get ripped to shreds by flying bullets.

All it would take would be one eager officer who'd had too much caffeine.

He had already placed his Browning on the pavement a good ten feet in front of him. It lay baking in the sun, roughly midway between himself and the closest cruisers.

The scene was one of utter bedlam. Officers leapt out of their cars, taking defensive positions behind their open doors and pointing their weapons at him. Everyone seemed to be yelling at once.

Bill could sense the people inside the plaza gathered at the door and the big plate-glass windows watching in fascination, not considering the fact that they were positioned directly behind him. They would be mowed down where they stood if the cops started blasting away.

It was hard to tell for sure with all of the officers screaming at the same time, but the general consensus seemed to be that they wanted Bill to lie facedown in the parking lot, a situation he really hoped to avoid. The temperature of the pavement had to be one hundred fifty degrees. He stood his ground, picking out the closest group of officers and raising his voice to be heard above the din.

"I'm unarmed," he announced loudly, making eye contact with the cop at the front of the phalanx of officers. He guessed that one might be in charge. "My weapon is on the ground in front of you."

The man hesitated, then edged out from behind the cover of his vehicle, holding his weapon eye-level in a two-handed grip similar to the one Bill had employed a few minutes ago. It was aimed dead center of Bill's body mass, right in the middle of his chest.

The shouting had died down, replaced with an expectant silence as all the other cops seemed to have decided at the same time to wait and see what happened next.

Bill was a little curious himself. He had known the cops would be twitchy when they got here; after all, they probably had been given no details other than something very bad had gone down at the travelers' plaza and guns were involved. They didn't know whether anyone was hurt or maybe even dead inside the building and they had no way of knowing whether Bill was any kind of threat. He had put the odds of getting through this without taking a bullet from a nervous cop's gun at about fifty-fifty as the sirens approached, but was beginning to wonder if maybe he hadn't been a little over-optimistic.

The police officer moved forward, tension written on his face. "Get your ass on the ground right now," he said in an almost conversational tone of voice. Bill had expected the man to scream, but he was maintaining a calming posture, clearly hoping to keep this situation from sparking into something deadly.

"The tar is too goddamned hot," Bill answered. "My weapon is on the ground in front of you. I'm unarmed."

"I can't be sure you don't have another weapon. Get on the ground and we'll have you back on your feet in just a couple of seconds."

Bill figured that was the best offer he was going to get. One way or the other, he was going to end up on that pavement. He could either do it on his own or with the help of a lead slug or a Taser.

He sighed and eased into a prone position. And he was right. The pavement was hot. He tried to keep his exposed skin out of direct contact with the burning tar.

The cops rushed forward the moment his body touched the ground, one sticking the barrel of his gun in Bill's ear as another patted him down roughly. When they were satisfied he posed no danger—a process that seemed to take much longer than the couple of seconds the guy in charge had promised—a third cop yanked him to his feet, where he stood surrounded by grim-faced officers of the law who suddenly seemed to have no idea what to do next.

The one who had lifted him off the pavement pulled Bill's hands behind his back and slapped a pair of cuffs on him, tightening the bracelets unnecessarily.

The officer in charge reappeared and asked brusquely, "Where's the other guy with the gun?" His disposition seemed to have worsened now that Bill was restrained.

"He's gone. He took off eastbound on the interstate in an off-white box truck, probably ten or twelve years old."

"Is anyone hurt inside?"

"Not unless they cut themselves on broken glass."

The officer turned and nodded to the cop who had patted him down, and Bill found himself being perp-walked to an idling cruiser. His escort dumped him into the back seat without a word—no warning about hitting his head on the car's roof like they always seemed to do on television—and slammed the door. Bill supposed the guy didn't watch much TV.

The officer then turned and walked back toward the plaza, where the rest of the cops seemed to be marshaling for an assault on the interior.

The cruiser's air conditioner was running and the coolness felt refreshing after the blistering heat radiating off the pavement. Bill sighed and closed his eyes. He tried to find a comfortable position, not an easy task with his hands cuffed behind his back.

It seemed like he was going to be here a while. He wished he had his coffee.

13

"What the hell were you doing inside that rest area with a loaded gun?"

Bill was seated in an interrogation room at the State Police barracks in Lee while a petite auburn-haired woman who had introduced herself rather perfunctorily as "Canfield" paced back and forth in front of him. She seemed angry, affronted that an ordinary citizen might carry a concealed weapon in a public place.

Bill assumed Canfield was a detective, but since she hadn't offered her status during the introduction, he couldn't be sure. One thing he *was* sure of, though, was that she was pissed off and more than willing to let him know it.

He had cooled his heels inside the State Police cruiser for close to forty-five minutes before officers returned and removed the handcuffs, apparently satisfied after speaking with the many witnesses that Bill was one of the good guys, or at least didn't represent the enemy. They had very respectfully informed him they would be driving him to the station—he waited for someone to say "downtown," like they always did on TV but was once again disappointed—where he was going to have to answer a few questions.

The police had been sure to stress he was not under arrest, nor was he considered a suspect in any criminal activity, and they backed up their claim by not cuffing his hands to the iron ring protruding from the middle of the scarred wooden table that dominated the interrogation room.

Aside from that courtesy, though, Bill doubted there was much difference between how he was being treated and how the I-90 Killer might have been treated, had he been apprehended.

Bill watched his interrogator as she stomped back and forth. It was like trying to follow a particularly spirited tennis volley. Canfield stopped short of adopting an accusatory tone but came close. She was clearly trying to lean on him, although for what purpose he could not guess.

Canfield—whether that was her first or last name was unclear, although Bill figured it was the latter, since she was very clearly a woman, and a good-looking one at that, and he had never known a single female with the first name of Canfield in his life—seemed to find it unlikely in the extreme that an ordinary citizen carrying a concealed weapon would happen to be inside the plaza at the exact time the I-90 Killer would try to snatch a girl.

Bill thought the kidnapper had probably found it unlikely as well, and tried to hide a smile. He failed and Canfield stopped right in the middle of a question to ask, "Do you find something funny about this, Mr. Ferguson?"

"Listen," he said. "I'm not the enemy here. I have a valid, up-to-date license to carry that Browning due to business concerns. Feel free to check, although I imagine you already have. I realize that, mathematically, the odds are against me being in the exact position to see an attempted kidnapping and then stop it, but that's precisely what happened. Obviously, the girl and her parents related the same story or I would be sitting in a holding cell right now. So why bust my chops? What do you think you're going to gain from that? I don't expect a ticker-tape parade from you people, but you don't need to flog me with a rubber hose, either."

Canfield leveled her best flat-eyed cop gaze at Bill, amazed by the outburst, her next question apparently forgotten. Then a trace of a smile seemed to tug at the corners of her mouth for just a second before disappearing. She turned without a word and left the room.

Bill waited fifteen minutes before Canfield—Officer Canfield? Detective Canfield? Agent Canfield?—returned and when she did, she was lugging a bulky tape recorder. She took a seat across from him at the table and set the recorder between them. She plugged it in and turned it on.

She recorded initial identifying information, including the date and their names, before starting on a formal interview. The mystery was solved. "Canfield" was FBI Special Agent Angela Canfield, lead investigator on the search for the I-90 Killer.

The FBI was extremely interested in Bill Ferguson as he was the first person they were aware of who had interacted with the elusive I-90 Killer and survived to tell about it, and the authorities wanted to learn every last detail of the encounter.

The other witnesses, all of the people inside the travelers' plaza at the time of the confrontation, were undoubtedly being interviewed as well, but the two the authorities were most interested in would be Bill and the young girl who had been the target. They had gotten closest to the man.

Agent Canfield's initial questions centered around a detailed physical description of the kidnapper. Then Canfield took Bill through a timeline of the attempted abduction from beginning to end. Where was Bill when he noticed something was wrong? What was he doing? What drew his attention to the kidnapper? Why did he feel something was amiss?

After that, Canfield spent a long time questioning Bill about the vehicle he had seen the I-90 Killer driving. He'd gotten a pretty close-up view of it and the authorities wanted as detailed a description as possible to add to the alert that had already been issued.

"It was pretty generic," he said. "A standard truck with an enclosed square cargo box on the back, like a small moving truck. It had obviously been repainted and its color was off-white. It looked like an amateur paint job to me, as the coloring was uneven and beginning to fade."

"What about identifying markings? Name of a business, telephone number, anything?"

"No," he said. "There was nothing on the truck at all that I could see, either on the side of the cargo box or on the passenger side door when he drove by. I can't speak to the other side of the truck but I'd be shocked if it were any different."

"What about the license plate?"

Bill shook his head. "I tried to read it, but there was so much blue smoke pouring from the exhaust on that piece of shit that it totally obscured the tags. I couldn't even make out what state the vehicle was registered in. In fact, I would say the smoke might represent the only real identifying characteristic of the truck. It needs a ring job very badly. Aside from that, the vehicle is completely anonymous. There are probably ten thousand trucks just like it all over the east coast."

From there the interview deviated into Bill's perceptions of the attempted kidnapper. The man had been evading capture by law enforcement for well over three years. Every time they got close he would frustrate authorities by simply disappearing.

"If you had to choose one word to describe this man, what would it be?" asked Canfield.

Bill sat quietly, thinking. The question surprised him. The agent didn't press him for an immediate answer; she seemed to have all the time in the world.

"Arrogant," he finally answered.

"How so?"

"Even when I had my weapon trained right on him, he seemed to feel he was in complete control. Looking back on it now I suppose he was, considering how it turned out. But at no time did he ever seem to doubt his own ability to escape from a situation that had to have appeared pretty hopeless."

"He wasn't nervous?"

"I wouldn't say that," Bill said. "He was definitely nervous; he was sweating up a storm and smelled like he hadn't showered for days. I feel sorry for the poor girl in that regard—he was hugging her like a second skin. But even though he was nervous, he acted like he believed he was smarter than everyone else in the room and could utilize that advantage any time he wanted, to fashion his escape."

Canfield paused, studying Bill. It had been a long time since an attractive woman looked at him that closely—definitely since before the divorce, probably since *way* before—and Bill wasn't about to complain. It seemed clear her interest in him was strictly professional, but still, he had to admit it felt kind of good.

Plus, it was obvious she was trying to formulate a question she didn't quite know how to ask, and he was happy to let her twist in the wind for a while as payback for leaning on him so hard about his gun at the beginning of the interview.

At last she cleared her throat. "Why do you suppose…"

He thought he knew what she wanted to ask but waited her out. Finally she finished, rushing through the question as if embarrassed about asking but still anxious to hear his answer. "Why do you suppose he didn't just shoot you and take the girl? He was holding a human shield, but you had no such protection."

Bill smiled. "I've been asking myself exactly that question since about five seconds after the guy drove away. I really don't have a clue. The only thing I can surmise is that maybe he was afraid shooting me would cause a mass panic and that the rest of the people inside the plaza might stampede wildly toward the door in an attempt to escape, blocking him in. He must have known the cops were on their way and that he had a limited amount of time to get out. After all, this State Police barracks is only a mile or so away from the plaza."

At last Agent Canfield turned off the recorder and unplugged it, winding the cord around the machine. She reached into the breast pocket of her chambray shirt and pulled out a business card, handing it to Bill.

"This has my office number as well as my private cell number on it. If you think of anything else, I don't care how small or unimportant it seems, please call me. Any time, night or day, I don't care. We want to catch this guy, and we want to do it before he takes another girl."

"How is she?" Bill asked.

"Who?"

"The teenage girl the guy tried to kidnap. I don't even know her name. How is she doing?"

Canfield thought about it and laughed. It made her whole face light up and Bill wanted to tell her she should do it more often.

"The girl is fine," she said. "She's a tough kid. Her mother, though, that's a different story. I don't think she's going to let that poor thing out of her sight again. Ever."

Canfield stood and picked up the recorder, indicating the interview was over. "I'll take you back to the travelers' plaza to pick up your vehicle," she said.

"Isn't that kind of a menial job for a big-shot FBI Special Agent?"

She laughed again and said, "We're stretched a little thin at the moment, as you might imagine. Everyone available is back at the rest area cleaning up your mess." She said it with a smile.

The pair walked out of the State Police barracks and the heat rolled over them. The pavement felt soft and mushy underfoot.

"Seriously, though," Canfield said, "nice work back there. You could have been killed but you managed the situation and now that seventeen year old girl is going home with her parents tonight when she could have been dead or God knows where facing an unthinkable fate."

They slid into an unmarked Chevrolet Caprice and Canfield cranked the engine. "I don't know if you've had a chance to think about this, but the media is going to be all over you when we get back to the crime scene. I called our people at the plaza and there are television trucks and reporters everywhere. We can't order you not to talk to them but would prefer that you don't—"

"Don't worry about that," Bill interrupted. "I have zero desire to be a reality TV star."

"Good. We will be behind most of the assembled media when we enter the parking lot, so with any luck you will be able to make it to your van unseen, but I wouldn't hold out too much hope on that score. I'm sure they're staking out your vehicle just waiting for you to come back to pick it up."

"If they know which one it is."

"They'll know."

The pair cruised westbound along the interstate to Exit 1, then crossed over the highway and turned back east. Less than five minutes later, Canfield eased the unmarked vehicle into the massive service area parking lot. She wasn't kidding when she told Bill the media would be buzzing around the location like bees at a honey pot. He pointed out his van and the FBI Special Agent pulled to a stop as close to it as she could manage without alerting the throng of reporters to their presence.

"Good luck," she said as he opened his door, "and remember what I told you. Feel free to call me any time if you think of anything else that might be helpful. No detail is too small."

Canfield handed him his gun with a smile. "I know it will be tempting, but try not to use this on those vultures out there." She nodded toward the gathered mass of television and newspaper reporters milling about at the front of the parking lot.

Bill secured the weapon in the shoulder holster under his jacket and stepped out of the car, walking casually toward his van, covering roughly half the distance before being spotted. The horde of media turned their attention from the front of the service plaza toward Bill as he picked up his pace. Television cameras tracked his progress; questions were shouted. He reached his van and yanked open the driver's side door as the speediest of the news people shoved microphones in his face.

"I have no comment," Bill said, grimacing and shaking his head at the chaotic scene. It occurred to him that he had felt safer and more in control with the I-90 Killer's gun stuck in his face than he did right now.

He eased the door closed, using his right hand to shove three stubborn microphones out of the way while he pulled on the handle with his left. He could have closed the door on the reporters' hands with no problem at all. These people were relentless.

The van started with a rumble and Bill pulled carefully around the men and women holding cameras, microphones and notebooks, making his way slowly toward the on-ramp and the freedom of the interstate.

Finally he broke loose from the crowd and accelerated away, anxious see Carli, who by now would be home from school. It was a weekday, so she would be at Sandra and Bob's home rather than at Bill's apartment, but he didn't think Sandra would mind him stopping by for a few minutes to chat with Carli. It was something he really needed to do right now.

That blonde teen who had come so close to being taken by the gunman at the travelers' plaza reminded him so much of his own seventeen year old child that he needed to see his little girl for himself, to hug her and tousle her hair the way she hated, to see her and talk to her and feel her. To convince himself she was okay and not the unwitting victim of some random act of violence committed by a mentally unstable nut with a gun.

Because you never knew.

That was the lesson of the day. You just never knew.

14

Martin Krall sat on his threadbare couch staring at the TV, a dirty glass of flat cola warming on the table next to him. The porn videos he had planned on watching were forgotten for the time being because something even more interesting had caught his attention. The moment he arrived home he had flicked on the television, certain he would be able to find breaking news reports from back at the travelers' plaza, but the scene that greeted his eyes he almost could not believe. The highway rest area was a madhouse. All the local stations had preempted their afternoon programming in favor of live coverage of the attempted kidnapping.

Apparently, the breathless reports went, a citizen inside the building had thwarted the I-90 Killer in his attempt to abduct another girl, his fourteenth over the past three-and-a-half years, the first time the infamous outlaw had ever been unsuccessful.

On the screen, reporters interviewed the victim's tearful mother as she stood in the shade of the overhang on the top step just outside the entrance to the travelers' plaza. Her arm was wrapped tightly around her daughter's shoulder and it appeared she had no intention of removing it. Ever. The blonde girl looked as though she would rather be anywhere else in the world.

Martin's heart ached. She was so beautiful. He already missed her immensely.

"It was incredible," the woman was telling an unseen reporter. "This man, Bill Ferguson they tell me is his name, he risked his life to save my little girl. He stared down the barrel of that lunatic's gun and saved her life. Then the police came and he just disappeared. I don't know what happened to him or where he went, but I didn't have a chance to talk to him or even thank him for the tremendous risk he took. Mr. Ferguson, if you're out there, you are a true hero. Thank you from the bottom of my heart."

Martin felt a tide of anger rising inside him as he watched the disgusting display on his television. He wanted to pull his gun out and shoot the woman right through the screen. That girl she was so obsessively hugging to her bosom should have been his. She *was* rightfully his, and she had been taken away by that fucking asshole busybody who didn't have a shred of common sense.

Why in the holy hell did he have to stick his nose into a situation that was clearly none of his business? Didn't a loaded gun mean anything anymore? Martin was flabbergasted. None of what had happened today made the least bit of sense.

The more he thought about, the more he realized he had been wronged, had suffered a personal insult. He was not about to take it lying down.

The old Martin Krall would have curled up in the fetal position like some pathetic loser when life dealt him a bad hand. No more. The new and improved Martin Krall knew you had to fight for yourself in this world. You had to go after *what* you wanted *when* you wanted it, because no one else was going to get it for you.

On television the cameras tracked the reluctant hero as he climbed into his vehicle, clearly anxious to escape. Questions were shouted at him from every direction and he ignored them all.

"No comment," he said as he pulled his door shut and started his van's engine. He pulled forward slowly and carefully, the reporters moving out of the way only with the utmost reluctance and only at the point of being run down.

The man's van lumbered left to right across the screen as he accelerated toward the on-ramp. He was driving a Ford Econoline panel van. Stenciled across the side in big gold block letters against a blue background were the words FERGUSON HARDWARE. Underneath, in smaller print, were words Martin could not make out. He assumed they were the locations and telephone numbers of his stores.

No matter. Bill Ferguson was the man's name. And even

though "Ferguson" was a fairly common name, Martin also knew he owned one or more hardware stores.

Question: how many Bill Fergusons could there be in the area who also owned hardware stores?

Answer: probably not many.

Probably only one.

Undoubtedly only one, in fact.

He took a sip of his warm cola and reached for the remote, changing the input on his television so he could watch a DVD. A long, lonely night stretched endlessly in front of him with no blonde teenaged companionship to help pass the time.

That was the fault of one person and one person only. But it was okay, because Martin had all the information he needed to begin rectifying the situation.

It was time for a little porn and some planning.

15

Bill stood on the oversized farmer's porch running the length of the colonial style home and rang the doorbell.

He hoped Carli would be the one to answer the door but knew it was unlikely. She was probably upstairs finishing her homework or listening to music or texting her friends.

The intense heat had barely abated even though it was now nearly dinnertime, and Bill was thankful for the shelter the porch provided from the direct sunlight. He hadn't realized until now how much the confrontation with the I-90 Killer had taken out of him. He felt shaky, washed out. As soon as he was done here he would drive straight home to his apartment in town and put his feet up, crack a beer, and watch the Sox game.

The door opened and Bill found himself staring into the face of his ex. Crow's feet had begun to show around her eyes and a touch of grey was making inroads on her blonde locks, otherwise Sandra and her daughter were dead ringers. He felt the familiar ache for just a moment and then swallowed it down, locking it away, pasting a pleasant smile on his face.

He never blamed Sandra for leaving; not even after the affair she had begun with her now-husband Bob while still married to Bill. Bill knew it wasn't easy being the wife of a small business owner, particularly when the business in question was a pair of hardware stores continually in danger of being forced into bankruptcy by the big chains. Thus far Bill had managed to keep his business afloat through herculean effort.

That effort came at a price, though. A steep one. All those late nights at the store, serving customers, ordering merchandise, paying suppliers, planning marketing and promotional campaigns designed to help his stores avoid becoming a victim of the chain operations with their fancy storefronts and huge advertising budgets; all of that translated into time spent away from home.

Time spent away from Sandra and Carli.

Eventually all those lonely hours and nights and weeks had become too much for his wife to endure. She began a relationship with an old high school boyfriend who still lived in the area. Bob Mitchell had never married. He was a successful dentist, complete with a thriving practice, a big house and a pool and expensive cars. Most importantly to Sandra, Bill knew, Bob Mitchell was home most evenings for his family, making him a considerable upgrade over her husband.

It had been two years now since Sandra left him, marrying Bob Mitchell six months after that, and even though most of the hurt had dissipated, even though he didn't blame her for doing what she felt she had to do, even though he told himself he had moved on with his life just as she had moved on with hers, there was always a momentary tug of sadness, of pain and regret, whenever he laid eyes on his former wife.

"Bill," she said in surprise, brushing a stray hair out of her eyes, stepping back into the foyer out of the unseasonable late-afternoon heat. "What are you doing here? Are you all right?"

"Sure, I'm all right. Why wouldn't I be?"

"Why wouldn't you be? You've been all over the news this afternoon. Fighting with that awful I-90 Killer. You could have been shot!"

"Oh, that, yeah," he said. "Sorry. I don't know why but it didn't occur to me you might have seen the reports. I mean, I saw all the news trucks and the reporters at the rest area, but it seemed a little unreal to me, like maybe if I ignored it all it might just go away. Guess I was wrong.

"Anyway," he said, suddenly feeling silly but not letting it stop him. "I was wondering if I could see Carli for a couple of minutes. It's been…I don't know…kind of a long day and I just wanted to say hi to her."

Sandra hesitated for half a second and then pulled the heavy door open wider. "Of course. Come on in out of the heat. Wait right here."

Bill stepped inside and his ex-wife pushed the front door closed. The house felt cool and comfortable, a far cry from the stifling temperatures he knew he would face when he went home. A window fan moving stale air around a second-floor one-bedroom apartment could not compare with the comfort of central air conditioning.

He stood awkwardly on the foyer's gleaming hardwood floor as Sandra brushed past, stopping at the foot of the stairway and yelling upstairs to his daughter.

To their daughter.

"Carli, your dad's here!"

From somewhere down the second story hallway came a muffled reply. "Be right there," it sounded like, but Bill could not be sure. She was obviously in her room behind closed doors. Sandra smiled at him and his heart ached.

"So, what the heck happened today?" she asked.

He shook his head. "It all went down so fast I'm not exactly sure. I was having a cup of Smokin' Joe's Coffee at the highway rest stop—"

She laughed. "You always loved that coffee and I never understood why."

"Hey, it's really good," he protested. "Give it a chance and you'll be hooked. Anyway, there I was, minding my own business, getting ready to go back out to the truck when this guy pulls a gun on a teenage girl. He was right in front of me when he did it, Sandra, and nobody else saw a thing. He was hustling her out to the parking lot and in about three seconds would have had her out the door and she would have been gone. And still nobody noticed. So I just reacted and did what I had to do. What anyone would have done, hopefully."

From the top of the carpeted stairway came a sound like a herd of water buffalo stampeding across the African plains. "Daddy, you're a hero!"

Carli bounded down the stairs like a whirlwind, taking them two at a time, launching herself at him off the bottom step and nearly driving him through the closed door and into the front yard. Bill laughed and caught her, grabbing her upper arms and swinging her around like he had been doing since she was a baby. Sandra turned and walked up the hallway toward the kitchen. "I'll give you two some privacy," she said as she rounded the corner.

"Daddy, are you okay? The whole school was talking about what you did today. Even the principal made a big speech during closing announcements at the end of the day about how you saved some girl from the I-90 Kidnapper, and guess what?" she said, her eyes shining with excitement.

Bill smiled. His day was looking up already. "Yes, I'm okay. And what?"

"Cody Small—he's the captain of the football team, Daddy— he came up to me and talked with me all the way to the bus. Cody Small has never paid any attention to me before; I didn't even think he knew who I was!"

"Well, then, it was all worth it." He looked his daughter in the eyes gravely. "Can I let you in on a little secret?"

"Of course. You know you can always tell me anything."

Bill laughed. "Hey, that's supposed to be my line. You stole it from me! Anyway," he said, "that was the whole reason I decided to help that poor girl. I figured you needed a little boost with Cody… what was his name again?"

"Small, Daddy, Cody Small."

"Oh yeah, Cody Mall. That's why I saved that girl, so Cody Mall would talk to you."

Carli laughed. "Small."

"Well, I'm sorry," he told her. "I can't do anything about his height. I've given you all the help I can with this Cody Mall character. The rest is up to you now."

His daughter shook her head. "You're hopeless," she said, but she was smiling widely and Bill knew the trip over here had been well worth it. She kissed him on the cheek. "I've got to get back to my homework."

"Yeah, sure," he said. "I know you're really texting Lauren, telling her this whole Cody Mall story, embellishing it and making up all kinds of cool details that didn't really happen."

She stuck her tongue out at him. "Maybe so, but I'm getting my homework done, too."

Bill opened his arms and gave his daughter a crushing bear hug. She might be seventeen and going off to college next year, but she would always be his little girl. "I love you, sweetheart."

"I love you, too, Daddy."

16

Writhing on Martin Krall's high definition flat-screen TV was a cartoonishly well-endowed blonde. She possessed the hard looks of a used-up young woman who had once been beautiful but was now, after years of drug and alcohol abuse—not to mention the rigors of filming dozens upon dozens of porn flicks—nothing more than cartoonishly well-endowed.

The barest shadow of a long-lost former innocence colored her features as she moaned and groaned, giving the performance an almost comic quality as three young men, probably years younger but cartoonishly well-endowed also, speared various parts of her anatomy with bored, half-attentive expressions.

It was a wasted performance, at least for now, because Martin Krall was engrossed in an Internet search and only paying the barest attention to his TV. He wasn't worried about missing the flick. He could always watch later.

First things first.

And the "first thing" tonight was the fascinating information Martin had been able to uncover about the asshole hero wannabe from earlier today; the guy who had stuck his nose where it didn't belong and in the process ruined a perfectly good kidnapping.

It was unbelievable how much an intrepid explorer could discover on the information superhighway if that explorer was properly motivated. In Martin's case, it didn't even take a whole lot of effort. After all, the TV news whores had given him a leg up on the search by flashing that beautiful, high-definition video sequence of the busybody leaving the scene of the failed kidnapping in his work van. The work van with FERGUSON HARDWARE stamped all over the side.

And just in case there was any doubt in Martin's mind who had fucked up his plan with the blonde teenager—like, say, maybe the guy driving the van was just an employee of Ferguson Hardware and not the actual store owner—the coiffed and blow-dried news pimps had very generously provided Martin with a name as well.

Bill Ferguson.

Of the aforementioned Ferguson Hardware empire.

Armed with that knowledge, finding out all Martin Krall had ever wanted to know about the busybody asshole had simply been a matter of taking the time to read the information generated by properly worded search engine requests. For example, he discovered that Bill Ferguson was the owner of a pair of independent hardware stores in the local area, one in the town of Canaan Center, New York, and the other—the home office!—located in West Stockbridge, Massachusetts.

Bill Ferguson was forty-three years old, two years divorced, with an ex-wife who had remarried not long after ending the relationship. He maintained an apartment in the local area in order to remain close to—and here was the best part, the deliciously-cosmically-perfect part, the juicy-cherry-on-top-of-the-vengeance-banana-split part—his daughter Carli, a seventeen year old slim, athletically inclined blonde high school senior.

The perfect replacement for the prize Martin had lost today, in other words.

The girl lived during the week with her mother and new stepfather, owner of a thriving dental practice, but spent most weekends with her father, the busybody asshole wannabe hero himself.

After just fifteen minutes of digging online Martin had already decided exactly what he was going to do and exactly how he was going to do it. He almost could not believe his good fortune. This was perfect. It was as if the gods of karma were telling him the little chickie he had tried to snatch this afternoon was simply not good enough for him, that another girl would be a much better fit.

And now he knew who that girl was. Her name was Carli Ferguson and, incredibly, she lived no more than thirty minutes away from this very living room. Over the course of the last three years plus, Martin had been careful to spread his kidnappings over a very wide geographical area, an area covering more than five hundred miles of Interstate 90. He was certain that caution—among other important factors—had resulted in the authorities not having the slightest clue as to the location of his home base.

They wanted him badly, but they would never find him, not even after today's massive fuckup.

The drawback to his cautious approach was that at times he was forced to spend days at a time on the road far from home, scoping out potential victims. It wasn't a big deal, Martin Krall had never considered himself a homebody, but the last thing he wanted to do after snatching a sweet, juicy girl was to spend upwards of an entire day on the road transporting his prize home.

Unfortunately, after the first couple of kidnappings he had been forced to do exactly that, even resorting to spending many extra hours traversing back roads rather than cruising the interstate, all to throw off the nosy-ass authorities. Even though Martin was just about positive his vehicle was unknown to the law enforcement community—at least until today—it had still become far too risky to transport his companions along I-90 after picking them up, what with those inconvenient Amber Alerts causing roadblocks, and suspicious police officers all along the east coast examining the interiors of passing vehicles with suspicion in their eyes and murder in their hearts.

So the fact that his soon-to-be special friend Carli Ferguson happened to live in the immediate area was one more stroke of good fortune, all of which lead Martin to the conclusion that she might actually be the perfect temporary companion, the one special girl he had been searching for all these years. Time after time he thought he had found her, only to discover upon closer inspection that the girl's eyes were placed too close together, or she refused to shut the fuck up when ordered to, or she was too tall or too short or weighed a couple of pounds too much.

It was always something.

None of that mattered in the long run, of course, since seven days was such a short period. It was a mere drop in the bucket of time, really. But Martin considered himself extremely discriminating, and although he could still have plenty of fun with a companion who possessed a few flaws, he had lived his life waiting and hoping that the perfect girl would eventually appear. The search had been exhausting, both mentally and physically, and there were times when Martin had begun to fear he would never find her, that she was nothing more than the figment of an overeager and overheated imagination.

But now, with the perfection of Carli Ferguson nearly in his grasp, Martin felt like climbing onto his roof and shouting out to the world, "Yes! Yes! This girl is the one!"

The world, of course, would remain for the most part supremely uninterested, but Martin didn't let that knowledge interfere with his enjoyment of the scenario.

He navigated to the website of Stockbridge High School. Carli Ferguson was an athletic-looking girl and Stockbridge was a small town, so Martin figured there was a better than average chance she played at least one sport at the varsity or JV level.

First he checked out the softball team's page. No luck. She was listed on the roster as a varsity infielder, but Martin didn't care about that. He was looking for a picture.

No luck under field hockey either.

Then he clicked on the girls' soccer link and smiled as his patience and hard work was at last rewarded. Filling the screen as a background for the listing of the Stockbridge Girls Varsity Soccer roster and a rundown of the team's wins and losses from the previous season was a full-color action photograph of none other than his angel, Carli Ferguson herself!

She had just scored a goal and was captured at the apex of an exultant leap in the air, high-fiving two teammates on a sun-dap-pled late-fall afternoon. Her blonde hair, pulled into a ponytail, hung perpendicular to the ground at the top of her leap, her cream-colored satin uniform jersey pulled taut against her smallish breasts. She featured the toned legs of an athlete, long and coltish, as her physique had struggled to keep pace with her body's growth.

In short, and just as Martin had already known, she was perfect. He admired the photograph of his soon-to-be companion, lost in his fantasies, still paying no attention to the artificial ecstasy play-ing out on the television screen in front of him. He mused about karma; about how he had spent such a long time this afternoon picking out the girl he had hoped would be *The One* back at the rest stop, only to have her wrenched from his grasp by that asshole with the gun who didn't have a clue how to mind his own damned business.

Now, though, it was obvious to Martin that the fates had been at work. The girl he had chosen back at the travelers' plaza was unworthy; he could see that with the benefit of hindsight. The one he had nearly been stuck with was not quite tall enough and her dishwater blonde hair was dull and lackluster compared to Carli Ferguson's, whose golden locks seemed somehow to contain rays of sunshine itself.

He stared at the computer screen, awestruck by the magnitude of what had taken place this afternoon; by the ability of the universe to maneuver people and events in its own way to accomplish the proper scenarios.

It was practically an epiphany. If Martin had been a religious man, he might have said it *was* an epiphany.

Martin would have been thankful for Bill Ferguson's interference, but for the knowledge that the hero wannabe had had nothing to do with this afternoon's good fortune. That had been karmically preordained: it happened because Martin Krall was meant to possess Carli Ferguson. There was no more or less significance to Bill Ferguson's appearance at the travelers' plaza than that.

He gazed at her photograph, imagining the things they would do together, and marveled that such an angel had been produced by the likes of Bill Ferguson, so clearly a representative of the shallow end of the gene pool.

And that was the best part. In addition to finally possessing *The One*—his soul mate, the girl who would worship him and serve him and make this whole dreary existence worthwhile, at least for a short time—Martin Krall would enjoy the added bonus of fucking with that gun-toting asshole Bill Ferguson.

Because even though it was preordained that he experience a week of bliss with the angel Carli Ferguson, he would still derive tremendous fucking satisfaction out of making that stupid bastard Bill Ferguson's life a living hell. The damned fool would regret the day he had ever stepped between Martin Krall and Martin Krall's objective.

Martin shut down his laptop, but only after making Carli's goal-scoring photo the background on his computer screen, so he might gaze upon the sight of his angel whenever he booted up the machine.

He discovered he was hard as a rock and horny as hell and why wouldn't he be? The visions dancing in his head of the things he and Carli Ferguson were going to do together would make a priest abandon his vows. Hell, they would turn a saint into a sinner, and as far as he knew, no one had ever accused Martin Krall of being a saint. Nor were they likely to.

He turned his attention to the big-screen television taking up most of one wall in his living room. The credits were rolling across a black background, something Martin had always thought was ludicrous. Credits for a porn flick? Okay, people might want to know the name of the star, so they could buy her other movies, but who the hell cared what the director's name was? It's not like anyone would confuse *Naughty Nurses Five* with a lost classic from Alfred Hitchcock.

Martin snickered to himself at the picture of fat Alfred shooting video of naked models, directing them on the proper technique for displaying their assets—"No, no, no, butt *higher* in the air, *higher!*"—and thumbed the "Play" button on his remote. Instantly the film began again, the same tired blonde with the same used-up features writhing and moaning in the same patently phony way, but Martin didn't care.

All he saw when he looked at the screen was Carli Ferguson, and she wasn't used up at all.

Not yet, at least.

17

The dream is always the same.

You're lying in bed, tucked under the covers, fresh from a bath, squeaky-clean and warm. You fall asleep almost immediately, because there is so much to do when you're eight or nine or ten years old and you're so tired at the end of the day. You're not sure of your age, exactly— it is a dream after all—but you know you're very young, of that much you're sure.

After midnight—it's always after midnight when it happens—your bedroom door cracks open and a sliver of hallway light flashes across your carpeted floor, followed immediately by the figure of a man. He is tall and bulky but he moves with surprising stealth and speed. He sits on the edge of your bed as you pretend to sleep. The springs squeal, protesting the added weight of his body, and he knows you are awake, that you are only pretending to sleep, but you do it anyway. You can't help it.

You know what's coming; it's the same thing that is always coming. You wish it weren't but wishes don't matter, even in dreams.

Especially in dreams.

The man places his hand tenderly atop your head and strokes your hair, gently, almost reverently. Soon his touch takes on a more insistent quality and he begins to caress your face. His hand feels fevered, sweaty.

"I know you're awake," he whispers.

You open your eyes at his words and shake your head in mute protest at what you know is about to happen but it doesn't matter. It never matters. The man traces the bony contours of your prepubescent body with his rough hands. He is breathing harder now, harsher. His respiration comes in gasp-like bursts; he is nearly panting.

Finally he hooks his fingers under the waistband of your flannel pajama bottoms—the ones with Aladdin and the Genie on them, they are your favorites and you wear them to bed whenever you can—and slides them over your hips and down your legs. Then he does what he came to do, finishing quickly and then leaving the room without a word. The door closes silently behind him and the room is plunged into darkness.

It's painful and terrifying and no matter how many times he does it—and it's a lot of times, two or three times a week, sometimes more—you never get used to it, it never gets any easier, and you press your face into your pillow and you want to scream, but you never do.

You never scream.

18

Martin sat patiently in his car as it idled on the side of the road. He had positioned himself roughly half the distance between Carli Ferguson's high school and her mother's home on the route he knew she would take after school. He knew because he had been watching her for days.

The first day of his surveillance, Martin had parked his little Nissan in the lot of an anonymous convenience store located not far from her neighborhood. He much preferred the comfort of his box truck with its specially fitted cargo hold when hunting, but he thought it might be expedient to stay away from the truck for a while. He'd parked it parked safely out of sight inside his garage, and there it would stay for the foreseeable future.

He had always known there might come a day when the cargo truck became radioactive. He had prepared for that eventuality, planning ahead as he always did. For years Martin had garaged his Nissan at his mother's home three towns away. The inconvenience was a hassle but now his foresight was paying off—he had a vehicle at his disposal known to virtually no one.

After pulling into the convenience store lot, Martin made his way inside and purchased a soda, not because he wanted one but because he knew it was unlikely the manager would chase him off the property—for a little while at least—if he sat in his car sipping a drink he had just purchased inside the store.

A few minutes later, a big yellow school bus came roaring by, traveling much too fast as school buses always seemed to do.

Martin made a mental note that if the bus was involved in an accident and any harm came to his angel before he was able to snatch her, he would research the name of the careless driver and extract his own form of justice.

He allowed the bus to pass the store, then started his car and followed at a distance, stopping and waiting as students exited, just another anonymous motorist stuck behind the bus. Eventually the rig arrived at Carli's stop, the one just down the street from her stepfather's house, and he watched closely, waiting for Carli to exit, but she never did.

Apparently she preferred walking home from school to riding the bus. Why that would be, Martin had no idea, but he wasn't about to complain. He hadn't finalized his approach yet, but knowing she sometimes went home on foot would add a few options.

Martin Krall was a big fan of options.

The following day, Martin had chosen a parking spot across the street and down the road from the high school, in the direction Carli would have to walk to get home. He hoped she was not going to visit a friend's house right after school and figured his chances were pretty good that she would not. His theory was that an All-American type like her would go straight home and complete her homework before doing anything else.

Problem was you could never be too sure in this day and age. Parents were just so lax.

But he was right.

As usual.

Five minutes after two, shortly after the kids spilled out the school's front doors like bees exiting a hive, Carli Ferguson had come strolling along the sidewalk, engaged in an animated conversation with another girl roughly her age. Martin assumed the girl must be Carli's best friend, and the friend wasn't exactly ugly—in fact, under normal circumstances, Martin would at least have considered her an intriguing possibility as his next companion—but he only had eyes for Carli.

She was dressed in tight jeans featuring torn denim across the front of both legs in the current style of teens everywhere. He didn't understand why anyone would pay good money for clothes that were already ripped and torn, but figured it must be a generational thing. The pants were skin-tight and accentuated her butt perfectly, so Martin wasn't about to complain. A loose-fitting white T-shirt with the words "Life is Good" framing a smiling cartoon face were tucked into the front of her jeans, with the shirttail hanging over the back, fortunately not obscuring the view too badly.

In short, Carli Ferguson looked like a typical high school girl. She could have been any one of a million similarly dressed girls walking home from any one of a thousand similar schools in any one of a thousand small towns across the country.

Except she wasn't typical, not even a little bit. She was Martin's angel; the girl who would help him rise above a mundane and ordinary existence. She would give him a week in heaven.

The pair walked right by Martin's car, passing a scant few feet away from him. He had told himself he would drive away as soon as he saw Carli approach but then had become so enthralled by the girl's natural beauty and innocently suggestive sexuality that he simply forgot to leave.

Not that it mattered; Carli and her friend were so involved in their conversation he could have played with himself as they went by and they would never even have noticed.

That was yesterday. Today Martin had chosen the convenience store parking lot again, for the simple reason it was closer to Carli's house. He knew that her friend, the cute one whose beauty paled in comparison to Carli's, lived somewhere between the school and his angel's home, although he wasn't exactly sure where. It was important at this stage that she have company when he approached, in order that he not unduly frighten her.

Sitting in the parking lot of the same convenience store twice in three days was by no means ideal. He knew he was exposing himself to a certain measure of risk, but the goddamned town Carli lived in was so small there weren't a lot of reasonable options.

Oh well, he thought. *Both times would be before the actual kidnapping, which makes it highly unlikely any of the sheep will notice anything out of the ordinary. And besides, anything worth having—particularly Carli—is worth taking a few chances to acquire.*

He had just taken a bite from his bag of chips and cracked open his soda when Carli and her friend rounded the corner, meandering down the sidewalk that would take them past the store and on to their homes. Like yesterday they were deeply involved in a conversation that seemed to take place to the exclusion of everything else; certainly to the exclusion of any significant awareness of their surroundings.

Martin wondered what they were discussing. Boys, probably, although that particular subject would become moot once she became his companion, and certainly when she moved on afterward. She would have no need for anyone else when she was with him, and no opportunity for anyone else after that.

Finally the pair reached the convenience store parking lot, heads together, both of them giggling at something Carli's friend had just said, and as they walked past, Martin opened his car door and strolled causally to a point roughly ten feet in front of them.

They still hadn't taken any notice of him, or anything else for that matter.

He held his soda can in one hand and a plain white envelope in the other. "Excuse me," he said in a voice just loud enough to be heard.

Both girls glanced at him simultaneously, their faces instantly drawing down into identical looks of sullen suspicion, the universal expression teens display when being addressed by an adult. Especially an adult they don't know.

Carli's friend looked around as if to be sure the older stranger was actually talking to them.

He was. Nobody else was within earshot.

For a moment no one spoke, and then Carli answered tentatively, "Yes?"

Martin's heart soared. He had hoped his angel would be the one to answer, and she had. Her voice was sweetly feminine, melodic and pleasing, just as he had known it would be, even despite the element of suspicion currently shading her tone.

Kids today were so distrustful. It was a damned shame. Martin blamed nervous parents for that.

This was where it would get interesting. Martin knew if he seemed too anxious or came on too strong he would spook his new companion and her friend. "Yes...uh..."

He tried to put just a touch of uncertainty in his voice. Kids ate up vulnerability. They were drawn to it. Martin called it the Lost

Puppy Principle. "Um, is one of you Carli Ferguson?"

The girls looked at each other uncertainly. "Why do you want to know?" his angel finally asked.

"I'm sorry," Martin said with what he hoped was a disarming smile. "I didn't mean to frighten you. I'm an old friend of Carli Ferguson's dad, Bill. We ran into each other recently and it got me thinking about how much fun it would be to get together after all these years. Unfortunately, I don't know exactly where he lives. I know his daughter attends Stockbridge High School, though, and I kind of thought one of you might be her. I just wanted to ask Carli to deliver a note to my old friend."

He held the envelope up for their inspection. "I guess I was mistaken. Sorry to have bothered you."

Martin turned and took a step back toward his car. After a hesitation of perhaps half a second, Carli said, "I'm Carli Ferguson."

Martin smiled widely and then once again rearranged his features into a look of bland disinterest before turning back around to face the girls. He held the envelope out. "I'm sorry, I didn't see who said that. Which one of you is Carli?"

19

Bill blinked in surprise when he saw his daughter waiting for him in the hallway outside his apartment door. "Hey, honey, this is an unexpected pleasure."

He crinkled his forehead suspiciously. "Wait a minute. It's not Friday, is it? Did I sleep through two days or something? Have I been Rip Van Winkled? Are you here for the weekend?"

"No, Daddy, it's not Friday." She shook her head with a grin. "Do I really have to wait until the weekend to see my favorite dad?"

"You don't even have to wait another second. Come on in." He opened the door with a flourish and Carli bounced inside.

He followed her in and then peered back out the door, down the dimly lit hallway. "Where's your mom?"

"At home."

"Well, then, how did you get here? Did you use her car?"

"Who needs a car? I walked, silly. It's not that far."

"Does she know you're here?"

"Of course."

Bill sighed. It was sometimes hard to believe how big his only child was getting. Hell, she was practically an adult.

When she was a baby he'd thought that most of the worrying would end as she got older. It turned out the worrying never ended; you just focused on different concerns. That was the dirty little secret about parenting—there was no finish line, you just kept going and going, hoping you were running the race properly but most of the time not knowing whether you were even still on the course.

He reached for his wallet. "So, how much do you need?"

"I'm not looking to borrow money."

Bill laughed. "That's a relief. I was bluffing. I don't actually have any cash on me. But I am curious why you're here hanging out with your old man instead of plotting with Lauren how to catch Cody Mall's eye. Not that I don't appreciate the attention."

He moved to the kitchen sink and filled a teapot with water, placing it on the ancient stove. "Tea?"

"It's Small, Daddy. Cody Small. And sure, I'd love a cup of tea. Anyway, I'm here on a very important mission."

"Really. A mission. Now I'm intrigued."

Carli handed him a plain white envelope with the words MY FRIEND BILL handwritten on the front in black marker in carefully constructed block letters.

Bill turned it over in his hands, puzzled. "Okay, I give up. What is this?"

"How would I know? It's addressed to you. That's why I brought it here."

"Well, I can see it's addressed to me. Where did *you* get it?"

"Your friend gave it to me while Lauren and I were walking home from school today."

"And what friend would that be?"

Carli heaved the exasperated sigh only a teen can master. "How should *I* know? It's your friend! Why don't you open it and find out?"

A vague sense of unease wormed its way through Bill's belly. He couldn't imagine a single old friend who would approach his daughter out of nowhere and hand her a letter addressed to him. Something was not right.

Bill set the letter aside on the kitchen table as a shrill whistle erupted from the teapot. He would open it later, after Carli had gone home.

She watched him with a look of incredulous disbelief. "You mean you're not going to open it? Aren't you curious? Maybe it's someone you haven't seen since, like, high school. Did they even have a real high school back when you were a kid, or was it just a one-room schoolhouse?"

"Yes, wise guy, they had a real high school when I was your age.

It was *two* rooms, for your information. And if this letter is from someone I haven't seen in twenty-five years, it won't hurt to wait another hour or so, while I enjoy the limited time I have to spend with my little girl. Let's have some tea, shall we?"

Bill chatted with Carli as they sipped their tea, asking about her grades, her friends, her plans for the rest of the day, all the while pondering the mysterious letter she had given him. He couldn't quite put his finger on what bothered him about it other than the certainty that no adult he knew would consider approaching someone else's child, especially a teenage girl, out of the blue if he didn't know her.

He wouldn't do it and he couldn't imagine anyone else doing it, either.

But what was the point of handing her a letter and then turning around and leaving? Bill found his curiosity mounting, along with his concern, and was almost relieved when Carli announced it was time to return home. "*I* have homework to do, you know. I'm not like you; I can't sit around all day drinking tea and hanging out."

"Oh, I know," he answered, carrying the empty teacups to the sink and dropping them in with a clatter. "The life of a modern teenager is just one obstacle after another."

"So true. I'm glad we understand each other."

"Come on," Bill said. "I'll drive you home."

"You don't have to do that. I told you, it's not that far, and it's a beautiful day. I'm not old like you, I can walk it with no problem."

Bill smiled, this time without conviction, his thoughts on mysterious letters and unknown men approaching teenagers on the street.

"No," he said firmly. "I'll drive you."

20

Hello, Mr. Ferguson, the letter read.

That's quite the beautiful young girl you have there. Carli is a fitting name, too. Pretty and distinctive without being overbearing.

Just like her, if I may be so bold.

It is not a name that says, 'Look at me, I'm cute and adorable!' But she has no need to shout to the world about how cute and adorable she is; everyone can see it, don't you agree? Of course you do, you're the proud daddy.

She strikes me as intelligent and independent, too, although of course I've not plumbed the depths of her personality and physicality yet as we've only just met. I'm sure as I get to know her better—more intimately, if you will—I will discover all the many endearing facets of her totality.

That is something I am so looking forward to.

You see—and I'm sure a smart man like you can already see where I'm going with this—thanks to your unnecessary interference a few days ago, I am now lacking companionship, and certain acquaintances of mine have had their delivery schedules disrupted. These are not people who readily accept such disruptions, either.

At first I was very angry with you, Bill. May I call you Bill? I know it seems a trifle forward of me, since we've only met the once, and at gunpoint besides, but sharing someone as close to both of our hearts as Carli by definition makes us close as well, don't you think?

Anyway, as I did a little research into the man who ruined my carefully laid plans the other day, I discovered to my surprise and delight that you didn't interfere with me at all!

No, Bill, it turns out you weren't responsible for stopping me from securing that young lady at the rest area. It was fate. And why would fate do such a thing, I asked myself, especially when fate had ensured success so many times in the past?

Well, Bill, I got my answer when I began checking into the background of that asshole busybody who refused to mind his own business (I am referring to you, Bill, in the unlikely event I'm not making myself clear).

By the way, it was awfully generous of the news media to provide me with all that breathless coverage of your heroic and selfless act. I was able to learn, right from the comfort of my own couch, who you are and what you do (Really, Bill, hardware stores? Really? How boring. How pedestrian. I would have figured you for, I don't know, dentistry perhaps. Oh, wait, I'm sorry, that's the profession of the man who took your wife. I so hope I'm not touching a raw nerve, Bill.)

Anyway, when I conducted my research into this man who had become an instant thorn in my side, you can imagine my surprise when I discovered that the asshole busybody who refused to mind his own business has a daughter of his own. An angel, seventeen years old, blonde, beautiful and—if I may be so bold, Bill—incredibly sexy as well!

That was when the pieces all came together in my mind. Fate knew, Bill! Somehow fate knew that the girl I had mistakenly selected as my latest companion was not right for me. So instead of allowing me to follow through on my plan and make a grievous error, fate selected you—the father of my true soul mate—to step in and interfere, in order that I might learn of the existence of the lovely Carli.

The logic is perfect and unassailable.

So thank you, Bill, for your role, however accidental, in preventing me from making that awful mistake. And even though I know you were an unwitting tool of the fates, a puppet with but a minor role in this developing love story, I still feel it is only appropriate to offer you my sincerest thanks.

Magnanimous of me, I know, but my heart is filled with such great joy at finally having my true angel within reach that the trivialities that in the past would have caused me anger are now but fleeting concerns, dust in the wind of my happiness, if you will.

I hope I have not bored you, Bill. I understand this missive has been long-winded, but I felt the need to share my joy with someone. Then it occurred to me: Who better to confide the depths of my love to than the man who introduced me to my beloved?

The father of the bride, so to speak.

In closing, Bill, thank you. I would much prefer professing my gratitude in person, but for obvious reasons that can never happen. Please know in your heart that I will watch over my beloved Carli diligently and tirelessly. She is truly my princess and after leaving my side will no doubt serve honorably, wherever she ends up. Of that you may rest assured.

Sincerely,

Your grateful friend

Bill's panic mounted as he read the letter until he sat frozen in terror after reaching the end. Finally he stumbled to the phone, hands trembling, struggling to keep the contents of his stomach from spewing out onto the floor. He punched in Sandra's number and waited impatiently, swearing at the delay as the line rang on the other end. Why the hell had he waited to open the letter? Carli had been right here with him, safe and sound. Now she could be anywhere. She could be gone already.

He paced his tiny kitchen as he waited for his ex-wife to pick up the phone.

He prayed to God she was home.

He prayed to God he was not too late.

21

"Hello?"

"Sandra, it's Bill."

"Bill? Are you all right? You sound terrible, what's the matter?"

"Where's Carli?"

"Carli? Why?"

"Where is she?"

"She's upstairs finishing her homework, Bill, what's wrong?"

"Are you sure?"

"Of course I'm sure. What the heck is going on?"

"When was the last time you actually saw her, Sandra? In person?"

"Jesus, Bill, I don't know, maybe an hour ago. What's happening? You're starting to frighten me and I don't appreciate it."

"I'm sorry Sandra, I really am, but I need you to go up to Carli's room and check on her. Do it right now. I'll hold."

Bill imagined Sandra clutching the telephone receiver in front of her face, staring at it in frustration as if it might hold some answers. Finally she set it down with a *thunk* and he heard her muffled footsteps walking away.

It wasn't his intention to give his ex-wife a fright, but the only thing that mattered right now was making sure Carli was still in her room. Making sure she was okay. Everything else could wait, including explanations. His nerves felt stretched to the breaking point and he wondered whether this was what it felt like just before you suffered a massive heart attack.

He heard the receiver being picked up again. "Okay, Bill, I just disturbed her as she was studying for her big Calculus final. Now do you think you could explain to me why I had to do that?"

She was annoyed.

Bill didn't care. The relief flooded through him and he slid with his back against the wall to a sitting position on the kitchen floor, legs splayed out in front of his body. He was immediately filled with a sense of exhaustion. *Carli was okay!*

"Bill! What the hell is going on here?"

He took a deep breath and proceeded to ruin his ex-wife's day.

22

Special Agent Angela Canfield leaned over Bill's kitchen table, studying the letter intently.

After explaining to Sandra that their daughter had had a close encounter with the I-90 Killer, Bill had hung up and frantically searched for the business card Agent Canfield gave him a few days ago, finally digging it out of his wallet and dialing her personal cell number.

He had no idea what she was doing when he called and didn't bother to ask. Whatever it was, she dropped it like a hot potato when he explained what had happened. Less than half an hour later she was knocking on Bill's door.

She read the letter all the way through without speaking, then immediately returned to the beginning and read it again. Then she tucked a stray hair behind her ear and read it a third time.

Bill watched without interrupting but wanted to see some action. He was nervous and impatient and pretty certain the letter wasn't going to say anything different on the third read-through than it had on the first two.

Canfield leaned back and looked at the ceiling, lost in thought. "We're going to need to speak with Carli," she said, almost as if talking to herself. "And Carli's friend, of course. What was her name again?" She finally looked at Bill.

"Lauren."

"Yes, Lauren. We'll need to talk with both girls as soon as possible."

"Of course," Bill answered. "But what can we do about ensuring about Carli's safety right now? This lunatic approached her on the street and could have snatched her right then and there."

Canfield nodded. "We're way ahead of you. We have already established a police presence outside your ex-wife's home. Carli won't be out of their sight. She will be perfectly safe, Mr. Ferguson."

"Bill."

"Okay, Bill. We'll make sure she's safe. I don't believe she is really in any significant danger, anyway."

Bill raised his eyebrows, stunned. "How can you say that? Didn't you read that letter? What the hell have you been doing for the last fifteen minutes?"

Agent Canfield raised her hands in a *calm down* gesture. "Whoa, easy, Bill. Yes, I read the letter, several times in fact, but think about it. If he really wanted to kidnap Carli his best chance would have been today, before she knew who he was and what he looked like. He had to know that once you read his letter you would react exactly as you did. Police and FBI would be notified, protection would be established, the letter would be analyzed. We'll need to take this, by the way, for forensic analysis. This is not a stupid man, Mr. Ferg— uh, Bill. Impulsive and rash sometimes, sure. Psychotic and delusional, definitely. But stupid? No.

"I believe his intention was to throw a scare into you. To establish payback, so to speak, for interfering with his abduction of Molly Acton, the young girl you saved at the rest area. Obviously, we will have forensics and a psych team analyze the letter, but it is my opinion that the I-90 Killer has accomplished his objective— taunting you—and will now move on to his next victim, and that victim will not be Carli Ferguson."

Bill was quiet. It was his turn to think. What Canfield said made a lot of sense. After all, if nothing else, Carli was now well aware exactly what the I-90 Killer looked like—assuming, of course, he had not been wearing a disguise when he approached her this afternoon, and it sounded as though he had not. He would never again be able to get close to her as easily as he had today.

Still, and he realized he was about as far from a psychoanalyst as it was possible to get, but when he read the letter, something he had done over and over since opening it, what he saw was a man consumed with extracting vengeance from the person who had disrupted his precious plan. And what better way to combine revenge with his sick, twisted little obsession than to kidnap Carli Ferguson?

Canfield carefully refolded the letter on its original creases and dropped it into a clear plastic evidence bag, along with the envelope Bill had sliced along the top.

"We'll need to keep the original," she said, "but will be happy to provide you with a copy if you wish."

Bill shook his head and chuckled, despite the circumstances. "That won't be necessary, Agent Canfield—"

"Angie."

"Excuse me?"

"I said you can call me Angie. After all, it's only fair if I'm allowed to call you Bill. Besides, I have a feeling we're going to be seeing a lot of each other until we catch this guy, so we might as well dispense with the formalities, right?"

"Okay. Angie then. Thank you. Anyway, it won't be necessary to provide me with a copy of that letter. I had every word of it committed to memory before you even arrived. I can recite it beginning to end if you'd like. Backwards, too, probably. I'm pretty sure it's all I'll be thinking about for the foreseeable future."

She nodded. "I understand, but try not to make it into more than it is. Like I said, I think he just wanted to spook you."

"Then he succeeded admirably."

23

The dream is always the same.

The man leaves your darkened bedroom after he has finished with you and the first thing you do—the very first thing, even before crying—is to swear that this time will be the last time. This time you will tell your mother. Morning will come and you will tell her what the man—who is supposed to take the place of your daddy—has been doing to you several times a week for as long as you can remember.

Then you cry. Only then.

You swear to yourself again, in the dark, with your head burrowed into your tear-stained pillow as if trying to escape the madness, that tonight was the last time he will get away with it. Ever. You will tell your mother what he has been doing to you and she will toss the bum out of the house and then call the police for good measure. The police will come to the house in their cool black and white cars with their sirens screaming and their blue lights flashing and they will take the man away in handcuffs and you will never have to see him again.

It is a satisfying fantasy and it never fails to calm your ten-year-old fears.

But the dream, the long-repressed memory, is always the same. You never do tell your mother. You never tell her because, if you're going to be honest with yourself, you are afraid, somewhere in the back of your frightened mind, that she already knows, or at least suspects. She knows or suspects what he has been doing and just won't admit to herself what she knows or suspects. She is either too afraid or too uncaring to take action.

The dream is always the same and you wake up screaming. Unlike during the real-life horrors of your childhood, when you were never able to scream, when you choked down the humiliation and terror, you wake yourself up screaming. Your throat is hoarse, it hurts from all the screaming, but you don't care. You scream.

24

Martin was exhilarated. He hadn't felt this alive since his first couple of successful snatches, and those had taken place years ago. He actually was beginning to believe he owed a debt of gratitude to this Bill Ferguson character for forcing him outside his comfort zone; for making him break away from the same tired ritual he had been performing over and over.

It was patently obvious that finding a new companion was now not going to happen the way he had been operating. He had been successful over a dozen times using the same scenario, but after the near-miss last week, he had to acknowledge that the authorities were becoming too familiar with the travelers' plaza gig.

But somehow that run-in with the busybody asshole who had refused to mind his own business had cleared his head. He had an objective and was totally focused on it: Carli Ferguson. And the best part was that he wouldn't have to go anywhere near a highway rest stop to get her.

Well, that wasn't entirely true. The *best* part was that he could fuck with the busybody asshole at the same time he was accomplishing his objective! He had known that handing the letter to his angel would make realizing his goal more difficult, but anything worth having was worth working for, as his father used to say.

Not that that loser had much personal experience with working.

Besides, the pleasure of a few moments interaction with his angel yesterday had made all the extra effort worthwhile. She had turned out to be everything he imagined and more. She was smart and pretty and exuded the sort of innocent sexuality that really cranked his engine. In fact, he could feel himself getting hard just thinking about her.

And, really, where was the fun in getting what you wanted if it came too easily? As a noted philosopher once said, "life is a journey, not a destination."

Or maybe it was a songwriter, but who gave a fuck? The point was still the same, and it was a good one. Maybe part of the reason he had ultimately been disappointed with his previous companions despite his initial high hopes was because they had all come too easily to him. There was no real challenge in stealing young girls from under the unwitting noses of grazing sheep.

Now, though, things were different. Now he had a challenge worthy of his skills. The authorities knew he was coming to sweep his angel off her feet and they thought they could stop him.

Martin knew exactly how they thought. They would be convinced he wasn't actually going to grab her after passing her that note, but, hey, that was their fucking problem, not his. This time when he welcomed a companion into his home it would be after outwitting the authorities, and even though that would not exactly take an Einsteinian intellect, the hunt would still provide a enough of challenge to maintain his interest.

Hopefully.

Martin looked at his watch and was astounded to discover it was now nearly ten p.m. He had been daydreaming about Carli for over three hours! He smiled at his foolishness; he was acting like a love-struck teenager.

It was okay, though, because a romance like his and Carli's came along only once in a generation. It was a story that inspired great poetry and there was nothing wrong with savoring that.

Still, he was never going to accomplish his goal and experience that romance if he didn't get down to work and make it happen. As enjoyable as it was to sit around and moon about his angel, what he wanted more than anything else in the world was to have her here, to enjoy her in the privacy of his home in all of the ways he craved but "society" said was wrong.

Who in the fuck was "society," anyway? And what right did "society" have to intrude on his love affair?

He felt the familiar rage beginning to bubble just below the surface of his consciousness, like an ocean swell building to a tsunami. He wanted to allow it to consume him; to lose himself in the rage, but with a great force of will pushed it back down out of the way.

For now.

Never mind the restrictions of a society that could not understand his needs. Who cared about them, anyway?

Martin thumbed his remote and a new porn DVD sprang to life on his big-screen TV. He loved porn. The X-rated action relaxed him and formed a backdrop for most of his best thinking. Some people listened to Mozart for inspiration; Martin enjoyed the artificial ecstasy provided courtesy of the adult film industry.

You say tomato, I say tomahto. The point was he had some serious planning to do if he was ever going to be together with his little angel.

Martin Krall relished the challenge. He sipped his drink and got to work.

25

Bill didn't think there was any way he would be able to sleep tonight. The adrenaline was still pounding through his body at a rate nearly as strong as when he first finished reading that taunting letter from the I-90 Killer. He knew at some point in the not too distant future all that adrenaline would wear off and he would crash, feeling headache-y and sick to his stomach.

But fall asleep? No way. It would never happen.

But then he did sleep, and when he did his dreams came all night, nearly non-stop. They were vivid and colorful, free-form, filled with jagged shapes and menacing shadows and threatening monsters. Enemies he could not see or feel or touch assaulted him from all sides. He could hear them, though, and they taunted him, telling him they were going to tear him apart slowly, so that he could feel every limb as it was ripped from his agonized body, count every drop of blood as it spilled from his torn arteries onto the floor.

Interspersed among these non-specific visions of impending doom were other, more detailed dreams. They were like subconscious commercials, breaking up the longer television show dreams that spelled out in excruciating detail Bill's demise or, he thought later as he considered their significance, the demise of someone close to him.

Carli, of course.

The shorter dreams were different; they felt more like flashes of something resembling memory than actual scenarios containing a beginning, a middle and an end. Repressed consciousness or some such similar bullshit, perhaps.

These shorter dreams consisted mostly of brightly rendered flashes of memory from that fateful two or three minute encounter with the I-90 Killer and its immediate aftermath. The dreams featured that familiar quality of cartoonish exaggeration unconscious visions always seemed to employ: edges were much sharper than they had actually been; movements were slowed and magnified in significance. The split-second of time that elapsed between Bill centering his Browning on the back of the retreating I-90 Killer and making the decision to warn the man rather than simply blow him to Hell seemed to elongate. It lengthened and stretched from maybe the half-second it had actually been into several agonized minutes, during which time Bill's gun remained trained on the man but he could not quite bring himself to shoot.

Later in the night, Bill had another "Flash-dream." In this vision of recollection he reached for Molly Acton to pull her behind him and shield her with his body. Just as he did, the I-90 Killer shoved her and sent her crashing into Bill, landing them both in a tangled heap on the floor. In the dream, that process of reaching toward her shoulder seemed to take forever to accomplish. It was no wonder the kidnapper had anticipated the move.

Finally, as dawn approached in his dream-disturbed slumber, Bill watched for what felt like hours rather than just a couple of short seconds as the man drove past in his repainted off-white box truck, the one with no identifying markings, the one that had obviously been repainted so it could NOT be identified. He stared and stared at the truck as it receded, hanging before his searching eyes forever as the I-90 Killer drove away. Something was not quite right but Bill could not put his finger on what it might be. He felt frustrated and angry, like he was missing something of importance.

These short snippets of the remembered encounter were the little mini-commercials interspersed with the longer dreams—the main event, nocturnally speaking—where his body was rent; ripped and torn apart painfully, agonizingly, his screams echoing on and on until they were all he could hear. They were everything. It was the longest night of Bill Ferguson's life.

He awoke to the sound of his dying screams echoing through the tiny bedroom, wondering how many neighbors were cursing him, wondering when the cops were going to show up and serve him with a Disturbing the Peace citation. But they never did. He listened to his heart hammering in his chest as he wiped the sour perspiration from his face with his bed sheet and turned his pillow over, trying unsuccessfully to escape the uncomfortable slick of hot sweat.

Eventually his hammering heart slowed and he again dropped into an uneasy slumber. When he did, the whole crazy cycle began again—the long, horrifying dreams of being pulled apart, broken up only by the shorter, ultra-vivid sequences of exaggerated remembrance from that fateful afternoon.

Finally, as the first hint of dawn's watery arrival began to insinuate itself into his bedroom, Bill raised the white flag of surrender against his subconscious. He threw off the bedcovers, listening to his joints creak and complain as he drew stiffly up to his full height, and stumbled into the bathroom to brush his teeth and face the day.

He wondered if he had gotten more than ten or fifteen minutes of truly restful sleep all night. He doubted it. The entire exhausting evening was nothing more than a jumble of half-remembered nightmares and confusing dream-sequences. Bill Ferguson was a man who rarely dreamed; or if he did, he certainly never remembered most of them. He normally awoke refreshed and reinvigorated.

Today, though, was just the opposite. He tried to make some kind of sense of the vivid nightmares as he dragged his toothbrush back and forth across his teeth and gums, doing his best to saw away the sickly taste of fear and foreboding. Obviously, the longer dreams—the ones featuring his bloody dismemberment—were a demonstration of his almost paralyzing terror at the prospect of losing Carli to the I-90 Killer; the fear that the kidnapper/murderer would take her and inflict upon her whatever horrible tortures he reserved for his victims before finally taking their lives.

Those dreams represented the fear that he would snatch her and hurt her and ultimately kill her and Bill would be left to suffer the knowledge that he could have avoided his baby's awful fate simply by killing the man when he had had the chance.

All of that was obvious; you didn't have to Sigmund Fucking Freud to figure it out.

But the shorter dreams, the ones that seemed as though they were nothing more than tantalizing memories of the actual encounter, those haunted Bill even more because he didn't understand their significance. They seemed to be trying to tell him something, to convey some cryptic message that he didn't understand or couldn't decipher and that he feared might be of the utmost importance.

He walked to his kitchen, the worn vinyl flooring cool and refreshing on the soles of his feet. He started the coffee machine, hoping a good strong shot of caffeine might reduce the pounding in his temples to a somewhat manageable level. If these dreams continued, he thought he might have to invest in a new coffee-maker, one of the fancy models with a timer so the coffee would be ready for him, hot and fresh, when he stumbled out of bed after suffering through eight hours of tortured sleepless misery.

The kitchen table felt foreign as he leaned on it with his elbows, holding the hot coffee with two hands in front of his face, blowing lightly on the steam rising in curlicue patterns off the top. The dreams were beginning to fade from his consciousness; already he could recall only the most terrifying selections from the evening's highlights—a greatest hits compendium of fear—and Bill felt a tug of annoyance. He was convinced there was a significance to them that he was missing.

He shook his head and sipped his coffee and thought about Carli, presumably safe in her bed inside Sandra and Bob's house. He wondered what the I-90 Killer was doing right now and prayed to God Agent Canfield was right when she said the crazy prick had sought out Carli and written the letter only as some sort of cruel mind-fuck.

He didn't care about being messed with; he welcomed it, in fact, if it was all the perverted bastard had in mind. Bill could live with the strange dreams and the frightening nightmares of half-remembered significance if it meant only *he,* and not Carli, was being targeted.

But the fact of the matter was he couldn't be positive that was the case. Sure, Agent Canfield was the professional. She had probably dealt with dozens of cases similar to this one or maybe, God forbid, even worse. And her take on the note made sense. But what if the madman really was spelling out his plans for the immediate future in that letter? What if he really was coming for Carli, as he had stated in plain English?

If the sick bastard was coming for Carli, then his reasoning was irrelevant. Whether he came to get even with Bill or because Bill's seventeen-year-old daughter really did fit his twisted image of female perfection wouldn't matter in the least.

Because it was all Bill's fault.

26

The dream is always the same. You swear you're going to tell your mother what the man is doing to you at night, in the dark, when he comes to you while she is fast asleep and safe in her bed. You swear you're going to tell her but you never do.

Instead you make a promise to yourself, to that frightened, humiliated ten year old huddled in the dark, crying into a pillow with no one to turn to. You promise yourself that you will survive and get even someday. Even if it doesn't happen until you are a full-grown adult like the man, even if it doesn't happen for twenty years—fifty—you will get even.

You lie in the dark hardening your heart, visualizing what you will do and how you will do it, and gradually, slowly, ever so slowly, your tears stop flowing and your sobs stop choking you and you begin to calm your frazzled nerves. You don't fall asleep yet, oh no, it is much too soon for that, you won't fall asleep for hours yet, your mother will wonder why you're always so tired although you will never tell her, but you begin to feel like you might actually be able to survive, to hold on for one more day.

Picturing the vengeance you will reap when you're older works for you. If you were an adult you might recognize you are experiencing what grown-ups call "transference," but you're not older. You are ten years old with no one in the world to turn to and you are just trying to make it through one more interminable night.

The dream is always the same. You are terrified and humiliated and in pain, so much pain, mental and physical pain, and you get through the night by promising to get even. Someday you will get even.

27

There wasn't really all that much to the plan. Even though he had spelled out his intentions, Martin still figured it wouldn't be that difficult to take Carli Ferguson.

The fact of the matter was he was a predator. He was smarter, better prepared, and far more motivated than the herds of sheep grazing in the verdant fields of civilization. Even if the sheep knew the wolf was coming for them, they still were only as bright as... well...*sheep.*

And sheep were no match for the cunning wolf.

So even though it would have been much easier to snatch Carli Ferguson two days ago when she had stood so tantalizingly within his reach, doing it this way would be much more satisfying. He felt like a cat toying with a mouse. Except that when he finished toying, he would have sweet Carli as a prize. And they would share seven days of unimaginable bliss together before she moved on to her final destination.

The time now was a little past noon, and the drive from his home to Stockbridge High School would take no more than thirty minutes. Dismissal time at SHS wasn't until just after two o'clock—that was one of the first details Martin had checked—so there was no need to rush. He had completed his prep work yesterday, driving to Stockbridge and following Carli's school bus as it completed its route, just another anonymous car in the long line of anonymous cars stuck behind the big yellow vehicle as it lumbered down her street.

He had figured, teenage obstinacy being what it was, that Carli would convince her mother to let her take the bus to and from school for the foreseeable future. Obviously she wouldn't be walking home any more, her mother would never allow that and neither would the police. He knew she didn't own a car and was pretty confident she would flatly shoot down any plan that required her to be picked up at the front door of the high school by mommy—that would constitute the most flagrant form of teenage humiliation imaginable.

Thus the school bus would be left as the only reasonable alternative, and after discussing the matter with the police, who were almost certainly staking out the Ferguson home, the reluctant mother would agree to allow her child to ride the bus. She would hesitate, but the police would eventually convince her that they could keep Carli safe as she walked the short distance from the bus to her front door.

Carli would insist she was not going to be picked up at school by her mommy—Martin smiled as he pictured his angel stamping her foot, hands on her hips, to make her point—and the mother would cave.

That had been his working theory and he'd been right on target. He waited in a lot around the corner from the store where he had met Carli—he wasn't crazy enough to park at the convenience store a third time—and as the bus turned the corner he pulled out behind it, three cars back but still with an excellent view of the exiting passengers.

When the bus had screeched to a stop in front of Carli's house, he watched intently as one solitary passenger—his angel!—climbed delicately down the steps and hurried across the front lawn and into her house.

The police were parked across the street in an unmarked blue Caprice, about as subtle as a sledgehammer to the side of the head. Of course the whole thing was just a show of force; they had no reason to believe he would be bold enough to try to snatch her here.

Or anywhere.

The cops were so intent on tracking Carli as she crossed her front lawn that they didn't pay the slightest attention to his vehicle when he drove past them after she disappeared into her house.

Idiots.

That was yesterday, and his little sortie behind enemy lines had given Martin all the information he needed. Today would be the day. It was very soon, some might say too soon, after giving the police and that busybody asshole the advance warning of his intentions, but the plan really was foolproof, so there was no reason to delay.

Plus, and here was the real reason he didn't want to wait, he absolutely ached with need. He missed his angel with an almost physical hurt, he was simply lost without her, and he knew he would continue to feel that way until she was at his side where she belonged.

Well, he wouldn't have to wait much longer.

Just a couple more hours.

* * *

Martin wondered why anyone would ever want to drive a school bus. Despite the fact that he was drawn toward teenage girls like a moth to flame, the notion of spending most of every day trapped inside a gigantic tin can with dozens of them, with their snotty attitudes and lack of manners and often deplorable hygiene, was more than he could stomach. He knew if *he* worked as a school bus driver kids would end up dead, probably before the end of the first run on his first day on the job.

He wondered about the apparent contradiction of a man who preferred the company of children—pedophile was the proper term, but he steadfastly refused to use or acknowledge that word; the girls he chose as companions were practically full-grown adults—choosing to avoid them for the most part.

Maybe that was why he would never be caught. He was very different from most others of his ilk; men who worked as schoolteachers or counselors or sports coaches or scout leaders or priests because of the opportunities those positions afforded to get close to children. Martin had never really enjoyed being around children, with the exception, of course, of the select few, the ones he picked out to serve as his special companions.

Thus far, three and a half years into his project, he had chosen well on some occasions and poorly on others, but he knew, he was absolutely one hundred percent fucking *certain*, that Carli Ferguson would be perfect for him.

And why wouldn't she be? He hadn't chosen her, not really. The fates had. And that made all the difference in the world.

Martin sat inside his idling car pondering these and other philosophical questions as he waited on the side of a quiet redneck back road somewhere in Stockbridge. He didn't know the name of the road but didn't care either. It was on the outskirts of town, the farthest fringes of Stockbridge, past the water treatment plant, on the very edge of civilization where the forest reclaimed the landscape.

The nearest house—besides the one he was watching—was probably a quarter-mile away, and that was assuming the broken-down double wide with the front door hanging halfway off its hinges was even inhabited.

This was where Carli's bus driver lived. Martin knew it was where she lived because he had followed her home last night at the end of her shift.

In this little town, as in small towns everywhere, the school bus drivers ferried kids to the high school first thing in the morning, then a few minutes later they ran the same routes all over again, this time bringing kids of a slightly younger age to the middle school, and then repeated the whole routine one more time a few minutes after that to bring the youngest children to the town's only grade school.

At the end of the school day they performed the same ritual all over again, bringing the kids back to their homes from the three schools in the same order: the high school classes ended first, followed by the middle school and lastly the grade school. In between, the drivers had a couple of hours to themselves and were allowed to park their buses at their homes rather than take them all the way to the bus company's lot and have to pick them up later.

The driver of Carli's bus, a squat, middle-aged woman with a massive head of frizzy brown hair and sweat stains under her armpits, should be walking out the front door of her dumpy little ranch-style home to begin the afternoon shift any second now.

When she did, Martin would be waiting for her. She had backed the bus into her gravel driveway after the morning shift, a fairly impressive feat, he thought, considering the relative sizes of bus and driveway. Now it loomed next to her house, a hulking yellow tin can, facing the road as if prepared for a quick getaway.

Right on cue, the front door swung wide and out waddled the frumpy driver. Martin gunned his engine, pulling the little car skillfully across the end of the driveway, coasting to a stop in front of the bus's grille as the woman watched, her mouth forming a surprised "O."

Martin could almost see the question mark hanging in the air over her head. She wasn't afraid, at least not yet, she was just curious. That was why he had come in so fast. He had discovered that if you caught them before they had time to realize they should be scared, the sheep were much easier to deal with. More compliant.

He put his best insincere I'm-just-a-huckster-with-some-swampland-to-sell-you smile on his face and stepped out of the car, crossing the front yard's burned-out brown grass in a few long strides. It was obvious the woman could give a shit less about the condition of her property. It was only late-May for chrissakes; the lawn shouldn't be in this kind of horrible condition for another two months yet.

"Excuse me, ma'am," he started out, "I'm so sorry to intrude, but I was wondering…" He was making it up as he went, riffing, enjoying the opportunity to fuck with a stranger. He hardly ever interacted with people and this was kind of fun.

I really should get out more.

By now he had almost reached the woman and it was just beginning to dawn on her that something was wrong. The shit-eating grin Martin had plastered on his face was only effective from a distance. Up close, people seemed to recognize that the smile was a put-on, because the good humor it implied never quite reached his eyes. Martin could see the exact moment the alarm bells started going off in her head, the panic beginning to blossom in her eyes, but by then it was much too late.

She took a couple of shuffling steps backward, wanting to turn and run for the safety of her house but afraid to turn her back on this man who was approaching her for some unknown purpose. It was the wrong move, although by now it didn't matter. By backing up instead of running she was missing the opportunity to prolong her lifespan by no more than two or three seconds.

As he arrived at a point roughly three feet from the now-terrified bus driver, Martin reached behind his back with his right hand and pulled a razor-sharp combat knife out of a leather sheath on his belt. He held it up with a flourish in front of the astonished woman's eyes as if performing a magic trick—"Watch me pull a rabbit out of my hat!"

She didn't "ooh" or "aah" or applaud like she might have done for a magic trick, but Martin hadn't really expected her to. Still, you never knew unless you tried.

What she did do, though, was draw in a great wheezing breath in preparation for a scream she would never get the chance to emit. With the grace born of practice and preparation, he sliced her throat deftly from right to left, severing her vocal cords, nearly beheading her, opening a great yawning chasm from which blood splattered like crimson water from a fire hose.

The woman knitted her eyebrows as if the events of the last thirty seconds were beyond her comprehension, which, given the circumstances, they probably were. She shot Martin a look of extreme reproach, as if he had farted in church or something, then finally staggered backward and reached for the spurting neck wound with both hands to try to stanch the flow of blood.

It wasn't going to work.

It wasn't going to come close to working.

Martin danced back out of range of the arterial spray, which was already weakening, and waited for the end. It didn't take long. The bus driver almost went down on her back, overcorrected, and finally collapsed face down on her front lawn. Martin wondered if she was sorry now she hadn't taken better care of it; the dry brown grass did little to cushion her fall.

Seconds after she fell she stopped twitching and Martin got to work. He had a lot to do and not much time to do it in. He hefted her over his shoulder, doing his best to minimize the amount of blood slopping onto his head and neck. The rest of his body he didn't care about; he had worn a long sleeved jumpsuit in expectation of this very occurrence. He would peel it off and shitcan it later.

The woman was sturdy, built like a block of wood, and Martin struggled under her weight as he trundled her body to his car. He popped the trunk with the remote control on the key fob and dumped her body inside, slamming the lid on the still-warm corpse.

There was nothing he could do about the blood staining the dusty yard where she had fallen. He just had to hope no one would come traipsing up to the front door for a while. She was too old to have school-age children, so that didn't seem to be an issue, but you could never tell when a neighbor might drop by to borrow a cup of sugar or discuss the stock market or do whatever the hell the sheep living in this miserable hellhole did to pass the time.

On the bright side, the area was relatively far from town and sparsely populated so the likelihood of anyone stopping in unexpectedly seemed remote.

Martin jumped behind the wheel and backed out of the driveway, moving quickly but being careful to avoid scraping the front of the bus. He drove the stolen Hyundai—he had jacked it off an old lady three days ago and would be sad to see it go; it had served him well but all good things must come to an end and all that—up the country road several hundred yards.

When he had gotten far enough to be out of sight of the murdered woman's house, Martin yanked the wheel sharply to the right and hit the gas, forcing the little vehicle as far into the woods as possible. It jounced and stuttered over uneven ground, finally coming to rest against a massive oak tree.

Satisfied the Hyundai was more or less screened from the view of anyone driving past on the road, Martin grabbed a backpack off the seat next to him, then opened the door and stepped out into the woods. He quickly stripped off the jumpsuit, balling it up and tossing it into the trunk with the murdered bus driver before slamming the lid back down. He wasn't concerned about leaving behind DNA evidence—there was none of his on file anywhere and in the unlikely event he was ever caught he knew he would never see the light of day again. So why worry?

Martin trudged out of the woods the way the car had come in, doing his best to straighten the crushed tree branches and scrub brush the car had smashed down during its short but violent cross-country trek. When he reached the pavement he peered back at his handiwork. It wasn't perfect, but the foliage above was so thick it was dark as a hooker's heart in there and unless anyone was looking directly at the car, it would probably not be discovered for a while.

And a while was all he needed. The camouflage job didn't have to be perfect. In another hour or so, Martin would depart this little shithole of a town for good, and by then it wouldn't matter whether anyone found the lady or not.

He jogged back along the edge of the road, thankful for small towns and people who valued their privacy. There wasn't one nosy neighbor to worry about and not a single car had passed by on this little out-of-the-way cow path the entire time Martin had been here, and that included the time he sat parked up the road waiting for the driver to come out of her house. The whole thing had all gone down so easy it almost didn't seem fair. But he wasn't done yet; the most challenging portion of the day's activities was still to come.

Martin retraced his steps to the scene of the murder and picked the bus key off the ground. The driver had been so busy dying she had forgotten all about it. It was slick with her blood and he was momentarily disgusted. Who the hell knew what nasty diseases the old bat had been carrying around? It was one thing to get her blood on his overalls, he could deal with that, but all over his hands? The idea was just repulsive. He wiped the key off as best he could on the ground, succeeding mostly in getting dirt and dead brown grass all over it. Ah, fuck.

Oh, well. You couldn't make an omelet without breaking a few eggs, as the expression went, and Carli Ferguson was going to make one hell of a tasty omelet.

28

"I think we should just take her and leave town, go on a vacation, do anything to get her out of the sights of that madman." Sandra Mitchell stood with her hands on her hips in the middle of her spacious kitchen, facing a group seated at the table that included her husband Bob, her ex-husband Bill, and the FBI Special Agent in Charge of the I-90 Killer case, Angela Canfield.

Canfield nodded placatingly, holding her hands up, palms out, as if trying to ward off an evil spirit. Bill felt a little sorry for her. He had been in similar situations many times during arguments with his ex-wife, and knew that getting her to change her mind when it was made up was like trying to stop the sun from setting.

"Believe me, I understand how you feel," Canfield said gamely. "But as I explained already, I believe this letter is nothing more than an attempt at misdirection. It's a chance for the perpetrator to put the unsuccessful kidnapping behind him while at the same time tweaking the man he holds responsible for his failure. He likely is very frustrated at the moment because he has never experienced failure before."

"You *believe* it's an attempt at misdirection, but you really don't know," Sandra countered. "Let's face it, Agent Canfield, if you really knew what was going on with this man you would have caught him years ago, and yet he is still on he loose, terrorizing innocent young girls. So you'll excuse me if I don't put a whole lot of stock in what you have to say."

Bob Mitchell rubbed his wife's shoulders possessively and Bill felt a stab of sympathy for him as well. He was stuck squarely in the middle of this situation just like everyone else, but the child in question was not his and the biological father was sitting just a few feet away. *Not an enviable position to be in*, Bill thought.

He also figured there was no way in hell the man would go against his wife's wishes in the matter—at least not if he knew what was good for him—regardless of where his true feelings might lie.

"Can I offer a compromise?" Bill asked. "There are only a few days of school left. Graduation activities start soon and it would be a shame for Carli to miss them after spending the last twelve years with her friends, right?"

Nobody argued, so he carried on. "How about letting her finish out the year, just those last few days, letting her take part in graduation, and *then* whisking her off to Europe or wherever you're planning on vacationing. You can disappear all summer if you'd like. I won't even put up an argument, custody-wise. Just let her finish out her high school career. She deserves that."

"Obviously it's your choice, Mrs. Mitchell," Agent Canfield added. "But you've seen the police presence we have established right outside your door, and I can assure you it is just as strong at the high school. Carli is safe, and it is our priority to ensure she stays that way."

Bill could see his ex-wife giving serious consideration to their words, turning them over in her mind, looking for flaws in their logic. He had spent nearly sixteen years married to Sandra and he could still read her expressions with ease. She would have made a shitty poker player.

It pained him to offer up a solution that would result in his not seeing his child for nearly three months. But he, like Sandra, was more than a little concerned for her safety, regardless of Canfield's assurances. If leaving the area for was what it took to keep her out of harm's way, he was one hundred percent in favor of the idea.

The kitchen was silent as Carli Ferguson's mother weighed the options. There weren't many. She'd made it clear she wasn't about to allow her daughter to be used as bait for some madman, so it was either pack up and take her away *now*, today, immediately, or wait a few days. One way or the other way she would be leaving.

The only reason she had even agreed to allow her to attend school these last two days was because she didn't want Carli home during these meetings.

She sighed and turned to her husband. "I want you to call the travel agent, right now, and book a trip for us. For the summer. Starting the day after graduation."

"Of course," he said. "Where would you like to go?"

"I don't care."

29

Martin felt strangely at ease as he sat inside the school bus, just another driver waiting outside the high school at the end of the day. The big vehicles rumbled, filling the air with the oily smell of idling diesel engines.

He had been a little concerned about the possibility of other drivers poking their heads into the bus with the intention of chit chatting with their dead friend while they waited for their passengers. Had been so concerned about it, in fact, he had prepared a bullshit story about being a newly hired substitute driver.

It hadn't turned out to be a problem. His fellow drivers sat behind the wheels of their rigs staring straight ahead through the tinted windshields like automatons.

Regulations, Martin decided. They probably weren't permitted to leave the cabs with their engines running just in case one of the budding young delinquents made a break for freedom early and decided to take a bus for a joy ride.

After disposing of the driver's body inside the stolen Hyundai and then hiking back to her house, Martin had pulled his disguise out of his backpack and hurriedly applied it. It was nothing elaborate, just a mullet wig—making him look like a 1980's vintage Billy Ray Cyrus—which he then covered with a green John Deere baseball cap pulled low over his eyes. He topped the disguise off with a fake brown mustache and decided he was good to go.

There was no point going overboard. It wasn't like he was trying to fool Sherlock Holmes, for crying out loud. All he had to do was alter his appearance just enough so a seventeen-year-old girl wouldn't recognize him, a girl who would undoubtedly be distracted and not paying the slightest attention to her surroundings. She would be engrossed in a conversation, or frantically texting a friend, or lost in the music of her iPod, or, more likely, all three at once.

Whatever.

The point was Martin felt confident Carli Ferguson would not walk onto the bus and examine the face of her driver to ensure it was not the same guy who had handed her the threatening letter two days ago. No one would expect him to take the bold step he was planning today, least of all a naïve small-town high school girl.

And that was exactly why he was doing it.

The front doors of the school opened and a swarm of students began to exit, moving faster and looking more alert than they probably had all day. After squeezing through the natural bottleneck of the doorway, the kids fanned out and began searching for their buses, scanning the long yellow row of vehicles parked along the access road leading from the street to the paved parking lot behind the school.

Each bus was equipped with a white placard placed in a side window with a unique number emblazoned on it. The students searched the row until locating the bus with the specific number corresponding to the route on which they lived, and then clambered aboard that bus.

It should have been chaos. Martin figured the process might take half an hour or more, but the last of the students boarded their buses no more than five minutes after the school's doors had swung open. It was a well-choreographed dance, as complex and impressive as any Broadway musical number.

Martin held a newspaper to his face and pretended to read as the kids boarded, confident in the anonymity his disguise afforded, doing his best not to watch as the teens climbed on. He was anxious and nervous but trying to project an air of routine boredom. It was not an easy expression to achieve, especially knowing that any one of the girls climbing the aluminum steps and brushing his arm on the way down the center row might be his angel, the girl with whom he would soon be enjoying a glorious week of unbridled passion.

The bus was roughly half full and things were progressing smoothly when one of the boarding students peered at him closely and asked, "Where's Mrs. Bengston?"

Martin's heart began hammering a staccato beat in his chest and for a brief moment he feared maybe the kid could hear it. His first instinct was to reach for the semi-automatic pistol concealed under the waistband of his jeans but he controlled it.

There was no reason to overreact. Yet.

He looked over the top of his newspaper at a pimply-faced boy of maybe sixteen, with curly hair a couple of days overdue due for a shampoo, and black horn-rimmed glasses that had slid halfway down his greasy nose and which he had made no attempt to push back up.

He shrugged. "I dunno, sick I guess."

The kid just stood there.

"I'm the substitute," Martin added lamely. Then he waved the kid down the aisle. "Let's go, kid" he commanded. The best defense was usually a good offense. "Move it, you're holding up the line."

Martin dropped his face back behind the open newspaper, ready to pull his weapon and wheel the big bus out of line and away from the school if necessary. He hoped he wouldn't have to, because he had no way of knowing whether his Carli was even on board yet.

Finally the kid shrugged and slouched down the aisle and the boarding process continued. No one else said a word to him or even acknowledged his existence, which was exactly what he had been counting on.

As the last of the kids filed onto the bus, Martin considered what might have caused the one teenager to question him. He wondered if maybe the kid had heard the story of the I-90 Killer approaching one of his schoolmates, but that scenario seemed unlikely. Martin assumed the authorities would be keeping a lid on the story, hoping to avoid a panic. Probably the kid was related to "Mrs. Bengston" or lived down the road from her or something; this hick town was so small it seemed the most obvious possibility.

Approximately two-thirds of the available seats had been filled when the last of the students shuffled in and sat down. Martin waited for the bus ahead of him to close its doors and begin pulling ahead, as he had seen the drivers do when he performed his surveillance. The urge to check the young faces in the oversized mirror looming above his sun visor was almost overwhelming, but he controlled himself. Patience.

Finally the conga line of vehicles began moving. Martin shifted into drive and eased down on the accelerator and the big diesel engine pulled the bus forward. He was almost there.

The only thing that could go wrong now was if Carli Ferguson had missed school today for some reason and was thus not aboard the bus. Martin refused to acknowledge that possibility. If she had attended classes yesterday, one day after being approached by the infamous I-90 Killer, Martin figured she almost certainly would have done so today as well.

Of course, there was always the possibility she had gotten sick or stayed home for some other reason. No matter. If Carli wasn't on the bus today, Martin would simply return home and develop an alternative plan. He was nothing if not resourceful.

The line of buses burst out of the school driveway, one after the other, half turning right and the other half left, as oncoming traffic ground to a halt in both directions, stopped by a police officer stationed in the middle of the road. Martin appreciated the courtesy.

He made the left turn as a low buzz of conversation filled the bus. The line moved steadily and one by one the vehicles in front of Martin veered off the main road onto side streets and began dropping off students.

When he had traveled roughly half the distance between the school and the convenience store where Martin met with his angel two days ago he pulled off the road, wheeling into the mostly empty parking lot of a strip mall that had seen better days. The tired-looking complex housed a hair salon, a donut shop, and an auto-parts store, as well as two empty storefronts standing as mute testimony to a sputtering economy in a struggling rural town.

Immediately after entering the lot, Martin cut the wheel to the left, rolling the bus to a stop parallel to the street it had just exited. This was not a scheduled stop and even the most unobservant of the children had by now realized something was not quite right. The first stop on this route was not supposed to occur for nearly another half-mile.

A jumble of confused but not particularly concerned voices drifted forward, some kids questioning the unexplained stop but most simply complaining about the delay.

"What the hell?"

"Hey, what's going on?"

"What is this?"

The questions were all directed toward the front of the bus in general and Martin in particular, but he ignored them. What was he going to say? "Oh, it's okay, none of you have to worry. Except, of course, for Carli, my sweetheart, my angel, my special girl!"

Instead of responding to the grumbling, Martin climbed to his feet. He pivoted to face the kids, a few of the more adventurous of whom had begun standing and moving into the aisle. What exactly they thought they were doing Martin had no idea, but he decided it would be wise to put a stop to the activity.

He drew his gun and held it up next to his ear so it would be clearly visible, even from the back. For now he kept it pointing at the roof.

Everyone froze. One boy who had been halfway to a standing position eased back down into his seat but he was the only one who moved. Everyone else simply stopped as all the kids did their damnedest to will themselves invisible. No one had yet screamed, although several girls seemed to be giving it serious consideration.

Martin used the silence as an opportunity to address the crowd. "No one has anything to worry about as long as nobody does anything stupid."

Silence.

"Would Carli Ferguson please stand up?"

Still nobody moved. Cars cruised past in the parking lot and people walked in and out of the stores at the other end of the pavement, none of them paying any attention to the drama playing out in the stationary school bus parked out near the road. Martin had known they wouldn't, but he also knew that if a police car should happen to drive by and see the bus parked where it didn't belong, the complexion of the entire scenario would change in an instant.

It was time to move things along.

He scanned the rows of drab green vinyl-covered double seats quickly and his heart soared when his eyes came to rest on his angel. She was there!

Carli sat by herself, cringing, pushing herself into the back of her seat as if she thought she might be able to disappear, her eyes wide and terrified. Apparently her friend Lauren had not taken the bus today. Martin wanted to tell her not to be afraid, that he would never do anything to harm his girl.

Provided, of course, she did exactly as she was told.

He began opening his mouth to tell her, "Look, I'm pointing the gun at the ceiling so nobody gets hurt!" when he sensed rather than felt furtive movement diagonally off his left. Immediately he brought the handgun to eye level as he turned and found himself face to face with a big kid, a junior or a senior, probably a football player pumped up and strong. Full of himself.

It was arrogant fucks just like this that had made Martin's life miserable back when he was in school, and this damn fool was obviously just as stupid as any of them had been. The moron had been going to make a play for Martin's gun, he was sure of it.

Martin leaned forward, jamming the barrel of the pistol against the middle of the hero's forehead, remembering his humiliation at the hands of that busybody Bill Ferguson who had refused to mind his own business. This guy was younger but otherwise just the same.

The kid whimpered, yanking his head back reflexively, smacking the back of it against the window, murmuring "No-no-no."

Through gritted teeth, Martin asked, "Something I can do for you?"

The kid shook his head. He looked like he was about to shit his pants. Maybe he already had.

"What part of 'Don't do anything stupid' did you not understand?" he asked, and the kid said nothing. His lips were trembling and his face was sheet-white and Martin said, "Sit down and don't you fucking move. Not one inch."

The kid nodded.

Turning his attention now back to Carli, Martin was surprised to see her standing in the aisle, hands raised with her palms held outward in a gesture of submission.

"Please," she said softly, as if afraid she might spook him. "Please don't hurt him and I'll come with you. I won't be a problem, I promise. Just don't hurt anybody, please."

The bus was as silent as a graveyard at midnight. Martin could hear the football player breathing heavily in the seat to his left. It sounded like he was sobbing. He could hear Carli Ferguson's footsteps as she moved slowly up the aisle, dragging her feet on the floor as if her body was resisting what her mind was telling it to do.

The students who had risen from their seats and moved into the aisle stepped aside en masse. They took their seats and cleared the way for their schoolmate to move toward the man with the gun. Any thoughts of heroism seemed to have disappeared, choked back by Martin's brutal response to the one alpha male who had attempted to interfere.

Martin backed toward the dashboard of the bus, pointing the gun in the general direction of the students. There was no real reason for caution now that he knew Carli's location. He had been afraid that if the gun went off he might strike his girl by accident, but there was nothing to worry about now on that score. He had no desire to hurt or kill any of the snotty brats, but no real problem with it, either, should it come to that.

By now Carli had reached the front of the bus and stood facing him. A look of terror marred her beautiful features but there was something else, too; a quiet dignity that surprised Martin. He had expected to have to deal with a screaming hysterical mess, but Carli Ferguson seemed composed beyond her years, further confirming Martin's conviction that she was special.

For a moment he had the strangest sense of déjà vu. Carli's father had faced him days before in virtually the same position at virtually the same distance, just before everything had gone sideways.

Even though he knew now that fate had been at work that day and that this girl was his destiny, he still felt a palpable sense of victory. He wished that asshole Bill Ferguson were here to witness this moment, but took solace in the knowledge that the testimony of an entire bus full of witnesses would ensure the busybody hero wannabe suffered through every last excruciating detail of his daughter's disappearance.

Martin smiled widely and a look of alarm filled Carli's eyes. This was not what she had been expecting.

"I'm not going to hurt you, baby," he whispered as he pulled the lever to open the bus's door.

Then he looked down at the kids cowering in their seats and said, loudly, "Don't anybody fucking move or I'll come back in here and kill every last one of you."

Utter funereal silence greeted this pronouncement and Martin decided the baby sheep might actually stay in their seats as long as he needed them to. All he required was a few seconds.

He nudged his angel down the steps and then followed her into the intense May heat, slipping the gun into his pocket as he moved. A couple of people glanced suspiciously at the bus but took no action, retreating immediately back inside their insulated cocoons.

Parked two car-lengths away was a maroon Toyota, nearly brand new, clean and shiny. Martin had stolen it specifically to impress Carli. It was slightly more conspicuous—newer and more expensive—than what he would normally steal, but it was still fairly unassuming. Nearly invisible to the sheep. And it seemed appropriate to let his angel know how much she meant to him.

The car had been sitting in the lot for a couple of hours now, but Martin had jacked it more than a hundred miles away and then slapped a set of stolen license plates on it before parking it here. He'd known it would be available when he needed it and it was.

He fumbled for the key fob in his pocket. Found it and flipped the automatic locks. "Get in the driver's door and then slide over to the passenger side," he muttered under his breath to Carli.

She complied without argument. "Just don't hurt anyone," she repeated, as if Martin were some sort of monster, an implication that cut him to the quick. He choked down the anger that rose like bile in his throat, resolving to show his little angel how deeply he cared and how hurtful it was that she didn't trust him or understand his motives.

The instant she had begun sliding over the center console, Martin climbed in behind her, pulling the gun out of his pocket and training it squarely on her back. He didn't think she would try to burst out the other side of the car and run but wasn't sure.

He needn't have worried. His angel settled into the passenger's seat and sat staring resolutely out the side window as if silently imploring someone, anyone, to come along and save her.

Fat chance. Martin had gone to a lot of trouble and taken more than a few risks to maneuver Carli Ferguson to his side where she belonged; he wasn't about to let her slip away now.

The Toyota started up on the first try and rolled smoothly forward. In seconds, Martin and his precious cargo had reached the parking lot's exit. He flicked his left turn signal, waited for an opening in the passing traffic, and then accelerated onto Main Street. In the rear view mirror he checked on the school bus, alone in the parking lot, its' red hazard lights flashing an automatic warning with the door hanging open.

The bus steadily shrank in size as Martin sped away until it disappeared from view. The Toyota passed the high school on the right and continued out of town, moving toward the interstate and anonymity. In five minutes Martin and his reluctant passenger had left Stockbridge behind.

30

Squad cars and unmarked police vehicles were everywhere as Bill approached the Mitchell home. Some officers had parked in the driveway, others had simply slewed to a stop on the side of the road, the ass ends of their vehicles sticking dangerously into the road. One SUV had been abandoned with all four tires sinking into the lush green grass of the front yard. It looked like someone had driven his car onto the eighteenth green at Augusta National.

Bill parked his FERGUSON HARDWARE van where he could and sprinted to the house. He entered through the front door without knocking.

Inside the scene was chaos. To the left, Sandra sat on the living room couch weeping, a damp towel pressed to her forehead by her husband. A police officer stood nearby, uncomfortable and clearly unsure of what the hell to do next. In the kitchen, Agent Canfield stood with a mobile phone pressed to her ear in the center of a cluster of officers and plainclothes people Bill assumed must be other FBI agents. He walked down the hallway and no one paid him any attention.

Bill shouldered his way through the group of people surrounding Canfield and said, "What the hell's going on? All they told me on the phone was that something has happened to Carli. Where's my daughter?"

Canfield mumbled something into her cell phone and snapped it shut. She turned her dark eyes on Bill and he knew.

"Oh no," he said.

"We'll find her."

"How did he get her?"

"We're still trying to sort that out," she said. "Right now it looks like he stole a school bus and impersonated the driver, taking Carli after driving away from the school grounds."

Bill stared at her in disbelief. "He stole an entire school bus? Filled with kids? He was parked right outside her school? How is that even possible? Weren't you supposed to be watching the school? Where's the real driver?"

"Slow down," she said, holding up her hands. "We sent a squad car to the driver's home a little while ago, so the officers should be reporting back soon. But beyond that, yes, it appears he waited outside the high school in the line of buses. After it was fully loaded, he simply drove away with the bus full of kids."

"Is anyone else missing?"

"No. When he got about a mile away from the school he pulled into a parking lot and took Carli off the bus at gunpoint. He hustled her into what we assume was a stolen vehicle and drove her away. No one else was hurt."

"YOU! THIS IS ALL YOUR FAULT!"

Bill looked toward the sound of anguish and pain and saw Sandra standing in the doorway between the kitchen and dining room. She held the damp towel in front of her with two hands like a weapon and stared accusingly at the knot of people in the center of the kitchen. Twin streaks of tears ran down her cheeks and her face was flushed and angry and she advanced on him like an avenging angel.

"This is your fault," she declared again with slightly less volume but even more conviction.

Agent Canfield turned and faced the distraught woman, prepared to take the onslaught. She stood tall, looking Sandra in the eyes as she approached.

"I understand you're upset," she said. "So are we. We're upset that we didn't see this coming. I never imagined this man would be so bold and break so completely out of the pattern he has established over nearly four years of kidnappings. But I promise you, Mrs. Mitchell, we will leave no stone unturned in the search for Carli. We are going to devote as much of our resources as possible to this search and will not rest until we find your daughter."

Sandra looked past the FBI agent as if she didn't exist and trained her gaze on Bill. "This is your fault," she said for the third time, her voice now low and cold and hard. "*You* had to be a hero. *You* had to interfere with that monster a few days ago at the rest area. *You* focused his attention on this family and now my little girl is missing. She's gone, Bill. She's gone and this is ALL. YOUR. FAULT. Working eighty hours a week and breaking this family apart, that wasn't enough for you. Oh no. You wouldn't stop until you killed Carli. You killed your daughter, Bill. She's gone and you killed her. I hope you're happy now."

Bill stood, shocked at hearing the words spoken out loud. They were identical to the ones he'd been castigating himself with ever since hearing the news that something had happened to Carli.

Sandra was right. It *was* his fault.

He had nothing to say because she was right.

Agent Canfield glared a look at Bob and he wrapped his arm protectively around his wife, steering her back into the living room. Bill watched their backs until they disappeared.

What could he say? She was right. He had protected a stranger, a young girl who was now safe and sound in the arms of her parents, and meanwhile he had led the monster directly to the door of his own child. His own teenage daughter who was now out there somewhere, lost and alone and afraid.

Assuming she was even still alive.

Agent Canfield spoke softly, seemingly fearful she might disturb Sandra in the living room and provoke another ugly scene. "There is no evidence to support the notion that Carli is not still alive. We have every reason to believe he has not harmed her. We can get her back, Bill, you need to focus on that."

He opened his mouth to point out that they had no evidence supporting the notion that she *wasn't* dead, either, to make the obvious assertion, just in case she had missed it, that this was a revenge kidnapping based on his idiotic split-second decision to save that girl a few days ago, and what better way for a lunatic to get even than by killing the child of the man who had spoiled his precious plans?

Bill opened his mouth but didn't get the chance to say anything, because at that exact moment Agent Canfield's cell phone rang, the tone shrill and brittle sounding and somehow offensive in the live-wire tension of the kitchen.

She flipped it open. "Go." The person at the other end of the connection talked for maybe a minute and then she grimaced said, "Okay, keep me advised."

The FBI agent then flipped her phone shut and addressed not just Bill but the entire roomful of law enforcement personnel. "That was one of the officers sent to the home of the school bus driver, Mrs. Leona Bengston. They found a significant spill of blood in her front yard and then located her after a short search. She's dead. The suspect cut her throat, nearly decapitating her in the process, and then stuffed her body in the trunk of a stolen car before stealing her bus. We need to get this guy sooner rather than later. He's coming apart at the seams."

31

Martin turned the stolen Toyota into his dusty driveway and glanced across the front seat at Carli. His angel's head was turned away from him and she stared out the side window, exactly as she had done for virtually the entire ride.

That was okay. It was to be expected. Martin knew it would take some time—probably a lot more than the scant seven days available—before she grew to accept him. It would be nice, though, if she were at least to acknowledge him. He had gone to a lot of trouble to unite the two of them and she didn't seem to appreciate his efforts at all.

"We're here," he said softly, reaching out and stroking his angel's long blonde hair. She cringed and shrank toward the window with a cat-like mewl of fear and disgust as the car rolled to a stop.

"Why are you doing this?" The question was spoken so softly it was barely more than a whisper, almost indecipherable by Martin and he was sitting less than three feet away.

Still, at least his angel had decided to talk to him. This was a step in the right direction.

"Why am I doing this?" he repeated as if not understanding the question. "Are you serious? Why did Romeo need Juliet? Why did Richard Burton need Elizabeth Taylor? It's fate, my angel. We're meant to be together."

"Is that why you held a gun to Jimmy Morrison's head? Fate told you to do that? He could have been killed!" Her voice was a little louder now as her anger flashed.

"He was gonna make a move on me. He was trying to be some kind of hero," Martin snarled, "and I couldn't let that happen. Besides," he said with his most charming smile—a waste of effort since Carli continued to face the passenger side window—"I didn't shoot him, did I? I didn't even hurt him."

"How can it be fate if you've never even met me? You don't know anything about me." The anger had dissipated and now she was practically whispering again. Martin loved the sound of her delicate voice; it was like the breeze rustling the tree branches outside his window at night.

"I know I can't live without you. I knew that the moment I laid eyes on you. That's what 'fate' means. I don't have to know you to realize how special you are."

Carli shook her head, still facing the side window but holding her head a bit higher. "That's bull," she said. "I know what this is really all about. I'm not stupid. My dad saved that other girl from you and now you're trying to get even with him."

A flash of anger bubbled inside Martin's chest and he nearly grabbed her by the throat. How dare she question his motives! Who the hell did she think she was talking to?

He sat perfectly still, breathing slowly in and out through his mouth until he managed to get his emotions under control. It wasn't easy. His angel was going to have to learn to keep her insolent mouth shut, but there was time to teach her that lesson. At least she was talking to him now, and Martin didn't want to lose the hard-won progress he'd made.

He thought for a moment about how to answer. The head Carli had lifted in defiance just a moment ago was now lowered, her shoulders raised in anticipation of the blow she expected to receive.

He kept his hands at his sides and finally said, "Have you ever heard of the word 'convergence'?"

Carli said nothing.

Martin continued. "The word 'convergence' means a coming together, a merging of groups that were originally opposed or different. Yes, I was angry with your father for interfering in a situation that was none of his fucking business, for sticking his nose where he had no good goddamned reason to put it. I'm not going to lie to you, my angel—I will never lie to you—yes, I am hopeful this hits him right in the gut and maybe teaches him a thing or two about minding his own business. That's something he really should have learned by now and I have to tell you I'm happy to be the one to teach it to him.

"But that is an entirely separate issue from you and me. In fact, if anything, I should probably thank him. He stopped me from making a very big mistake. Because if he hadn't interfered I would never have looked into his background and I would never have learned of your existence.

"That girl I almost got stuck with at the rest area last week was not a good fit for me, I know that now. *You* are a good fit for me. So don't tell me what my motives may or may not be, Carli Ferguson, because you have no idea.

"Anyway, please allow me to return to my original point, which was this: my act of removing you from that school bus this afternoon is what is known as a 'convergence.' It combines my primary goal—to enjoy your company for as long as possible before moving you along to your final destination—with a very pleasant secondary goal, which is to teach your father an important and obviously long-overdue lesson. Do you understand?"

Carli's shoulders were shaking and he knew she had begun to cry, although she still refused to face him.

"At some point," he continued, "you will appreciate my position and see that what has happened today is for the best; of that I am sure. Anyway," he said, opening the driver's side door of the stolen vehicle, "let's go inside and get out of this heat."

He left the car parked nose-in to the closed door of the single-stall garage. It was already hiding his box truck, the vehicle for which the police would be searching most diligently. Leaving the Toyota in plain sight was risky, but there were no neighbors within a mile in any direction and this end of the long, winding driveway could not be seen clearly from the road, so Martin was confident it would not pose a problem.

"We are destined to be together, my angel, you'll see." He opened Carli's door like a gallant suitor trying to impress his girl on their first date. She stepped out of the car slowly, reluctantly, and Martin wrapped an arm around her waist. He could feel her entire slim frame shaking like a leaf and she continued to sob quietly.

Ahead the house loomed, creaky and silent and empty. Siding rotted away in places and long strips of peeling white paint hung from the window frames. Martin walked his angel up the front steps and into her temporary home.

32

Bill felt dazed, disoriented, like he had gotten disgustingly drunk last night and was now suffering a massive hangover. He almost wished that were the case. At least maybe then he could have forgotten about his entire life crashing down around him in the last few hours.

He glanced at the clock hanging over the kitchen sink. It was 5:20 p.m.

Carli was gone and it was his fault. Sandra had said so, attacking him in front of the police and FBI personnel, and she was right. He had brought the I-90 Killer down on them by his actions.

He still didn't regret saving that girl. Would it be any better for her parents to be suffering right now as he and Sandra were? Of course not. But by the same token, there was no point in even attempting to make the argument that he was not directly responsible for the events that had followed.

Carli was gone. Maybe she was already dead. Agent Canfield had stressed to him the FBI's position: that she was still alive. That the I-90 Killer would keep her alive for a while—days at least, maybe even weeks—before finally tiring of her and succumbing to his own psychosis, his compulsion to kill.

But then again, Agent Canfield had believed the psycho bastard's aggression would end with his letter, that he had been taunting Bill and trying to frighten him, but that he would turn his attention elsewhere once he had accomplished that goal. Bill had feared otherwise but had given her the benefit of the doubt as a professional, had given more weight to her gut feeling than to his own, and look what that had gotten him.

He paced his tiny apartment, wanting to do something, *needing* to do something. Canfield and her team of Feebs—an apt description if ever there was one—and local law enforcement had exited Sandra's home at the same time as Bill following the blowup with his ex-wife. The agent had spoken quietly to him for a moment in the front yard in a vain attempt to take some of the sting out of her words.

"She's just upset," Canfield said. "Understandably so. But she's taking her fear and frustration out on you. Try not to take it to heart."

"I don't care about any of that. I just want my little girl back. Besides, how can I even think about arguing with her when she's right?"

Canfield shook her head and Bill thought she was going to try to press her point when she changed the direction of the conversation entirely.

"We're splitting up the investigative teams now," she said. "The locals have been tasked with interviewing all of Carli's schoolmates who were on the bus this afternoon to try to get a handle on this guy. Maybe he inadvertently let slip where he was taking her or made some other mistake we can use to our advantage."

Bill nodded. He was glad to hear something, even for just a moment, to take his mind off Carli and the gruesome scenarios running rampant inside his head. "Makes sense. And what are you going to do?"

Agent Canfield made a face. "I'm taking my people out to comb that poor bus driver's property for evidence."

That was two hours ago. Canfield had taken off and Bill walked back to his van. He immediately called the office of his West Stockbridge store, leaving assistant manager George Bentley in charge. He filled Bentley in on the situation and advised him he would not be returning to work for the foreseeable future.

Then he called his other store and repeated the exercise with Stefanie Wilson, the manager of that location.

Now he wondered if he had made a mistake. He couldn't imagine working while Carli was missing, but it would likewise to be impossible just to sit around this little shithole of an apartment waiting for the authorities to tell him they had discovered the lifeless remains of his child.

The hot dead air circulated listlessly, affected only slightly by the single overmatched ceiling fan mounted in the living room. For the hundredth time, Bill considered how nice it would be to bring an air conditioner home from work and stick it in his window, but he had resisted doing that for the completely irrational reason that doing so would signify a permanence to this residence that he simply did not want to acknowledge. The notion that a man well into his forties, a successful businessman at that—if you could consider barely avoiding bankruptcy "successful'—could make his home in an apartment so shabby any self-respecting crack whore would turn her nose up at it, was so depressing Bill had been determined to avoid doing so at all costs.

The house he had Sandra had shared with Carli prior to the divorce was nowhere hear as palatial as Bob Mitchell's, Bill wasn't about to kid himself otherwise. But it had been warm and cozy and comfortable. Three bedrooms. Roomy kitchen. Casual dining area. Comfortable living room and two-and-a-half baths. Nice. Nothing spectacular, but nice.

After Sandra left, Bill tried staying in the house, but he quickly discovered the memories were too close and too overwhelming to allow him to stay. They smothered him. They were everywhere. Each square inch of the place reminded him of the life he had shared with Sandra and Carli back in happier days.

The weight of all those memories, plus the severely restricted cash flow of a man paying alimony and child support with the income from two barely sustainable businesses, convinced Bill Ferguson in short order that a change would do him good.

He put the house on the market at a reasonable price and it sold quickly. His share of the profit from the sale went in the bank, and the hell with the tax consequences. The IRS would tax the shit out of the money in two years if he didn't roll it into another home, Bill knew that, but he wanted to put it aside as a head start on paying for Carli's college, which was coming up faster than he could believe.

Bill found this apartment after a brief search and immediately rented it. It featured the only he was looking for in a residence: it was close to Carli. The building was ancient, with creaky stairs and cracked linoleum and crumbling plaster and substandard wiring and Bill Ferguson didn't care about any of that. The place was close to Carli and that was good enough for him.

And now Carli was gone.

Bill sipped a soda, not because he was thirsty but because he needed something to occupy his hands as he paced the kitchen floor, over and over, back and forth. Carli was gone. It was his fault. He had to do something.

He looked at the clock. 5:30 p.m. Ten minutes had passed since he last checked the time. He was miserable.

He had to do something.

There was nothing to do.

He continued to pace.

33

Carli sat handcuffed to a bed, trying to force stale potato chips down her throat. She wasn't hungry but knew she should eat, if for no other reason than to keep up her strength. Her dad would be coming for her, she was sure of it, and she had to be prepared.

Her kidnapper had confiscated her watch and her phone, so she had no idea what time it was, but presumably the chips were meant to be dinner. It seemed unlikely that steak or spaghetti or chicken chow mein was on the menu for later, so she slogged through the bag, washing the stale snack food down with water from a greasy plastic cup.

Where her kidnapper was right now and what he might be doing she had no idea and no real desire to find out. Whatever it was, it couldn't be good for her. She wondered how long her body could continue dealing with her sky-high stress level before it finally crashed. Adrenaline coursed through her, not that it was doing any good.

The man had told her his name was Martin, which was a very bad sign if he was telling the truth. Carli had watched enough television and read enough books to know that when the bad guy lets you see him without a disguise and then follows that up by telling you his name he has no plans to release you.

Ever.

As soon as Martin cuffed her to the bed and retreated up the basement stairs, Carli had set to work, twisting and turning the handcuffs, probing for a weak spot, searching for a way out. One side of the bracelets was fitted snugly around her slim wrist, and the other was attached to the headboard of the bed frame, which was stark and depressing but made of iron and, as far as Carli could tell, uniformly solid and well-made.

A short length of metal chain, a couple of inches in total, connected the two bracelets. The links were thick and heavy. They were thinner than, say bicycle chain links, but much too strong for her to break. She knew because she tried, yanking her hand insistently, succeeding only in tearing her skin and raising a painful bruise on her wrist.

She bent to examine the cuffs more closely, squinting, concentrating on those three metal links, certain that if there were a weakness to be exploited, it would be found in the links. But there was nothing. The steel seemed shiny and strong, with no hint of corrosion, no fortuitous gaps in the ovals that could be pried open, nothing.

Her right hand, sweaty and throbbing from her aborted attempt at snapping the links, slipped suddenly off the headboard's iron rail. It fell behind the bed, causing her to scrape the backs of her knuckles painfully on the cement blocks of the side wall, further bruising her wrist as the cuffs snapped her hand back.

Tears filled Carli's eyes and she yanked her hand reflexively, using the palm of her free hand to rub the sting from her knuckles. Blood stained it when she stopped. She would have to be more careful because the same thing would happen if her hand slipped off the damned iron post again, that was how close the headboard had been placed to the cement wall. The scrape hurt like hell and her skin stood no chance against that rough surface.

Then a thought occurred to Carli, and with it the barest glimmer of hope: if the rough concrete surface could damage her skin so easily, why couldn't it have the same effect on the shiny silver steel of the handcuffs? There was very little play in the bracelets, just a couple of inches, but she had already proven—painfully—that she could reach the wall. Now all she needed to do to test her theory was twist her arm so that her wrist faced the wall, then rub it back and forth, scraping the small round circle of steel against the cement blocks.

It was uncomfortable, with Carli's wrist twisted at an unnatural angle, but she smiled as she felt the cuff's metal ring contact the wall. She eased her arm toward the floor and felt friction, heard a tiny whispered scraping sound. In less than a second the chain had been pulled taut, sending a pulse of pain radiating outward from her already injured wrist.

She let out a hiss of pain from between her clenched teeth and pulled her arm back.

Examined the handcuff.

Still strong, still shiny. But—there! A little scratch, almost invisible but definitely there, defaced the steel on the ring where Carli had run it along the cement. It was nothing more than a tiny blister; an irrelevant imperfection in the die cast steel. It certainly wasn't enough to magically allow Carli to snap the cuffs apart.

But it was a start.

She breathed deeply and tried again.

* * *

A short time later the man returned and when he did, Carli's heart began hammering like a runaway freight train inside her chest. She hadn't thought it possible to feel even more afraid than before but she was wrong.

She shrank against the bed's uncomfortable iron headboard, eyeing her captor with suspicion and fear. What was he going to do to her? In his hands he held the potato chips and the dirty cup, which he placed on the small table next to the bed, within Carli's reach, then turned and climbed the stairs again, still without speaking a word to her.

She forced herself to choke down another chip. Her breath tasted sour and she wished she could brush her teeth. She thought about the frightening scene on the school bus, when Martin thrust the barrel of his gun between poor Jimmy Morrison's eyes. Carli had thought at that moment the man was going to pull the trigger and blow Jimmy's brains all over the side window of the bus.

It was then that she had stood and walked into the aisle. There was nowhere to hide anyway; it was crystal clear the man would find her soon enough, so why risk a bloodbath by remaining slumped down in the seat?

Carli Ferguson was coming of age in the new millennium, and as a twenty-first century teen, she'd seen plenty of news coverage of school shootings, had even studied the phenomenon in her Civics class. She figured that if the guy with the gun started shooting, he probably wasn't going to stop until either he ran out of ammunition or everyone inside the bus was dead.

So it was a no-brainer. She had stood and identified herself to the man with the gun. It wasn't because she cared about Jimmy Morrison, not exactly; he had always been kind of a jerk to her, actually.

But at that moment he had been trying to help her and didn't deserve to be gunned down for it. She wasn't trying to be heroic; she simply did what she had to do. In that sense her actions had mirrored those of her father a few days ago in the travelers plaza almost exactly.

The disguise the driver had been wearing was ridiculous and mentally she kicked herself for not being more observant. The moment she took a good look at him she recognized him as the man who had handed her the letter, the man with the bullshit story about being her father's old friend.

The I-90 Killer.

Of course that moment had come far too late to be of any use.

Carli knew the fact that she was now a prisoner of one of the most notorious and brutally successful kidnappers and suspected mass murderers in recent memory should have terrified her beyond reason, but surprisingly that wasn't the case.

She was fearful, there was no question about that, but knowing the identity of her captor didn't seem to make it any worse. She had already come to the conclusion he was never going to let her go—just listening to his loony fantasies about destiny and romance told her that—so the terror she experienced from that scenario alone was about as complete as she could imagine it being.

She swallowed the soggy potato chip and reached for another but couldn't bring herself to take one more. The salt was making her thirsty and she looked dubiously at the cup, which didn't appear to have been washed since the turn of the century. She couldn't afford to become dehydrated, though, that would be the quickest route to weakness. And "weakness" was another way of saying, "death."

She screwed up her courage and took a hesitant sip. The water tasted cool and refreshing despite the nasty appearance of the cup. She drank more, hoping her nervous stomach wasn't going to mix the water and stale chips together and send everything back up.

She needed to pee and tried to ignore it. Her mind wandered to her mom and dad and even to Bob, her mom's new husband, who tried really hard but had no clue how to relate to a teenage girl.

Placing the cup carefully back on the bedside table—it was gross but the water was good and the cup wasn't yet empty—Carli examined her right wrist, the one trapped inside the damned handcuff. It throbbed in time with her heartbeat and already boasted an impressive array of colors, from purple to green to a kind of off-yellow that reminded her of the summer squash her mom planted one year, just before it turned and went bad because she forgot to harvest it.

The wrist looked sore because it was, but that pain was nothing compared to what she knew she could expect from the twisted loverboy upstairs. She eased her right hand through the space between the iron bars and began scraping the inside of the hand-cuff up and down against the cement.

Scree...

Scree...

Scree...

The noise was minimal, she knew there was no possible way the crazy bastard could hear it unless he was standing right next to her, but still the thought of him catching her was terrifying.

How he might react if he found her attempting to escape Carli had no idea, but she knew it wouldn't be pleasant. All the more reason why she had to try.

Scree...

Scree...

Scree...rubbing the cuffs against the wall, wincing in pain after every stroke, as the bracelet pulled tightly against the worsening bone bruise.

Across the basement was a single dirty window, through which the sunlight had fought a losing battle to penetrate since her kidnapper had deposited Carli down here. Now the weak light began to dim. It would be night soon.

It was late May, only a month away from the longest day of the year, and Carli figured the time must be a little after eight-thirty if darkness was approaching. Martin had left the lights off the last time he went upstairs, and now it was getting dark inside as well as outside.

What would happen when the sun went down? The basement was dank and creepy, undoubtedly filled with spiders and who knew what other insects. The prospect of sitting here chained to this disgusting bed in the pitch-dark basement of this lunatic's house in the middle of the night frightened Carli almost as much as the idea of being a victim of the I-90 Killer.

Scree…

Scree…

Scree…

She pulled her hand through the bars to give her aching wrist a break and examined the cuff closely. Right there! Was that a little more damage to the steel bracelet or was it just her imagination?

She leaned back against the cardboard-thin pillow the man had provided and closed her eyes, willing herself to listen and concentrate. Immediately after the man brought her dinner—if you could call it that—she had heard him moving around upstairs. The house was old and the floorboards creaked and for a long time she had heard him walking around on the first floor. It sounded like maybe he had been pacing.

Quite a while ago, though, the noises had stopped and Carli assumed he had gone away. Maybe he had a job, maybe he was off looking for other girls to kidnap—who knew?—but she was pretty sure he wasn't up there at the moment.

She yanked her hand in frustration as tears welled up in her eyes and the cuffs rattled against the thick iron bar of the headboard, pulling painfully against Carli's wrist and further deepening the ugly bruise. Where was Dad? She felt the heavy weight of hopelessness descending upon her and she felt a gut-wrenching sob building.

She closed her eyes, just for a moment. Despite the intense

fear and near-constant jittery adrenaline buzz, Carli began to feel drowsy as her body finally gave in, reacting to the hours of unrelenting stress.

Almost instantly and without realizing it, Carli Ferguson drifted off to sleep, transported to a world of jangling and terrifying dreams, of men with guns, and giant spiders, and horrors yet to be experienced.

34

A single bulb mounted on one of the beams crisscrossing the basement's ceiling flashed on and Carli jerked awake in the middle of a nightmare. In her dream, she was being devoured by a gigantic scabrous spider, and she awoke confused, shaking and afraid. Her bed felt hard and lumpy and her pillow smelled of old drool and the anguish of countless victims. It was the pillow that reminded her where she was and what was happening.

After her dad finished reading the letter she delivered two nights ago, he had called her mom in a panic and come over for a visit a few minutes later, despite the fact it was very late on a school night. The entire family gathered around the kitchen table, talking deep into the night, discussing the I-90 Killer. Dad explained how saving that young girl had resulted in his family now being targeted for revenge by the unstable kidnapper.

The police showed up a few minutes after her dad, and FBI Special Agent Canfield a few minutes after that. Canfield was young and pretty and very much in charge. She had explained, and Dad had agreed, that the letter was probably nothing more than a way for the frustrated lunatic to take out his anger on the man who had thwarted his plans, and that in all likelihood Carli would never see or hear from him again.

Mom had been dead-set against Carli going to school but she had insisted on finishing out the semester. She had worked hard for twelve long years, why should she have to miss the last few days before graduation with her friends just because of something no one believed was even going to happen?

In the end, her mom had reluctantly agreed to allow Carli to attend the final week of pre-graduation activities, based on Agent Canfield's recommendation and the concurrence of her dad.

Now she shook her head, trying to loosen the cobwebs, and the awful events of the day came rushing back—the kidnapping, the man with the gun nearly blowing Jimmy Morrison's head off, the handcuffs clanking against the iron bed frame, and oh, God, the fear.

Especially the fear.

She had fallen asleep while the man was gone and now he was back. He had to be back because the light was on. It seemed much brighter than it should after the all-encompassing darkness, and her captor descended the stairs slowly.

The basement window revealed nothing of the world outside. It was now pitch-black out there and she wondered what time it was. As the man approached her bed, Carli saw a horrifying look on his face. It was a look of anticipation with maybe just a touch of nervousness mixed in.

And she knew.

She had intentionally avoided thinking about this scenario but she knew.

She was about to be raped.

And, really, it was inevitable, wasn't it? After all, this was why he had kidnapped her. The romantic fantasy he painted of the two of them together, fate and destiny and all that crap he had spouted while holding her in the car at gunpoint and then cuffing her to the bed, it was all just a smokescreen to keep her calm.

Or maybe he really believed his lame line of bullshit. He certainly seemed nutty enough to think it was normal for a grown man clearly in his mid-thirties to be paired up with a seventeen-year-old high school girl.

But regardless of what he really believed, regardless of the weird notions bouncing around inside that twisted skull, the man's intention was now to rape her. It was written all over his face. This was the scenario she had carefully avoided thinking about for fear that it would drive her to a screaming panic attack and now that scenario had arrived.

She knew she had to think but she couldn't think because here he was, approaching the bed like some nervous groom on some sick twisted wedding night and the panic she had feared was here and it filled her head and her heart and threatened to explode and oh god here he was and he was fumbling with the buckle on his belt, getting ready to slide his jeans down and—

And she smiled at him.

And he stopped and stared, thunderstruck, clearly unprepared for this reaction from her.

In a voice shaking with what she prayed he would think was desire and not barely controlled panic she said, "Is this how you want our first time to be?"

35

Bill almost missed the knock on his apartment door.

Nobody ever visited him here except for Carli, and she obviously wouldn't be dropping by any time soon. Maybe not ever again.

So he paced and turned and paced some more, lost in his thoughts—self-recrimination was a lot more draining than he would ever have imagined—and almost didn't hear the knock when it came.

It was soft and hesitant—timid, if a sound could be described that way—and he paused in mid-step, head cocked to the side, listening, uncertain at first that he had even heard anything.

After a moment the sound repeated itself and Bill turned toward the entrance to his tiny apartment. Who the hell could it possibly be?

It wasn't going to be Carli, obviously, and it certainly wasn't going to be Sandra, not after her devastating dressing-down of Bill a few hours ago. Beyond those two, he couldn't think of a single person who might visit him here.

He swung the door open and blinked in surprise. Standing in front of the door, fanning her face with her hand in a vain attempt to generate a little airflow in the sweltering heat of the oven-like hallway, was FBI Special Agent Angela Canfield. She looked tired and drawn, like she hadn't been sleeping well, and it occurred to Bill that he wasn't the only one feeling the weight of responsibility for Carli's disappearance.

Despite her exhausted countenance and the haunted look in

her eyes, she flashed a bright smile when he pulled open the door.

Bill stared, shocked into inaction, and Agent Canfield finally said, "What does a girl have to do to get a drink around here? Do I need to show more leg?"

Bill laughed despite himself. "I'm sorry," he said, "but I don't often get visitors here. Actually, I *never* get visitors, except for Carli. Come on in. Oh, and for the record, the leg thing sounds great."

He took her by the elbow and ushered her inside, easing the door closed behind them with his foot.

"I don't have a lot to offer you in terms of drinks," Bill said apologetically. "I hardly ever eat at home. Would you like a ginger ale?"

"That sounds great, especially if you have something stronger to add to it."

Bill smiled. "In the movies, the cops and the FBI agents always say, 'Thanks, but I can't drink while I'm on duty.' When did they change that rule?"

Now it was Canfield's turn to laugh. The sound was light and airy and reminded Bill of birds chirping in the early morning. It was completely incongruous, given the gravity of the situation.

"No," she said, "they haven't changed that rule, but my work day is over. I've been going for about sixteen hours straight and I need to take a breather. I left my partner, Mike Miller, in charge at the home of the murdered bus driver and gave him instructions to call my cell if anything significant turns up.

"In the mean time," she said, looking up at Bill, "I thought it might be a good idea to see how you were holding up. That was a pretty rough scene between you and your ex this afternoon."

Bill dropped ice cubes into two glasses. The tinkling sound the cubes made reminded him of Canfield's laugh. Then he added three fingers of whiskey to each and finished up by filling the glasses to the brim with ginger ale.

He handed one to the agent and took a sip from the other. Their fingers touched and Bill was surprised how cool hers were. It contrasted with her sweat-stained shirt and the beads of perspiration working their way out of her hair and dripping slowly down the sides of her face.

The bitter taste of the whiskey on his tongue was refreshing and Bill was suddenly glad Canfield had shown up. If he had been asked five minutes ago, he would have said he wanted to be left alone, so he was more than a little surprised at the intensity of his reaction to her presence.

"It was a bad scene," he agreed, "and it didn't feel good to be screamed at in front of all those people, but I can't really disagree with her point. It *was* my fault. Sandra wanted to keep Carli home where she would be safe and I convinced her to let our baby go to school. I caused this heartache, plain and simple, and I don't blame Sandra for reminding me of that."

"There's plenty of blame to go around," Canfield reminded him. She took a big sip of her drink—almost a gulp, really—and sighed in satisfaction. "Don't forget that I put my stamp of approval on the whole thing, too. I offered my assurance as a law enforcement professional that Carli would be safe."

Despite the dark circles under her eyes and the clear evidence of stress on her face, Special Agent Angela Canfield looked beautiful and Bill felt the strong pull of attraction. It was ridiculous given the circumstances, but he couldn't help what he felt. A stray lock of sweat-damp auburn hair hung in front of her eyes and she tucked it behind her ear in an unconscious gesture that made her look young and vulnerable.

"I know," he said. "But if I had disagreed with you, there is no way Sandra would have given in. None. Pointing fingers now, though, is irrelevant. The only thing that matters is getting her back."

"That will happen if I have anything to say about it," Canfield said, and took another pull of her drink. Her glass was already more than half empty.

An awkward moment of silence followed as they faced each other in the sweltering kitchen.

Bill said, "I'd offer you the nickel tour of my apartment, but there isn't really a whole lot more than this. A postage stamp living room, a bedroom that's probably the size of your walk-in closet, and that's it. The place is barely more than a studio and it's not really meant to be permanent."

He felt a vague sense of embarrassment. This beautiful young

FBI agent had a lot on the ball, that much was obvious, and she probably owned her own tastefully decorated home with a three car garage, two-and-a-half baths, and a couple of dogs.

No husband, though, Bill thought as he took note of the bare ring finger on her left hand, which at the moment was wrapped tightly around her drinking glass.

Canfield smiled sympathetically and as soon as she did it was as if a spotlight had come on inside the dingy kitchen.

"Divorce sucks, doesn't it?" she said softly, taking a sip of her drink. She gazed up at Bill with eyes clear and jarringly ice blue.

He nodded mutely. Took a half step toward her, lost in those incredible eyes.

She matched his advance with a step of her own and now their bodies were almost touching. Their drinking glasses jangled together and the ice inside them tinkled suggestively.

This was crazy. Carli was missing and he was going to—what? Screw the agent in charge of the investigation?

She reached for his big hand with her smaller one and it occurred to him that, yes, that was exactly what he was going to do.

His fear and anger and frustration intersected, exploding into a hunger, a desire for Special Agent Angela Canfield and he gripped her left hand with his right like a drowning man reaching for a lifeline.

He reached behind his back with his other hand and dropped his glass awkwardly on the kitchen counter. The contents sloshed around and spilled onto the surface and he didn't care. With his suddenly free left hand, he circled Canfield's waist, drawing her slim body into his and she pressed into him with an unspoken need that matched his own.

Her damp hair drifted down over her eyes again and he moved it tenderly back behind her ear, wiping the sweat from her forehead with the back of his hand. Then he kissed her hard and she returned his kiss with one of her own. Their tongues danced and darted and her body was warm and sweaty and desirable as it molded to his.

Bill pulled his lips from hers reluctantly. "We shouldn't be doing this," he managed, "for a hundred very good reasons."

"I know," Canfield responded, "maybe a thousand."

Then she unbuttoned his shirt. She took firm hold of his shirt-tail and led him down the hallway to the bedroom.

36

"Is this how you want our first time to be?" Carli said, and Martin stopped in his tracks.

He stood at the side of her bed, hands on his jeans where he was preparing to unzip them, and gaped at his angel in astonishment. The words she had just spoken were the very last things he had expected to come out of her mouth, with the possible exception of a declaration of undying love.

He wasn't an idiot. It was possible, of course, that she was fucking with his head in an attempt to delay the inevitable. Likely, even.

But this reaction was so different from anything he'd heard while approaching one of his girls for the first time that he was thrown off his stride. Could this high school girl really possess the inner strength and character to sit there smiling her angelic smile, speaking those captivating words, without truly meaning what she said?

He cleared his throat and said, "Excuse me? What do you mean?" It was imperative he not allow this young girl, destiny or not, to realize how badly she had rattled him just through the force of her personality.

"Well," she said, squinting up at him, "I've been in these clothes all day and they're dirty and wrinkled and I've been sweating and nervous and…well…I really have to go to the bathroom. Would it be all right if I washed up first, before we, well, you know?"

Martin smiled. All his past failures, all the girls who were impure or unworthy, all the times he had been forced to suffer the crushing disappointment of discovering his companions were not as he had imagined them to be, all of that paled before this moment with his little beauty.

All of the aggravation, the nearly four years of searching and trying and suffering, had been worth it, because it had all led up to this moment, with his lovely Carli shining her big blue eyes into his, asking to clean up before consummating their love.

"Of course," he replied. "Of course. How thoughtless of me."

He walked forward slowly, fumbling in the right front pocket of his jeans for the handcuff key. He bent down and stroked his angel's flaxen hair and as he did he felt her stiffen reflexively and saw her eyes widen in fear. The ever-present anger began welling up inside him at her response to his touch and he forced himself to maintain control.

She's not the same as the others, he told himself. He worked to clamp down on the rage before it could begin to consume him. *She's just nervous. She wants this as much as I do, but she is young and inexperienced, like a virgin bride on her wedding night. Of course she feels a little overwhelmed. It's to be expected.*

He reached forward and inserted the key into the cuff encircling the bedpost. He opened it and left the other bracelet securely fastened to his angel's wrist. There was no point in taking chances. He held his arm out and helped her to her feet, steadying her when she wobbled slightly. It had obviously been a long day for her and she was exhausted.

The strange-looking couple moved slowly to the crumbling basement stairs and began climbing into the main house.

37

It hadn't occurred to Bill that Agent Canfield—Angela—might dress and walk out the door in the middle of the night, but then again, he hadn't really been thinking rationally, had he? Their love-making had been frenzied, aggressive, an almost violent encounter, with both partners taking turns leading, a carnal dance made up of equal parts desperation and desire.

They had both been exhausted, mentally and physically drained. But then they touched hands in the kitchen and it was as if a hurricane had blown through. They moved down the hallway toward his bedroom, undressing each other along the way and dropping the clothes as they went, leaving behind a messy trail of shirts, trousers and underwear. By the time they reached his bedroom both of them were naked and fueled by raging sexual passion.

Angela was an unusual lover, not that Bill had had much experience in that regard since the divorce. At one moment she would seem forceful and bullying, taking charge and leading him where she wanted him to go, leaving no doubt as to her desires.

Then in the next she would back off, become submissive, almost seeming to fear his advances. In the end, though, they climaxed simultaneously and she fell on top of him, their bodies dripping sweat as she laid her head on his chest.

After a time she rolled off him and they lay side by side, not an easy feat to manage given that they were sharing a twin bed. Her breathing gradually slowed to normal as she played with his chest hair, running a tiny finger in complex patterns over his skin.

His right hand rested lightly on her bare belly and he said, "Wow."

She smiled. "Yea. Wow is right. I think they call that stress release."

"They can call it whatever they want, I'm in favor of it. In fact, I'm about ready to take that call again."

Angela grinned at him and kissed him hard, and they lost themselves in each other once more.

It was almost enough to make Bill forget his constant aching fear for Carli.

Not quite, but almost.

* * *

The second time around was only marginally less frenzied than the first. Once again, Angela continued her strange form of lovemaking; aggressively, almost violently taking charge and then without warning holding back. Bill thought the first part of the equation coincided perfectly with her personality—forceful and straight-forward. The second part, though, the meek submission, the hesitancy, seemed so unlike her that it was jarring, almost off-putting.

He could see how it might cause problems in a long-term relationship—the mixed signals were confusing—but for tonight it was a non-issue. There was no long-term relationship. In fact there wasn't any kind of relationship. Once Carli was located and returned safely to her family—Bill tried not to acknowledge any other possibility—Special Agent Angela Canfield would disappear, either continuing her search for the I-90 Killer, or moving onto another case if they were fortunate enough to catch the crazy bastard.

One way or the other, she would soon be gone, and Bill would go back to his old life, managing his two hardware stores in anonymity, just the way he wanted it.

For now, though, it was obvious that Angela Canfield needed him as much as he needed her. Maybe she was looking for a temporary respite from the pressures of her job, just as he wanted a short-term escape from the awful gnawing fear for his child, not to mention the knowledge that he was to blame for what had happened to her.

Their second session of lovemaking was longer if not less passionate, and when they finished, again dripping sweat and flopping next to each other on his small bed, Bill could barely keep his eyes open. He expected Angela to drop off into a deep sleep next to him—she certainly needed it, based on how exhausted she had looked when she showed up at his door a couple of hours ago—but instead she rolled her legs over the side of the bed and stood.

She began padding toward the bedroom door, naked but completely un-self- conscious.

"Where are you going?" Bill asked, surprised.

"Gotta pick up my clothes. In case you've forgotten, you left them scattered all over your apartment in your haste to seduce me."

Bill laughed. "That's funny," he said. "I seem to remember you pulling me down the hallway like the kitchen was on fire. Or maybe like *you* were on fire."

"Well, it seemed like the thing to do, and I couldn't think of a single reason why I should waste any time."

"Amen to that," Bill agreed.

"In any event," Angela continued, "I really have to get back to my motel and crash for a few hours. If I stay here it's patently obvious neither one of us will get any sleep. I think you'll agree that starting the day exhausted wouldn't be the most effective way to get Carli back. And to get to the motel, I need my clothes, since driving through town buck naked might undermine my authority a little if I were to get stopped by the local police."

"Hmm. I wouldn't be so sure of that," Bill said, smiling in appreciation of Canfield's firm, toned body. "It might actually give you *more* authority. If I was a betting man, I'd wager any male who encountered you in your present state would do pretty much anything you said, no questions asked."

She turned and gave him a hard stare. Bill could have sworn the look in her eyes was one of…suspicion.

Then she laughed and the look was gone, if it had even been there in the first place. Her laugh was light and musical, and she rounded the corner and disappeared into the hallway, bending to pick up her panties.

She seemed pleased, her mood exactly the opposite of a few hours ago, when she had showed up at Bill's door defeated and downcast.

"You're really going to retreat to your lonely motel room?" he asked and looked at his watch. "Why don't you just stay here tonight? I'll even promise to leave you alone, not that it will be easy. You'll be wide-awake and ready for whatever tomorrow throws at you. No one wants Carli back safely more than I do, so the last thing I want to do is interfere with your rest."

She was pulling on her dark blue slacks as she reappeared in the doorway. Somehow she looked completely put together, clean and refreshed, as though she had just stepped out of the shower instead of rolling around in the sack in the ninety degree heat with the father of the kidnap victim for whom she was leading the search.

"I told you already," she said softly. "If I stay here I won't be able to keep my hands off of you. Or any other part of me off you, for that matter." She bent down and kissed the tip of his nose lightly. She smelled wonderful.

"That's a good start but it's not nearly enough," Bill told her, reaching around the back of her head with one big hand and drawing her face down to his, kissing her long and hard.

She returned the kiss with equal force and Bill tried to ease her down on top of his body and back into bed, but she slipped away like a summer breeze, ducking out of his grasp with a wink and a giggle.

Then she hit the door and was gone.

38

Bill hadn't been worried about suffering a repeat performance of the bizarre dream sequence he suffered through the other night because he was certain he would be unable to fall asleep. How could he possibly expect to rest with Carli missing, in the grip of a brutal serial killer, in grave danger and possibly—hell, never mind possibly, *probably*—dead?

Add to that this new reality, the beautiful young FBI agent who had quite literally shown up on his doorstep and taken him to bed only to disappear into the night, and Bill was convinced that sleep would be a stranger for hours, if not the remainder of the evening.

But he *did* fall asleep. It took a long time and plenty of tossing and turning, but eventually sheer exhaustion overtook him. And the dreams did come back, in all their strange, colorful, jangling glory, torturing Bill with near-remembrances and tantalizing flashes of hinted significance.

The vivid sequences, with their too-bright colors and knife-sharp edges, were similar to the ones he had suffered through a couple of nights ago, long, non-specific nightmares in which he was torn apart, suffering and anguished. The enemy in these dreams remained the same faceless, shadowy nemeses as before.

Interspersed among these dreams were once again shorter visions, the ones he had thought of as "dream-commercials." These were more like slow-motion replays of his actual confrontation with the I-90 Killer, snippets of memories from those fateful two or three minutes that refused to leave him alone.

It was these shorter dreams that caused Bill to bolt awake in bed, sweating and shaking, straining to remember details and yet unable to manage it. There was something of significance hidden among all the distorted images his brain was showing him; something that would make a difference in some way, something that would matter. He had no idea *how* it would matter, only that it would.

The dreams kept coming. The dreams were like Grade-B horror movie zombies, shambling stiff-legged toward some seemingly random destination.

Bill would suffer unconsciously as long as his mind could stand it, screaming inside his head for rescue that would never come. Finally his mind would force his body awake and he would sit in bed desperately attempting to recover the rapidly receding memories of his nightmares, trying to ignore his pounding headache long enough to uncover the nugget of significance he knew was there.

Eventually his pulse would slow and he would lie back on his sweaty pillow, eyes drooping, the exhaustion returning, and he would once again drop off into a troubled slumber.

Almost immediately the nightmarish dream sequences would begin again.

That he was dreaming didn't surprise Bill, he had expected the night terrors to return, especially with Carli missing.

But the frustration of having to suffer through them time after time without gaining any insight into their significance was galling because Bill felt certain they contained the secret to rescuing Carli if only his conscious mind could read the clues his subconscious mind was trying to feed him.

There he was, watching himself draw down in slow motion on the back of the I-90 Killer as the man attempted to spirit away the young girl at the rest stop. He knew he should just shoot the fucker but he never did. Instead, every time, he issued the shouted warning to stop, the warning he now regretted with his entire being.

There he was, reaching for the girl's shoulder to pull her to safety, knowing the I-90 Killer was going to shove the girl at him to make his escape but unable to change the sequence of events.

There he was, in stifling heat more appropriate to August than May, leaping down the four steps leading to the rest area parking lot, desperate to catch up to the I-90 Killer, knowing he could not but trying anyway.

There he was, watching helplessly as the man motored past him toward the safety of the interstate in his shabby box truck, at least a decade old and carelessly repainted, and—

There!

There it was!

Bill sat up in bed, ramrod stiff, not sweating and frightened this time but sweating and excited.

Hopeful. Insanely, unreasonably hopeful.

He forced every detail of this latest snippet of the remembered encounter with the I-90 Killer into his memory banks, knowing he was hanging halfway between wakefulness and sleep, determined not to lose what he had just seen to the fading half-light of consciousness.

Electricity coursed through his now-wide-awake body.

What he had just seen might hold the key to saving Carli.

39

Carli Ferguson was her father's daughter.

She admired Bob Mitchell and understood that he provided a measure of support for her mother that her dad never could, but although she accepted Bob's place in the lives of her mom and herself, there was only room for one dad in her heart.

And that dad was her real one. That dad was Bill Ferguson.

Carli had understood immediately why her father took the action he did at the rest area last week, despite her mother's tongue-clucking disapproval as the live TV news reports came in. Mom watched intently, shaking her head and making comments under her breath.

"He could have been killed," Mom had said.

"What if that man had shot the girl, or some of the other restaurant patrons, or, God forbid, your father?" Mom had said.

Carli understood that he had done what he did because he had no real choice, that it was how he was wired. Her dad was not someone who could stand idly by while an innocent person—particularly a defenseless girl—was abducted and taken to face God knows what sort of horrible fate.

The fact that he'd been carrying his gun at the time went a long way toward bringing the situation to a successful conclusion—at least as far as the victim and her parents were concerned—but Carli believed he would have stepped in even if he had left his Browning home that day.

It was simply what her dad was about, for better or for worse.

She understood that about her father, which was how she knew he would come for her. She didn't know whether he had a clue as to the identity of the I-90 Killer, she didn't know if he had any idea where the man had taken her, but Carli was certain of one thing: he would come for her.

And, knowing this, she also knew she had to be ready. She had to delay the inevitable as long as she possibly could and wait for her dad, because he would eventually come.

So she did what she had to do. She smiled and pretended to accept his advances. She tried to convince him that the thought of him putting his disgusting hands all over her body was anything other than repulsive; that the thought of having sex with a stranger—and a sociopathic serial kidnapper/killer at that—who was more than twice her age was anything other than sick.

So she smiled at him and told him she wanted to clean up first.

And that much, at least, was true. She did have to pee and she really, really wanted to wash up. She had sweated rivers, first from the unseasonable May heat and then from terror. Her clothes felt damp and filthy and although there wasn't much she could do about that, the notion of running a washcloth over her face and maybe under her arms seemed like heaven.

But most importantly, if he agreed to allow her to freshen up, it would delay the inevitable moment when he would place his nasty, disgusting rapist hands on her and do the things to her that she could not bear to think about.

And every second she delayed was one second closer to the moment when she would look up from her dirty, disgusting bed and see her dad. That's what she told herself because that's what she knew to be true.

She was marginally surprised when he actually agreed to her request. She had been certain he would snicker and tear her clothes off, doing the things he wanted to do without regard for her desires. After all, he had kidnapped her in order to do these things, why would he suddenly consider her comfort?

But he *had* agreed. He actually seemed to believe this elaborate fantasy he had constructed where the two of them were some bizarre modern-day Romeo and Juliet, holding hands, partnered together against the rest of the world.

That was fine with Carli. Maybe she could continue to use his insane fantasy against him.

He approached her and actually removed the handcuff fastened to the bedpost, and even though he left the other side attached to her wrist and kept a death grip on her arm, still, it represented progress.

She gave a momentary panicked thought to the marks on the cement wall behind the headboard. She'd continued relentlessly scraping her handcuff against the rough surface in what was likely the weakest and most fruitless escape attempt in the history of escape attempts, and if he happened to see those marks and make the obvious connection, she knew he would punish her in some bizarre but undoubtedly painful way.

But he didn't see. He wasn't even looking. He unlocked the cuff from the bedpost and led her to the basement stairs, supporting her by the elbow like some twisted suitor, like some undead freak straight out of a Roger Corman movie.

She tried to pretend not to mind. She tried to pretend the feel of his hand on her body didn't make her skin crawl; that it was not the worst, most horrifying thing she had ever experienced.

She needed to focus on the positive: Her diversion was working. It was working! He was bringing her to the bathroom to clean up, which meant he was not raping her.

Yet.

And every minute that passed where he wasn't raping her brought her one minute closer to being rescued by her dad.

She believed it. She had to believe it.

They reached the wooden door at the top of the stairs and the I-90 Killer nudged it open with his shoe.

"So, what's your name?" she asked, hopefully in a voice that sounded calm and sincere, trying to keep him occupied, trying to show an interest and feed his romantic fantasy. He had already told her, but the silence was terrifying and she couldn't think of a single other thing to say.

"Martin," he said immediately, and his answer scared the shit out of her.

Again.

She hoped by making a connection with him she would be

humanizing herself to him, maybe making herself a little less disposable. She knew it was unlikely. Carli Ferguson had seen plenty of news reports over the last three and a half years about the I-90 Killer. He had kidnapped, raped and, the authorities believed, murdered over a dozen girls and those were just the ones they knew about.

How do you humanize yourself to a monster?

He told her his name. He allowed her to see him without that stupid disguise he had worn on the school bus.

Carli wasn't an idiot; she recognized the significance of all of that. He would never release her, never allow her to describe him to the police or tell them his name or in any way implicate him. He would use her, and when his bizarre fantasy began to bore him, he would send her off to her "final destination," as he had put it.

Undoubtedly that meant killing her and dumping her body into a shallow grave as he had presumably done so many times in the past.

But her plan was working. She told herself to focus on that. It was working. Take it one second at a time, because every second that passed brought her one second closer to rescue.

She took a deep, shaky breath and walked through the door and into the madman's house. It looked as though a tornado had passed through, disturbing only the kitchen before lifting off and disappearing.

Dirty dishes were piled in the sink.

A layer of grime covered the kitchen floor, which looked like it hadn't seen the business end of a mop since before Carli was born.

Dozens of empty frozen dinner boxes littered the kitchen, some resting inside a grimy trash barrel but most scattered around the floor in the vicinity of the trash container as if Martin couldn't be bothered to take the time to aim properly. It looked as though a bomb had gone off at the box factory and their stock had come floating down in a random pattern, like snowflakes during a blizzard, landing in the man's kitchen.

This guy was a pig. Carli didn't know why that should surprise her. She already knew he was a kidnapper, a rapist and a murderer, why would she expect him to be some sort of Martha Stewart where housework was concerned?

Martin led her across the room toward a dimly lit hallway, which terminated at a door, probably the front door. To the left was a staircase and to the right, Carli couldn't tell. Maybe the bathroom. It would make sense, since that was where she had requested he take her.

She didn't know what she expected would happen when she reached the bathroom. She would go pee, certainly. She would wash up, definitely, taking as much time as possible. But then she would be right back at square one, trapped in a decrepit house with a lovestruck psycho waiting to rape her.

She tried to think. There had to be a way to more fully develop her plan. "Gee, honey, I want to wash up before we make beautiful music together," was a start, but it wasn't going to buy her much more than a couple of minutes.

She was making this up as she went along, and she was rapidly running out of ideas. The biggest problem was the nearly crippling terror that had gripped her since seeing the man with the gun on the school bus. That fear, which threatened to overwhelm her, made thinking straight a nearly impossible proposition.

As hard as she tried, she could not seem to force her mind to get beyond the horrifying visualizations of what might be in store for her.

It was kind of funny, in a sickly ironic way. Carli Ferguson was a virgin. She had had a couple of different opportunities to rectify that situation with a couple of different guys, but neither one had been special enough. She had wanted her first time to be something more than the stereotypical. nervous fumbling in the back seat of some boy's mother's minivan.

And now, the thought that not only would her first time not be special, but rather it would be a rape committed by a thirty-something murdering pervert was causing Carli's brain to seize up and cease functioning.

It was kind of like what had happened to the engine on her dad's car a few years ago. One minute it had been running, humming along like nobody's business, and the next it had bucked and complained a couple of times before dying with an awful, metallic screech. That was exactly how her brain felt right now.

As she passed the crazy bastard's kitchen table, everything crystallized in an instant.

She almost could not believe her eyes.

Nestled among three dirty plates caked with some sort of hard-packed glop that looked like it might have been spaghetti sauce in a former life but was now practically unrecognizable, a couple of dirty glasses, some silverware and, eww, an old Penthouse magazine—what was an old Penthouse magazine doing on the kitchen table?—was a single steak knife.

This was her chance. Never mind washing up in preparation for her impending rape, suddenly she had been presented with a legitimate chance to fashion an escape if she played her cards right.

It might be the only chance she was going to get.

The knife had a serrated blade, maybe six inches long, with a pearl-white handle and some kind of strange-looking metallic ball on the end. Carli had about a half-second to decide what to do and then she would be past the table and her chance would be gone.

The I-90 Killer was paying no attention to his kitchen table. He was paying no attention to anything; he was probably anxious to get her into the bathroom and back out again so the fun could begin.

Carli made her choice.

It was no choice at all, really.

She yanked her arm hard, pulling the open end of the hand-cuffs out of the man's grasp and ignoring the pain radiating outward from her already injured wrist. She leaped for the table and grabbed the knife.

Then she spun on her heels and faced her attacker, lunging with everything she had, aiming at his midsection. She was going to gut him like a fish.

40

Bill concentrated on securing the contents of the dream, memorizing the important parts like he was studying for a test back in high school.

In the dream he was standing in the parking lot of the travelers' plaza, searching for the man who had tried to kidnap that young girl. He scanned the lot but it was choked with cars, not full but still clogged with vehicles. Then the would-be kidnapper passed Bill almost close enough for him to touch. He was escaping, driving a beat-up old box truck toward the interstate and freedom.

The truck chugged by, blue plumes of exhaust pouring from the tailpipe and hanging in the fetid air. Bill squinted and stared, trying desperately to make out the numbers and letters on the license plate but no matter how hard he tried, the goddamned pollution coming from the back of the vehicle stymied him.

Out of the corner of his eye, though, and somehow retained in a remote corner of his brain, he finally saw what he had been looking for. It was the key to finding his missing child. His subconscious mind must have been trying to show it to him all along in these crazy dreams.

The truck drove by and Bill concentrated on the license plate, but as he did, he took note of the obviously amateur paint job. The side of the truck was a riot of fading off-white vehicle paint, sprayed in overlapping strokes. Some areas were still covered completely. But in others the paint had begun fading badly, to the point where a series of blocky green letters from the truck's previous incarnation were beginning to show through.

It was the sort of thing where if you looked directly at the side of the truck's cargo bed you would never notice it, like one of those optical illusions where you couldn't see the real picture until you concentrated your attention elsewhere and viewed the picture out of the corner of your eye. But Bill wasn't looking directly at the side of the truck; he was looking at the back, where the license plate was fastened to the bumper.

His conscious mind had missed the detail about the lettering, probably because he had been so frigging concerned about getting the license plate number. He missed it again during the series of nightmares two evenings ago, too. Who knew why?

Tonight, though, he saw it and when he did he wondered how he could ever have missed it. It was exactly like the reaction you had when you looked at those stupid visual illusions.

The faded blocky green letters on the side of the truck had obviously been put there by the original owners to advertise their business. Then the kidnapper purchased the vehicle—why he needed a box truck to kidnap teenage girls was anybody's guess, but apparently it had been important to him to have one—and either painted the cargo box himself or maybe paid a friend to do it, since obviously kidnapping girls in a truck with a name on the side wasn't the best avenue to achieving a long and successful criminal career.

The I-90 Killer had been in business for three and a half years, and over that time the harsh northeastern winters and hot summers had done a job on the paint, to the point where now, Bill could now distinctly recall seeing the letters SPE FAR KET on the side of the crappy truck, hovering beneath the remains of the crappy paint job.

The portions of the cargo box where the painter had overlapped the spray were still not visible, but that didn't matter.

Bill had seen SPE FAR KET and that was something.

He reached for his wallet and pullet out the business card Special Agent Angela Canfield had given him and looked at the clock.

3:18 a.m.

He dialed her cell number and hoped she wasn't a heavy sleeper.

41

Carli spun and lunged at the kidnapper, swinging the knife with no real skill but plenty of adrenaline-fueled enthusiasm. She wasn't sure where to cut him and knew she would never get a second chance, so she aimed for the center of mass—his belly.

Immediately everything went to shit.

She swung the knife in a wide arc, angling for his stomach, planning to put him down with the first thrust and take him out by any means necessary after that.

But he was quicker than she had anticipated. He raised an arm to defend against the slashing blade and stepped back at the same time. He moved quickly, twirling on the balls of his feet like one of the male dancers in the production of *Cats* she'd seen with her folks a couple of years ago on a rare vacation in New York City.

The knife dug into his outstretched arm. She felt the resistance as it sliced all the way to the bone. Blood spurted, an impressive fountainous arc and he yelped, a guttural grunt that seemed to signify surprise more than pain.

Carli had put everything she had behind her thrust, driving forward with her legs and putting all of her one hundred five pounds into the parry. The knife ricocheted off the man's arm and the force of her momentum caused her to lose her balance.

She stumbled forward, falling to her knees as the man screeched and clutched his wounded arm reflexively to his chest. She scrabbled on the floor, trying desperately to get under control so she could strike again before he had time to recover, but once again his reflexes were much faster than she expected.

The blood continued to waterfall from the man's left arm, but after his initial cry of surprise and pain he rallied. He dropped the useless arm to his side and advanced on Carli quickly.

She regained her footing and turned to launch another strike, but the angle was all wrong and he was coming at her too fast and she didn't have sufficient time to wind up and get any kind of torque behind her swing.

Martin easily danced away from the weak thrust, his hard eyes glittering. Carli's only advantage—surprise—was now long gone and wasn't coming back, and he grabbed her wrist with his still-strong right hand, squeezing the small bones together until she cried out, first in fear and then in agony.

The knife clattered to the floor and she sank to her knees as bright pain flared in her already throbbing wrist.

He released his hold and bent down, snatching the knife up off the floor. He was incredibly quick. He spun the weapon expertly in his hand until the blade, now slick and black with his blood, faced inward toward his body.

Then it was his turn to swing the steak knife. He lifted it high in the air as Carli dropped to the floor and shrank away, scuttling like a crab, her hands and feet slipping on the grimy surface.

He brought his fist down diagonally sideways, knife-handle clutched in his hand with the steel knob protruding from under the meat of his palm. It smashed into her skull with the full force of his swing, tearing the skin open, and she crumpled onto her side, her head bouncing off the linoleum with a loud *crack!* Her blood splattered, mixing on the dirty floor with Martin's, which continued to gush from his arm.

Carli groaned and her arms and legs continued swinging for a moment in her reflexive attempt to escape her attacker, but her eyes had closed and she couldn't seem to force them open.

Then her brain shut down and the world fell away.

42

Martin stumbled to the kitchen pantry and grabbed the last clean dishtowel. He swore and screamed in frustration, surrendering to the rage, letting it wash over him. How could he have been so stupid? How could he have fallen for that little slut's silly song and dance? "Oh, I've been sweating and nervous all day; I don't want our first time to be like this!"

He felt like a world-class fucking idiot, like some stupid junior high sap played for a fool by the cute girl in class. He glared accusingly at her, motionless on the floor, blood leaking out of her head, and the urge to finish her off welled up inside him like lava preparing to blow the top off some long dormant volcano.

He was humiliated and angry and she should goddamn well pay.

But he was also injured, and from the looks of it, quite badly. He lifted the dishtowel gingerly from the arm to examine it more closely and winced when he did.

There was no pain, not exactly, not yet, but he knew that was thanks solely to the adrenaline rushing through his body in response to the sudden altercation with Little Miss Academy Award over there. Soon enough the adrenaline would evaporate or disappear or whatever the hell it did when the threat was gone and the pain would come rushing in to take its place.

He was fortunate in one regard. The fucking little bitch had swung the knife diagonally, holding it high, starting her swing up in the neighborhood of her shoulder, an error in judgment that had given him the split-second he needed to react. When she struck his arm the knife had sliced into the fleshy outside part.

If she had come at him from down low, swinging upward as she should have, she probably would have sliced his belly open and his innards would be scattered all over the kitchen floor, or he would even now be staggering around, dying, fighting a losing battle to hold his guts inside his body.

Although angry and humiliated and even now beginning to suffer a little of the pain he knew was about to wallop him, Martin was proud of the self-control he had exhibited once he had begun beating on the girl in response to her attack. Every ounce of him wanted to kill her, to slice and stab and fillet the little traitor.

After fucking her good and hard, of course.

But he had stopped himself, and it had not been easy. This girl was special, regardless of how badly she had played him. Even more importantly, his contact would be more than furious if he murdered a perfectly good girl just because she'd become a little feisty.

And that in turn might have jeopardized the entire setup he had enjoyed for the last three years.

Martin knew something else instinctively as well. This clusterfuck was his fault, not hers. He was still convinced that this beautiful little thing sprawled unconscious on his kitchen floor was the one; she had to be the one, the fates had spoken, and he was determined to enjoy the remainder of his allotted seven days with her.

But goddammit, the fact of the matter was that he had allowed his emotions and his dreams to rule his actions. Sure, she was special, but she had only just arrived; he should never have trusted her, should never have allowed himself to believe she would do anything other than try to escape. She was still a teenage girl, after all, unused to the ways of the real world.

Martin's arm began to throb, lobbing the opening volleys in what he knew was only the beginning of the war. The little bitch hadn't done any irreversible damage—at least as far as he could tell—but the wound was deep and he was losing blood and the pain was going to get a lot worse before it got better.

He needed to get to a hospital and get his arm sutured, that much was clear, but he had work to do first. Hopefully he could complete it before he lost so much blood he passed out on the floor.

Slipping and sliding through the blood to the bathroom— God, there was blood everywhere!—Martin knelt and rummaged through the cabinet under the sink. He picked through spare toilet paper, boxes of tissues, a hand towel, even a box of tampons he had purchased for one of his previous angels when she was suffering through that time of the month. He threw it all on the floor behind him and then finally spotted what he was looking for: a rolled up Ace Bandage.

He grabbed the bandage and as he did he noticed his hands were shaking badly. Then he stood and a wave of nausea and lightheadedness caused him to stumble and he grabbed the edge of the sink for support. He looked in the medicine cabinet mirror and the man staring back at him was white as a ghost and Martin knew he was slipping into shock. He had to hurry.

He opened the medicine chest, grabbing the rubbing alcohol, marveling at how far away from his body his hand seemed to be when he wrapped his fingers around the bottle. It was as if his arm had magically elongated, like he was some sort of superhero.

Rubberman or something.

In his ears a buzzing noise had begun and was growing steadily louder. It reminded him of a mosquito flying around his head at night.

The rubbing alcohol slipped from his shaking hand and fell into the sink. *Thank God this shit's packaged in plastic bottles now and not glass like it used to be.* He really would have been fucked—and not in a good way—if the bottle had shattered, spilling the precious disinfectant down the drain.

Martin slapped himself in the face, hard, and it seemed to help a little. His eyes focused and the buzzing noise receded slightly, like an army falling back to regroup.

How long he could keep that army at bay he did not know. Probably not long.

He unrolled the bandage, anchoring one end on top of the sink as the rest trailed away onto the dirty floor. Then he reached into the basin and lifted the bottle of alcohol, uncapping it with his teeth as he pressed his injured arm to his belly to keep the dishtowel secured firmly over the wound.

It wasn't easy, but he finally managed to screw the top off the bottle. Martin placed it next to the end of the bandage on the sink. He breathed deeply and then lifted the towel, now soaked crimson red, off the knife wound. Blood gushed and there was no way to reliably gauge the severity of the injury.

But the pain was building.

He sucked in his breath again and, gritting his teeth against what he knew was coming, poured the alcohol straight from the bottle over the open knife wound. The liquid hissed and bubbled and Martin sucked air in through his teeth, trying not to scream.

He failed. The pain ballooned and mushroomed, detonating in his arm like a nuclear explosion. Bright white spotlights danced in his vision and for the second time in minutes he had to grab the sink for support. His arm throbbed and he felt like he was being stabbed again, over and over and over.

When he could stand it no longer Martin grabbed a fresh towel—the last clean hand towel in the bathroom—and wrapped it as tightly as he could manage around the wound, doing his best to pull the two halves of sliced flesh together. It wasn't an easy trick to manage using just one hand.

He packed the towel as tightly as he could over the wound and then pressed it once again against his side. Picked up the end of the bandage off the sink. He anchored the towel over the wound by rolling the bandage around and around, beginning at his wrist and running all the way to the elbow, then returning to his starting point, pulling it tight.

He was panting and sweating, the pain rolling off his arm in waves that crested with each beat of his hammering heart. Martin sank to the floor and examined his handiwork with a critical eye while he tried to get his breathing under control and avoid passing out.

Under the circumstances he felt he had done a pretty impressive job of emergency first aid. Further blood loss should be minimal, although it continued to soak into the thick white cotton.

The urge to lie down and sleep was strong; Martin was exhausted. He had no doubt whatsoever that he could ease onto his side right here on the bathroom floor and sleep until morning. But as tempting as that thought was, there was still more to be done.

He struggled to his feet and waited for the accompanying wave of dizziness to pass, then reached once more into the medicine cabinet, this time pulling out a bottle of ibuprofen. His arm seemed to have returned to its normal length, at least for the time being.

After dry-swallowing five of those fuckers, Martin stumbled back into the kitchen, half expecting that sneaky little bitch—she might be his destiny, his little angel, but she had a lot to learn about loyalty and about not biting the hand that feeds you—to be waiting for him, awake and alert, and to come at him with another steak knife in her hand for Round Two of the World Extreme Knife-Fighting Championships.

He rounded the corner and was relieved to see her still motionless on the floor, exactly where he had left her. She was moaning softly and her eyes were open, but they remained unfocused and she stared straight ahead. The blood continued to flow from her head where he had hit her with the wrong end of the knife and it was clear that although he had clocked her pretty good, she was in no real danger.

Maybe she had a concussion or some such shit.

Good, if that were the case. Served her right. She could consider this the first lesson in the retraining process that was obviously going to have to take place. It would begin right here and now and continue wherever she finally ended up, until she had learned her place.

He knelt next to her and slapped her across the face, just as he had done to himself a few moments ago. She blinked rapidly and peered up at him, confused at first. Then terror blossomed in those beautiful eyes as her memory clicked in.

She began moaning, "Oh, oh, oh . . ."

Martin nodded. "Yeah, 'oh, oh, oh' is right, bitch. You ever come at me with a knife again, you better fucking kill me with the first swipe because this was your one and only mulligan, little girl. Next time I'll take the fucking thing and shove it up your ass, and then I'll put it other places you don't want to think about. Are you with me on this?"

Carli moaned again but nodded at the same time and Martin knew he had nothing to worry about. Not for a while, at least. His angel wasn't about to cause him any trouble for the foreseeable future. Maybe this little shitstorm would end up being a good thing in the long run. Maybe some time in the next week he and Carli would look back on this moment and laugh.

Probably not, but you never knew. She might be a fast learner.

At the moment, though, it wasn't very funny. The pain continued to ratchet up in Martin's arm and he felt more like swearing than laughing. When the hell would that fucking ibuprofen start to work?

He reached under Carli's armpit and pulled, and even in his weakened state was able to lift her to her feet using just his good arm. She really wasn't very big. He dragged/pulled/walked her to the basement and brought her back to her bed, shoving her down on it roughly and snapping the cuffs into place on the metal frame. She lay down in the fetal position and closed her eyes.

Martin thought briefly about getting her some of the ibuprofen from upstairs. He didn't think her head injury was severe but figured she must be suffering from a massive headache.

Then he decided, fuck it, she brought this on herself, it wouldn't hurt her to suffer a little bit. Maybe it would reinforce the message he thought she had probably received loud and clear: *don't fuck with Martin. He might want you, but he'll kill you if he has to.*

He watched for a moment as her respiration smoothed out and her breathing became slow and steady. She was asleep.

Lucky bitch. She caused this disaster and now she got to sleep like a baby, while Martin still had things to do.

Life was so unfair sometimes.

He sat and watched his angel for a while, filled with love and longing despite the trouble she had caused tonight.

Finally he rose unsteadily and headed to the stairs. It was time to get to the hospital, preferably before he passed out and bled to death.

43

It was barely 5:30 a.m. Agent Canfield had told Bill to meet him at one of the only places available at that time of the morning—a coffee shop located in the tiny town of Union, just off the interstate, not far from the travelers plaza where this whole mess had begun.

He had been surprised at how quickly Angela answered the phone when he called, given the fact that it was the middle of the night and he knew how much energy they had expended together in his apartment before she left.

She must sleep with the damn cellphone next to her head on the pillow, he thought, because it had barely begun to ring when she was on the line. And she sounded awake and alert.

"Canfield."

Bill paused for a second, actually pulling the receiver from his ear and staring at it in surprise. He had expected it to ring a while.

"Yes…uh…"

Now that he had her on the phone, what the hell should he call her? He decided to stick with formalities. He didn't know whether the FBI was in the habit of monitoring the calls of its agents, but figured Angela would not want anyone else knowing how she had spent those few hours last night and figured it was better to be safe than sorry.

"Agent Canfield, this is Bill Ferguson. I'm sorry to bother you at this ungodly hour, but you asked me to call if I thought of anything helpful, and, well, I have."

A moment of silence followed and Bill could hear the rustling of covers in the background. He pictured the pretty agent sitting up in bed, hair tousled and falling in unruly masses around her face, nightgown riding up her long legs. It wasn't an unpleasant image.

She coughed and cleared her throat.

"Okay," she said. "What is it?" She sounded distant, preoccupied, and for some reason that surprised him.

"You remember I told you the guy drove a piece of shit truck out of the plaza parking lot after the failed kidnapping? And that it had been repainted and the paint job was fading?"

"I remember. So?"

"Well, there was green block lettering, three rows of it, on the side of the cargo box. The lettering was just beginning to show through the fading amateur paint job. I remember now what it said."

Now she sounded focused. All business. "How soon can you meet me?"

"Just tell me where and when. I'm not going back to sleep now, that's for sure."

The FBI agent had then suggested this coffee shop. Bill was aware of its existence—after all, he had lived in this area for nearly twenty years—but had never stopped in. It looked like a hole in the wall and wasn't conveniently located on the route between his two stores.

They sat facing each other across a small table, steam rising from their cups. Canfield had ordered some kind of latte thing and for Bill it was his usual, basic black coffee. They were alone in the cramped dining area of the little coffee shop, but Bill figured within a few minutes business would start to pick up as all of the people working early shifts began stopping in to fuel their mornings.

"So you saw portions of the original paint job?" Agent Canfield stared at Bill with an intensity he found equally fascinating and disturbing. She was dressed in a loose-fitting t-shirt that did little to hide her figure, and a pair of sweat pants like the ones college kids wear with the name of their school running down one leg. Instead of a school, though, Agent Canfield's said "FBI" in gold lettering.

She had obviously thrown on the first things she dug out of a bag, but still she looked stunning. The stress of investigating the I-90 Killer case and the lack of anything resembling a good night's sleep hadn't done much to diminish her natural beauty.

"Yes," Bill nodded. "There were three rows of green block lettering painted diagonally down the side of the truck's cargo box. None of the rows were completely visible on their own, but I could make out a few letters in each row."

"And they were?"

"The letters in the first row were 'SPE,' and in the middle row were the letters 'FAR,' with the letters 'KET' running along the bottom."

Agent Canfield wrote the notations down in a small spiral pad Bill hadn't noticed until just now. He wondered where she had been keeping it since she wasn't carrying a purse or any kind of bag. Probably the sweat pants had pockets.

Although she wrote quickly, Bill could see, even from the upside down position of the pad, that her handwriting was neat and legible. While she wrote his mind wandered to their time together inside his apartment and he wondered whether hers was doing the same.

She wrote the letters in a descending diagonal pattern on the page, then spun the notebook on the table so he could look at her handiwork.

It looked like this?" she asked.

"Yes, that's right."

She flipped the notebook around again and stared at it, taking a sip of her latte. Her eyes never left the page as she drank.

She shrugged. "Okay, I give up. What does it mean?"

"I'm not sure." Bill shook his head, frustrated. "I feel like I've seen this before, or something similar, on a vehicle in the area, but nothing is coming to me. I've been thinking about it non-stop since I called you and I just keep drawing a blank."

The agent looked up at Bill appreciatively. "It's okay. Keep gnawing at it and if you really have seen it before, eventually it will come to you. In the meantime, we'll get the rest of the federal task force together this morning along with the local cops and run it past everyone. Maybe something will shake loose with someone.

Either way, it gives us something to look for other than a plain white box truck. Within the hour this description will be sent to every law enforcement agency on the east coast. If the guy is still driving this truck, someone will see it."

"Do you really think he's still using it?"

She shrugged again. "Who knows? It seems like a strange choice of vehicles for a kidnapper to use. It's slow and cumbersome to drive, but for whatever reason he seems to prefer it. In some ways, it's not a bad option from his perspective. Those vehicles are pretty much invisible. They're all over the roads and who pays attention to them?

"Nobody," she said, answering her own question. "Hopefully we'll get lucky and he won't realize you saw him driving it."

Bill shook his head. "I wouldn't count on that. He knows I saw him. He looked right at me as he drove by. I could almost have reached out and touched the bastard, that's how close he was to me."

She took another sip of her latte and licked foam off her upper lip. Bill wished he could have done it for her.

"We'll just have to wait and see. Maybe he'll make a mistake. But I have a question for you." The agent looked deeply into Bill's eyes, her direct gaze boring into him as if she could see straight through his soul.

"Yes, I'll sleep with you again," he said, waiting for a laugh, or at least a smile.

Her only reaction was a momentary look of annoyance. It crossed her pretty face and then disappeared.

So that was how it was going to be.

She continued to probe his eyes with her own, and her mouth was drawn down into a tight frown. "How could you have missed this lettering when I talked to you right after the attempted kidnapping?"

"You mean when you interrogated me?"

Now she smiled. It was like the sun breaking through the mist on a foggy morning. "Okay, yes, when I interrogated you."

"I'm not sure, exactly. When he first drove by I was so stunned I mostly just stared at him. Then, after he passed me, as he was heading for the highway, all of my attention was devoted to trying to get the license plate number or at least part of it. But that damned blue smoke was so thick it obscured the plate very effectively. And the lettering on the cargo box is barely readable. It's very faint. I think the only reason I even noticed it at all is because I wasn't looking directly at it. If I had looked right at the side of the truck I probably would have missed it entirely."

Agent Canfield continued to stare at the letters she had written on the otherwise blank page of the note pad as if she might be able to decipher their meaning by the sheer force of her concentration. Bill wasn't entirely sure she couldn't.

He cleared his throat and she glanced at him expectantly. "Don't you think it's odd," he said, "that in over a dozen kidnappings—"

"Fourteen," she interrupted, "Fourteen if you include the attempt you broke up last week."

"Okay, fourteen. Don't you find it a little strange that in fourteen kidnappings, no one else has ever seen this truck? Even though the lettering is faint and obscured and difficult to read, it's hard to believe in all that time nobody else would have noticed it."

Canfield sat for a moment pondering the question. "You have to remember, the other kidnappings were completed successfully. As far as we know they all went off without a hitch. To the best of our knowledge, until last week no one had seen the kidnapper get into his vehicle with any of his victims. Once inside the truck, he basically became invisible for the very reason we already discussed. Nobody notices those box trucks. They're everywhere."

"I suppose," Bill said, still unconvinced. Then he shrugged. "So, what happens now?"

"We transmit this information as widely as possible and continue working the case. If this guy is still using his truck, we'll get him. I like our chances. These slimeballs are creatures of habit; they like to stick with what has worked for them in the past. Either way, though, we keep on keeping on. This is one more piece of evidence. A big one."

"Did the search of the murdered school bus driver's property turn up any usable evidence?"

"I really shouldn't be discussing this with you."

"Come on, I bought you a latte; that's got to count for something at 5:30 in the morning." He didn't mention last night because she obviously didn't want to hear it. Second thoughts, Bill supposed, and decided he couldn't really blame her.

She smiled. "Fair enough. I can tell you this much. We found plenty of prints on the stolen car the guy used to get to her house and to dump her body. They were all over the steering wheel and gearshift, as well as on the door handle and the trunk."

"That's encouraging."

"Well, yes and no," she answered. "Incredibly, there's no match in the system. This guy's never been in the military and he's never been convicted of any crime as far as we can tell. So the prints will help us convict him when we finally catch him, but they're useless to us in terms of actually running him down."

Bill was incredulous. His voice hitched as he pictured Carli, alone and afraid. "This guy kidnaps and murders teenage girls and he's never even been caught jaywalking?"

"I know it's hard to believe. It was hard for us to swallow, too. It is unusual but it's not unheard of. Apparently the guy has led a pretty low-key life and was able to function in society relatively normally for years before giving in to his destructive urges."

"Carli's dead, isn't she?"

Agent Canfield was silent for a moment. "I don't believe that," she answered, placing her hand on Bill's arm as he grasped his cup on the table. He felt an electric charge run through his body at her touch and wondered whether she felt it too.

She said, "I'm going to tell you something, but if I do, you have to promise me you'll keep it to yourself."

"Of course. I promise. You can trust me, Angela," he said, referring to more than just the case.

"The media has been trumpeting this whole 'I-90 Killer' thing for years, and we've never done anything to dissuade them from the theory that this man is kidnapping and then killing the girls he takes. But we believe he might be into something else."

"Like what?"

"What do you know about human trafficking?"

He blinked in surprise. "Human trafficking? You mean slavery? We fought a civil war to end that sort of thing a hundred fifty years ago, didn't we?"

"Yes we did," Canfield agreed, "but the slave trade still exists.

In fact, it's flourishing. It can be an extremely lucrative under-taking, especially where young, pretty American teenage girls are concerned."

A creeping sense of horror dawned on Bill as he began to see where Angela was going. "He's *working* for someone? Kidnapping girls and—what? Shipping them out of the country? To whom? Where do they go?"

"Our theory," Canfield said, "is that he is just one link in what is probably a very long chain of conspirators. We believe he started out as a kidnapper, and in the beginning he did in fact sexually assault and murder his victims. We found their remains, so we know that to be true."

Bill winced.

She said, "Sorry. Would you rather I not go on?"

He shook his head. "I need to hear this."

"That's what I thought. Somewhere along the line this dis-turbed man who was kidnapping and murdering teenage girls was co-opted by players much bigger and more frightening than he. How this connection was made and how extensive the ring is we don't know. But now we believe he satisfies his compulsion, taking the girls and probably getting some sort of time limit within which he can enjoy them in his own way as long as he doesn't damage them irreparably."

Bill stared in horror. He couldn't take his eyes off her face as she continued. "Then he passes them along to a contact, who smuggles them out of the country, probably to buyers in Russia or the Middle East."

"Oh my God, that makes me sick." Bill's hand shook and coffee slurped over the side of the cup, overflowing the saucer and pool-ing on the scarred table.

"I know it's hard to hear," Canfield said gently, "but the thing you should focus on, and the reason why I told you, is that we believe Carli is still alive. And just as importantly, we believe she is still in this general area. If we catch a break or two, like we seem to have done with your memory about the truck, we just might be able to nail this twisted bastard before Carli is shipped out of the country. But if we don't find her before that happens…"

Her voice trailed off. There was no need for her to continue.

Bill hung his head, thinking hard, trying to digest the implications of this information. Carli was alive. He held onto that nugget of hope like a drowning man clinging to a life raft. She was alive, and if she was alive she could be saved. That was what he needed to focus on, not the horrifying scenario Angela had just laid out.

"Hang in there, Bill. As long as there is no evidence to the contrary you have to assume your daughter is still alive. She needs you." It was as if Angela Canfield had read his mind. He supposed it was not all that hard to do at the moment.

He nodded and gazed across the table. Canfield looked beautiful and desirable, of course, but also calm and capable. Professional. The FBI agent finished her coffee, setting the cup down on the table with a jarring clatter that sounded much too loud.

"I've got to get this information out to the unwashed masses. Thanks for calling, Bill. It goes without saying this is a huge break. If you think of anything else, let me know immediately. I would prefer if you only called me. A single contact point makes things much on my end."

"Of course."

"Thanks for the coffee." Agent Canfield rose from the table and glided out the door without a look back. Bill watched her through the big plate glass window as she got into a plain Chevy Caprice sedan and drove away.

He sipped the last of his coffee. He wanted to scream, to hit somebody or something. He didn't feel the information he had just given Agent Canfield was huge. If it didn't help capture the son of a bitch, what good was it, really?

Bill knew in his heart the I-90 Kidnapper was no longer driving around the east coast in that ratty old box truck; he couldn't possibly be stupid enough to continue using it after Bill had seen him in it as plainly as day. The guy had successfully kidnapped thirteen girls before making his first and so far only mistake. He was too smart to keep using the vehicle the only witness had seen him driving.

Not only that, but Bill realized something else after this morning's conversation—Special Agent Angela Canfield was sexy as hell and he felt a strong and growing attraction toward her. He had wondered whether last night was a mistake; a result of the stress of Carli's disappearance and the fact that he felt so helpless to do anything about it, or maybe because he blamed himself for the whole goddamned mess.

But whatever the reason, he couldn't deny his attraction—almost animal in nature—for the slim and pretty agent. It appeared she did not feel the same way toward him, based on her reaction this morning when he referenced their encounter, but perhaps that was nothing more than her way of compartmentalizing things while on the job.

And as far as using the available evidence to convict the I-90 Killer after his capture, Bill couldn't care less about that. Fingerprints, DNA evidence, the lettering on the bastard's truck, none of it mattered to Bill Ferguson, at least not in terms of using it to attain a conviction in a court of law.

Bill didn't give a shit about a winning a trial or incarcerating the lunatic or anything else.

Beyond finding Carli alive and rescuing her, what he wanted more than anything else in the world was the I-90 Killer dead and buried. It was a visceral need, the intense thirst of a man lost in the desert. He had missed his chance to put the fucker in the ground once; he wouldn't make that mistake again if he ever got another crack at him.

He drained his cup and stalked out of the coffee shop.

44

Carli's head pounded relentlessly. It felt like the USC Marching Band had taken up residence inside her skull and was practicing for their next halftime show. She had suffered on and off from migraines ever since young childhood, so Carli Ferguson knew headaches, and this one was off the charts.

She kept her eyes closed and began turning over in her bed, ever so slowly, moving onto her left side. Sometimes curling up in the fetal position with her right arm covering her eyes helped block out the light a little bit better than just lying on her back, and with this massive headache attacking her she was ready to try anything.

But as she pulled her right arm to place it over her head she was unable to move it. It was stuck. She couldn't move her right arm.

She pulled harder and still the arm refused to cooperate, and this time she could hear a clanking, like the creepy noise of the chains poor Marley was forced to tote around in the stage rendition of *A Christmas Carol* she had gone to see with her class in Boston last December. The actor playing the doomed financier had carried real chains, a lot of them, and the sound of them rattling together and dragging on the ground had been terrifying.

"Ponderous," the man had said.

This noise was similar, only not quite so extensive. What the hell would chains be doing in her bedroom?

Carli tried to open her eyes and then the reality of her situation penetrated her consciousness. She groaned, partly out of fear and frustration and partly from the pain pounding in her head.

She was here, wherever "here" was; in the basement of the lunatic's house. She had grabbed the grimy knife off the kitchen table in a desperate attempt to slice open the kidnapper and escape and had actually, for just a moment, thought she might manage it. She had even sliced open his arm. Then he overpowered her and grabbed the knife and—what? Did he cut her with it? In the head?

She didn't think she would still be alive if he had used the business end of the steak knife on her head, or anywhere else for that matter. And the almost unbearable pain thundering through her head led her to believe she was, in fact, still alive.

Either that or Hell was a real bitch.

Whatever Martin had done to her had been brutally effective. She reached her left hand, the one not handcuffed to the bed frame, tentatively up to the right side of her head and gasped in pain when her fingertips touched the open wound.

He had hit her with something. That was it. The skin on her skull was torn and raw and blood oozed from the open wound. The blood had seeped into her hair making it messy and sticky and then it had dried, clumping great tufts of hair together until it felt matted and disgusting and foreign against her head.

The blood had flowed in a tiny crimson river into her eye, crusting on the lid and sealing it shut.

The blood stained the dirty pillow and threadbare sheet her kidnapper had provided for her.

It seemed like a lot of blood. It was a frightening amount of blood to have all come out of her head.

On the bright side, though, if this nightmare could actually be considered to have a bright side, the blood flow seemed mostly to have stopped. What would happen when she tried to get up was anybody's guess, but with her head pounding and throbbing the way it was, she didn't think she would be jumping up and running the Boston Marathon any time soon anyway.

Plus you're still handcuffed. Let's not forget that.

And she had peed herself sometime during the night. Half-dried, sticky wetness covered her butt and the insides of both thighs and the worst part was she needed to go again.

Note to self, she thought groggily: *Wait until* after *your kidnapper takes you to the bathroom to attack him with a dirty steak knife. This sort of information is invaluable and will really come in handy the next time you're kidnapped at gunpoint off the school bus by a stark-raving-mad lunatic.*

Carli eased her good eye closed again, grateful for the resulting darkness, as the pounding in her head seemed to lessen slightly. She wondered what time it was, how long she had been unconscious, and most importantly, where the crazy kidnapper had gone and when he would be coming back.

Weak, watery daylight struggled through the dirty basement window so she knew she had been lying unconscious on the bed for quite some time. It was the middle of the night when she tried to play ninja with her kidnapper, and now it was daytime.

Without fully realizing it, Carli drifted back into an uneasy half-slumber.

*   *   *

Martin sat on the bottom step of his basement stairs and watched his angel quietly as she fidgeted on the bed. She explored her head wound, which had bled like a bastard as head wounds always do.

Martin still figured the injury was not too serious. He was something of an expert on inflicting damage on teenage girls and he guessed she may have suffered a slight concussion and probably had a doozey of a headache, but that was likely the extent of it.

The skin he had torn open with the butt end of the knife had more or less stopped bleeding. It probably required nothing more than a few stitches, not that he was about to bring her to the hospital. The scar would be almost invisible under her luxurious mane of blonde hair, so his contact would not be *too* upset, and the wound might serve as a handy reminder to her of what would happen if she tried to fuck with him or her next owner even again.

He would let her suffer for a while with her bloody face and pissed pants—it was exactly what she deserved after her treachery last night—and later, after she had had a chance to meditate on her foolishness, he would bring her upstairs to clean the cut on her head and allow her to shower.

While he watched, of course, as a security measure.

Clean clothes wouldn't be a problem. After hosting more than a dozen girls, all roughly her dimensions, for anywhere from a few hours in the beginning to seven days more recently, Martin had built up quite an extensive collection of stylish clothing favored by the twenty-first century teen girl. All the hot brands—t-shirts, sweat shirts, jeans, skirts, tank tops, and, of course, pretty underwear—he had everything, stacked in piles in the back of his closet, all waiting for the perfect girl to wear them.

Carli would be the one.

She was perfect.

Eventually he would do all that. For now, though, he was content to sit unobserved and watch his little angel as she began the process of adjusting to her new way station and her new situation. As angry as he had been at the moment of the attack last night, Martin now realized he had brought it upon himself. He never should have trusted her. It was just so hard not to.

The 4:00 a.m. trip to the hospital had been interesting. Martin drove himself to the emergency room, of course, his sliced-up arm screaming in protest, even after he had swallowed all those ibuprofens. The road in front of the windshield wavered and shimmied as if he were driving drunk, sometimes disappearing entirely for a second or two as his body dealt with the shock of the serious wound, before swimming back into focus, more or less.

At the nearly empty emergency room, first the nurse and then the doctor who eventually stitched him up took one look at the chunk taken out of his arm and eyed him suspiciously. The injury had "domestic dispute" written all over it, and the concern of the medical staff was clearly for whoever had been on the other end of the knife, and the fate she might have suffered.

Martin chuckled, watching as his angel tossed and turned on the bed in obvious discomfort. The medical buffoons assumed it was a domestic dispute, and in a way they had been spot on.

But of course, Martin had known what conclusion they would jump to and was ready with a story. He had been replacing the muffler on his car.

"The wrench slipped," he said, the picture of innocence, sincerity in his eyes, "and I gouged my arm on a loose piece of exposed sheet metal."

"You were working on your car at three o'clock in the morning?" the doctor asked sarcastically, making no attempt to hide his disbelief.

Martin didn't blame him, really; the scenario was about as flimsy as they come. But what could the doctor do? Martin stuck to his guns and in the end they had done the only thing they *could* do—suture the wound and give him a prescription for some high-quality painkillers, and then send him on his way.

They were suspicious, of course they were, and for good reason. They knew his story was bullshit. But there was not a goddamned thing they could do about it. Even if they decided to alert the authorities, their efforts would be wasted. The license and insurance information was all bogus—fakes provided by his contact for use in the event of just such an emergency.

By the time he walked back through his front door daylight was dawning, although the sky was overcast and moisture hung in the air like evil intent. Martin was exhausted. He had stumbled into the basement and checked on Carli, still passed out on the filthy bed, and then gone back upstairs and taken two Percs.

He had slept like a baby. A baby high on prescription pain meds.

The disappointment of not being able to consummate his burgeoning relationship with Carli last night was fresh in Martin's mind, but after participating in a knife fight, enduring the cleaning and suturing of a serious stab wound as well as the accusatory stares of the hospital personnel, and being up all night to boot, Martin decided it couldn't hurt to wait another few hours for the Big Moment.

He wanted to be able to enjoy it, after all, and right now, with his forearm throbbing and barking at him, the sex wouldn't be that much fun anyway. It would be nothing more than fucking, animal rutting, and he wanted it to be special. He wanted it to be something they could both remember with fondness as the years went by, despite the fact they would never see each other again.

There was still plenty of time, after all. He had six more days and Carli Ferguson wasn't going anywhere until that time was up. He watched her sleep for a few more minutes and then rose and ascended the stairs. It was time for more Percocet.

45

SPE

    FAR

        KET.

Nine letters clustered in three groups of three, placed diagonally, running from upper left to lower right, down the side wall of a truck's cargo box. Nine random-looking letters that obviously weren't random at all. They had at one time during the truck's previous incarnation signified something.

The question was: what?

Bill chewed endlessly on their significance. Nine little letters, along with their partners he couldn't see, were the key to finding Carli.

Assuming she was even still alive.

Thus, nine letters were all he could think about. Over and over, he considered letter combinations that might precede or follow those tantalizing green blocks of paint in ways that would make sense.

He pictured the pattern of letters as he paced his tiny apartment.

He pictured the pattern of letters as he walked the neighborhood under glowering skies, the air so heavy with moisture and the promise of rain that he felt as though he was practically swimming.

He pictured the pattern of letters as he brewed coffee and sat on the john and stood in the shower.

It was the worst form of torture. The significance of the puzzle hung just out of reach. He was certain he'd seen the letters before and felt if he just concentrated hard enough the shroud of mystery would fall away and the answer would reveal itself to him.

Bill suspected that if he could just let the matter drop for a while and think about something else, everything would click into place in his subconscious, just as it had done with the dream, and the meaning of the nine letters would become clear.

But how could he do that? How could he pretend his seventeen-year-old child wasn't missing, that she hadn't been kidnapped by a mentally disturbed man with a penchant for raping and murdering teenage girls?

It simply wasn't possible, and the knowledge that if Carli wasn't found she would likely be sold into a lifetime of sexual slavery didn't make things any easier. So Bill Ferguson went in endless circles in his mind, a merry-go-round of insanity, the frustration growing with the passage of time, knowing the longer it took to find his little girl the less likely it was that he would ever see her again.

And then he knew.

He was in the middle of vacuuming out his van—not because the carpeting was dirty, but because he needed something to do and thought re-washing his already clean dinner dishes from last night would be pointless, and so would re-dusting his spotless living room—when the significance of the letters revealed themselves to him.

The resulting vision of the truck was so clear that Bill could hardly believe he had been unable to summon it from his memory for this long. The breakthrough came in the form of a mental picture, sort of a waking version of the dreams he had suffered through the last few nights.

He thought he had seen the letters before because he *had* seen them before, and when the vision clicked on in his brain, he could picture the truck as it existed prior to the sloppy amateur paint job every bit as clearly as if it were parked in the driveway in front of him.

In its earlier incarnation the truck had been used as a delivery vehicle for a small produce supplier called Specialty Farmers Market, LLC. The company was local and independently owned, supplying grocery stores and markets in the area with fresh produce and vegetables.

Bill had seen the trucks occasionally for years, driving as much as he did between his two stores. He wasn't positive, but he suspected he might have done business with the owner, supplying the company with tools and small power equipment on several occasions.

The design of the company's logo had not changed as far as Bill could remember. He guessed that at some point within the last few years the owner of Specialty Farmers Market must have upgraded his delivery fleet and sold off his old truck or trucks.

And the I-90 Killer had purchased one of them. Obviously he could not drive around kidnapping teenage girls with foot-high identifying letters emblazoned on the side of his getaway truck, so he had done a quick repainting job, and now that paint was beginning to fade.

It was a huge blunder for a man who had escaped capture for nearly four long years.

Now that Bill could clearly picture the vehicle, the sixty-four thousand dollar question was this: had the owner of Specialty Farmers Market sold the truck to the I-90 Killer himself, or had he involved a middleman such as the dealer from whom he had purchased his new vehicles?

There was one way to find out.

Bill intended to do so.

*   *   *

In addition to trucking their produce to various area locations, Specialty Farmers Market operated an independent store, in which they offered their own products for sale, as well as basic grocery staples like bread and milk.

The market was housed in a long, rectangular-shaped rustic log building that looked like a cross between an ice arena and a steroidally enhanced version of Abraham Lincoln's boyhood home. A mammoth concrete and aluminum warehouse protruded out the rear of the store, angling away to the left, with a paved employee parking lot located at the rear of the property.

Bill had never been inside Specialty Farmers Market but had driven past it on numerous occasions and was thus familiar with its location. He figured the store was as good a place as any to begin the process of tracking down the company's owner.

He was well aware that his first move should be to alert Agent Canfield to the critical piece of information he had recovered. He had promised her he would, and common sense dictated he should.

He also knew he was going to do no such thing.

Bill Ferguson had spent a lot of time agonizing over the I-90 Killer since his meeting with the FBI agent at the coffee shop this morning, and the more he kicked it around in his head the more a surprising realization began to solidify.

He was going to rescue Carli himself. The authorities could go to hell. He was sick and goddamned tired of playing the victim.

This lunatic, this "I-90 Killer," had targeted him specifically, had set his twisted sights on Bill Ferguson's family solely because Bill had interfered with his attempt to kidnap an innocent girl at an interstate rest stop. He had taunted Bill, approaching his daughter on the street and spelling out in a letter exactly what he intended to do with her, and then he had gone and done it just days later.

The authorities, the same ones he was expected to now trust with the job of rescuing his child, had analyzed the letter after its delivery and concluded the I-90 Killer was full of shit, that he was boasting and bragging but would do nothing.

Well, he had turned out not to be full of shit. He had done exactly what he said he was going to do. He had taken Carli, and right out from under the noses of the very people who were supposed to be protecting her.

And now the FBI, in the form of Special Agent Angela Canfield, was telling him to do nothing, to hand over any information that might be helpful in the search for *his* daughter, and then to just stay the hell out of the way.

Let the professionals handle the search.

For the man they had been hunting without success for nearly four years.

With Carli's life hanging in the balance.

No way.

No. Fucking. Way.

Bill didn't care how sexy and alluring Angela Canfield was, he was not about to run to the phone and pass along the information he had finally managed to recover, then step aside and wait for Canfield or one of her FBI flunkies to report back at their convenience regarding the fate of his only child.

The I-90 Killer had snatched Carli Ferguson for a reason, and it was a reason above and beyond the fact that he was a perverted murdering oily slave-trading bastard.

He had targeted Bill's child and Bill would to get her back.

Or die trying.

* * *

Business was brisk at the retail home of Specialty Farmers Market, LLC. Cars filled the customer parking lot nearly to overflowing and people entered and exited the front doors in a more or less continuous flow.

Bill wondered what the hell the place could be selling that was so popular. It was too early in the season for most fresh veggies, but he supposed since the store was open year-round they must offer some other enticing homemade food products as well.

He walked across the lot under slate-grey skies that had been threatening rain all day but had not yet delivered. The moisture in the air was so heavy and thick it felt almost as though the skies had already opened up even though the rain had yet to begin falling. One helluva thunderstorm was on the way and would be arriving later this afternoon; that much was clear.

Bill followed a paved walking path from the front customer parking lot along the length of the log structure and eventually arrived at the smaller employees' lot adjacent to the warehouse in the rear.

Backed up flush against an elevated concrete loading dock was a white box truck with SPECIALTY FARMERS MARKET emblazoned on the side of the cargo area in green block letters. The truck was similar in size and style to the repainted one he had watched the I-90 Killer escape in last week at the travelers' plaza, just newer and less worn down.

He stared at it for a long moment before retracing his steps to the front entrance.

Bill walked into the store and approached the lone cash register. The checkout area was located next to the door, and operating the register at the moment was a girl roughly Carli's age. She was maybe fifteen pounds overweight, sporting jet-black hair with a maroon stripe dyed into the bangs, and wore a look of intense concentration as she dealt with the line of shoppers waiting to pay for their purchases.

"Excuse me," he said, stepping up to the counter. "Could you please tell me where I might find the manager?"

The customer currently waiting while her purchases were being rung up glared at him like he was planning on cutting the line and he ignored her. He doubted a homicidal maniac was holding her daughter captive.

The cashier looked up at him defensively, as if he had just caught her with her hand in the till. Bill figured she must assume he wanted to talk to the manager because he had a complaint. Maybe about her.

"Straight ahead, all the way to the back of the store on the left," she said testily, before returning to her work.

Bill nodded his thanks, a waste of effort since she was no longer paying any attention to him. The customer continued to eye him closely. Maybe she feared his question was some sort of diversionary tactic; that he would leap in front of her as soon as she let her guard down and check out his nonexistent goods, beating her out of the store and celebrating his victory by high-fiving a cheering crowd.

He weaved through the shoppers to the back of the building. A cold case filled with milk, juice and soda, and maybe the best selection of beer this side of the average college student's dorm took up most of a rear wall.

To the left of the case, though, was an open doorway giving on to a short corridor. Halfway down the length of the corridor on the right was a unisex bathroom and on the left, the manager's office.

The office door was propped open and inside a grey-haired man worked on a computer that took up most of the space on his desk. Whatever he was doing involved a lot of typing and Bill was impressed by the speed he was able to manage, particularly given the fact he was typing with just one finger on each hand.

He knocked on the open door and the man waved him in, glancing up for about a half-second before returning his attention to his project.

"Be right with ya," the man said. "Take a seat if you like." He gestured vaguely with his left hand at a single chair placed in front of the desk and continued typing with his right.

Bill sat. The man pounded the keyboard for perhaps another three minutes, finishing with a grunt of satisfaction, before lifting a pair of eyeglasses to his face from a chain around his neck and peering at Bill.

"How can I help you?"

"Pretty busy out there." Bill gestured toward the front of the store.

"Yep. We're very fortunate to have customers who swear by us, even in a down economy. But I doubt you came to discuss the health of Specialty Farmers Market. What can I do for you, Mr..."

"Ferguson. Bill Ferguson."

"How can I help you, Mr. Ferguson?"

"Well," Bill said, unsure of where to start, "I assume you're the manager here?"

"You could say that," the man answered with a wry smile. "This is my business. I own it. Ray Blanchard," he said, leaning across the desk and offering his hand.

Bill shook it and said, "Nice to meet you, Ray. I can see you're occupied so I'll get right to the point. I wanted to ask you about your trucks."

"About what?"

"Your delivery trucks. How many do you have?"

"Just the one. Listen, Mr. Ferguson, as you said yourself, I'm quite busy here. Are you an auto salesman or something? If so, you should know I'm not in the market for a new truck and don't expect to be for quite some time."

"No, sir, it's nothing like that. And I'm not trying to waste your time, but this is extremely important. Is it possible I may have seen one of your old trucks on the road recently?"

"I suppose so," Blanchard answered. "When I bought my current delivery vehicle about three and a half years ago, I sold the old one. It was still running well at the time, so if it's been properly maintained it is entirely possible that truck's still on the road. What is this about?"

"Did you go through a middleman, like a dealer, or did you sell the truck on your own?"

"I sold it on my own. I thought I could strike a better deal that way, and I did. Y'know, I'm just about out of patience here, so I'll ask one last time: What is this all about?"

"Well, Mr. Blanchard, I need to know the name of the person you sold your old delivery vehicle to."

The market owner lifted his glasses off his face and chewed on the end of one of the earpieces. It was clearly a subconscious act. Bill could see that the plastic had been destroyed by countless similar moments.

Finally Ray Blanchard shook his head. "I can't tell you that. For all I know you're some sort of serial killer. Why would you possibly need that information, anyway?"

Bill almost laughed out loud, despite the gravity of the situation. This guy was worried that *he* was a serial killer.

"It's nothing like that," he said. "It's about my daughter. You see, she was involved in a serious car accident, and the owner of the truck I'm referring to stopped and offered his assistance when she really needed someone's help. The problem is he never told her his name and he left before I arrived. I just wanted to meet him and offer my gratitude for all he did for my daughter."

Bill wondered if he was laying it on too thick, but one way or another he had to get the information he needed from Ray Blanchard. If he spelled out what was really happening, he feared the store owner would either think he was a complete lunatic or, more likely, insist on involving the authorities.

The man hesitated and Bill was certain he was going to send him packing. Then he leaned back and rolled his office chair the three feet or so to the back wall and opened the bottom drawer of a small metal file cabinet.

He riffled through papers for a couple of minutes, muttering under his breath, and then, "Aha!" He lifted a single sheet of computer paper out of the cabinet and placed it face down on the desk between them.

"This is the bill of sale I made up when I sold the truck, complete with the name and address of the vehicle's purchaser." He sat looking at Bill expectantly, his weathered right hand resting lightly on the paper.

Bill waited and the man made no effort to show him the document. He thought maybe he had not made his request clear and said, "May I have a look?"

"Maybe," the produce market's owner said. "If you decide to tell me what's really going on. I want the truth. The man who bought this truck deserves his privacy, and that story you told me about him pulling your daughter out of a damaged vehicle is complete and utter bullshit. No offense. The look on your face when you talked about this fellow here," he held up the bill of sale, "was one of pure hatred, not gratitude, and you're not getting a look at this bill of sale unless and until you tell me what this is really all about."

Any thoughts Bill may have had about putting something over on this man disappeared. *He may look like a simple farmer,* Bill thought, *but he's smart as a whip and probably saw through my act the minute I walked into this office.*

He took a deep breath and made a decision. For once it was easy. He had no choice. "Okay, fair enough. I assume you're familiar with the I-90 Killer?"

Ray Blanchard nodded. "Of course. The authorities have been chasing him for years. You'd have to be blind, deaf *and* dumb to live in these parts and not be familiar with that sick piece of garbage."

"Well, I'm more familiar with him than most. At least I am now."

Bill went through the whole story, leaving out nothing, beginning with the chance encounter last week in the travelers' plaza, emphasizing the kidnapping of Carli, and finishing up with his finally deciphering the significance of the green letters barely visible on the repainted side of the I-90 Killer's truck.

"That explains it," Blanchard said, snapping his fingers. "I was sure I had seen you somewhere before, I just couldn't place where.

I saw you on the TV news after you saved that girl's life."

"That's right, and it was that damned news coverage that resulted in the I-90 Killer piecing together enough information on me to take my daughter. I intend to get her back, and that bill of sale is how I'm going to do it."

Ray Blanchard placed his glasses back on his nose and peered into Bill's eyes. "This is a matter for the police. Why aren't they here requesting this information?"

"Honestly, Mr. Blanchard, I haven't informed them yet what I deciphered about the truck. They are busy attacking the case from another angle and I figured I would determine for myself whether this was a dead end before taking manpower away from other avenues of investigation."

"I see. And you wouldn't be planning to go after this man all by your lonesome, now, would you? I know if it was my daughter that psychopath had taken, I'd be storming his front porch myself."

Bill smiled uneasily. The clock was ticking and all of this gamesmanship was wasting valuable time. He was tempted just to rip the paper out from under the farmer's hand and leave with it—that's exactly what he *would* do if it became necessary because he certainly wasn't leaving without the address of the man holding Carli—but he had come this far, so he decided to play nicely just a little longer and see where it led.

"Of course not," he said. "Me sticking my nose where it didn't belong was what resulted in this whole mess in the first place. Once I have the man's name and address, I'm going to bring that information straight to the lead investigator, FBI Special Agent Angela Canfield."

"How sure are you that the man who purchased my truck is the man you're looking for?"

"Well, I can't be one hundred percent certain. After all, maybe the man who bought your truck resold it or maybe it was stolen some time afterward by the killer, but it's a solid lead and it's something that absolutely must be investigated, and the sooner the better."

"By the FBI."

"Absolutely. By the FBI."

Ray Blanchard waited a long moment, again sizing up Bill, giving him an appraising look.

Then he stood and said, "Follow me." He squeezed past Bill and out the office door, turning left and opening a bigger door that led into the massive warehouse connected to the loading dock Bill had seen when he first arrived. Standing in one corner was a copy machine. Blanchard fired it up and ran off a copy of the bill of sale for his old truck, which he then handed to Bill.

"Good luck," he said, "I'll be praying for your daughter's safety."

"Thank you, you may have just saved her life," Bill answered with a confidence he wished he really felt. "I've really got to be going, every second might literally represent the difference between life and death. Thanks again."

He hustled into the store, turning in the open doorway and looking back. "By the way, Mr. Blanchard?"

"Yes?"

"Tell all your friends to pray, too."

The store owner smiled and Bill walked quickly through the market, past the register next to the front door, and into the moist heavy air of the parking lot.

*   *   *

Ray Blanchard watched closely through the small office window as his visitor drove away.

He drummed his fingers on the desk in front of his computer keyboard.

With a frown, he reached for the telephone on the edge of the desk.

46

Bill studied the bill of sale and noted the name and address of the truck's purchaser. It was a man named Martin Krall, and he lived in a small town called Mason, New York.

Mason was located no more than thirty minutes away.

Unless Martin Krall had moved and assuming he was the I-90 Killer, there was every possibility Carli was at this very moment just a short half hour drive from here.

If she was even still alive, of course.

Bill had told Blanchard he wasn't one hundred percent certain the purchaser of the truck was the man who had kidnapped his daughter, and that was true as far as it went, but the pieces fit together perfectly. Blanchard had sold the vehicle roughly three and a half years ago. It was currently late-May 2011 and the first victim—at least the first one to come to the attention of the police—was kidnapped and subsequently murdered just before Christmas, 2007.

Three and a half years ago.

Bill had seen the I-90 Killer, clear as day, driving the box truck out of the traveler's plaza after the botched kidnapping. Assuming the kidnapper tried to keep to his routine when snatching his victims—and one thing the criminal profilers all seemed to agree upon was that he was a creature of habit—that would mean Blanchard had sold the truck at virtually the exact time the kidnapping/murder spree had begun.

Bill shivered.

This was the guy. He could feel it.

He felt badly about lying to Ray Blanchard and telling the man he would bring the bill of sale directly to the FBI, especially after the farmer had shown faith in him by giving him a copy of it in the first place. By all rights, Blanchard should have called the cops or the FBI right from his desk while Bill sat in his office.

And the man was one hundred percent correct in what he had said. This *was* a matter for the authorities, who had to be more adept at dealing with a dangerous and unstable serial kidnapper/murderer than the owner of two floundering hardware stores living in a ratty apartment after the dissolution of a failed marriage.

Agent Canfield was probably very good at her job. Bill was willing to give her a pass on the miscalculation about the I-90 Killer's next move after handing the note to Carli on the street. Bill hadn't seen the kidnapping coming either, so how could he blame someone else? And the agent was sexy and appealing, too, in a Megan-Fox-plays-Sergeant-Bill-Friday kind of way.

Bill thought about how she had covered his arm with her hand at the coffee shop and wondered if maybe, given enough time, he might have had a chance at developing a real relationship with her.

There was no point in worrying about missed opportunities now, though. Anything that might have been with Angela Canfield was irrelevant. Because after she found out he had run down this information and acted on it himself, she would be thoroughly and righteously pissed off, and the only touching she would do to his arm would be to slap handcuffs on him, probably.

It didn't matter.

Nothing mattered.

Carli came first and he was going to get her back. Period.

He drove the back roads to the nearer of his two hardware stores. He had some shopping to so before rescuing his child. Above his head, the clouds continued to roil, black and threatening, building to what was clearly going to be an impressive explosion.

47

Carli eased her good eye open slowly, hesitantly, waiting for the sledgehammer of migraine pain to strike. She had no idea how long she'd been asleep, but recalled vividly the intense headache that had threatened to overwhelm her earlier. Sleep had been fitful, an on-and-off dozing filled with bizarre and frightening dream sequences and the occasional hazy interludes of vague semi-consciousness.

In those moments, Carli was aware on some basic level that the pain of her headache continued to lurk around the fringes of her consciousness. It was like the sun hanging over a blanket of fog, she thought. You knew it was there, dimly visible, but its full force was diminished, in this case by the fuzziness of sleep.

Now, though, her entire body remained motionless except for her eyelids—or, more specifically, her left eyelid, as the right remained crusted shut by dried blood. Her eye slid open as she cringed inwardly in fear of the crushing pain.

Five seconds passed. Ten. Nothing happened. There was none of the dizziness or nausea that normally accompanied an onset of a migraine and that she had experienced earlier.

There was still pain, but Carli felt confident now that it was a different sort of pain than before. What was currently banging around inside her head felt less like "migraine" and more like "close call with a steak knife-wielding psychopath."

She doubted that was the precise medical terminology, it seemed a bit wordy to be correct in a professional sense, but it did the job as far as she was concerned.

The important thing was that the migraine appeared to be gone, which meant she might actually be able to function in more than the barest minimum fashion. Thank God the lunatic kidnapper hadn't come back and engaged her while she was feeling so ill; he probably would have finished her off simply because she was so damned unresponsive.

Of course, the sick bastard has his own problems to worry about. She smiled to herself in grim satisfaction.

The memory of last night's frightening confrontation came flooding back. The feeling of the steak knife slicing the man's arm down to the bone, the savage satisfaction she felt from hearing his cry of pain and seeing his blood fly.

She had come *so close* to escaping. If he hadn't been so quick on his feet, maybe she would be free right now instead of chained to this damned bed with a bloody head and pissed-in pants that stunk to high heaven.

Reflexively she pulled her right hand, testing the handcuff in what was becoming an almost unconscious action. She was entirely unsurprised to hear the clanking of the metal bracelet against the heavy iron bed frame.

Immediately the pain flared in her wrist. Now, not only did it hurt from yanking on the damned cuffs, there was a fresh wave of agony from where her captor had squeezed her bones together so tightly, forcing her to drop the knife, the action which had led directly to her recapture.

The bruising was extensive. She tilted her head back and squinted through her one useable eye at the impressive and ever-expanding range of rainbow-like colors radiating outward from her wrist: there were now various shades of green, purple and brown. Even the dull yellow of nearly rotten summer squash had graduated to the brownish-orange of nearly rotten pumpkin.

Some of the damage had been caused by last night's fight, but most of it was a direct result of her nearly obsessive scraping of the handcuffs against the cement wall, as she hoped over and over that *this* would be the time she would somehow pull against the bed frame and break free of her bonds.

Carli had once read a statement doing some research for a school essay that defined insanity as doing the same thing over and over, hoping for a different result. *If that's true*, she thought to herself, *I must be darned close to clinically insane by now.*

She yanked her wrist, listened to the *clank* of bracelet against metal, and whistled through her teeth from the accompanying pain as a half choked-off sob escaped through her clenched jaw.

The basement seemed dim and washed-out. The light filtering through the dirty window was much more diffused than when she had awoken earlier. Carli thought it must be nearly dusk again, meaning she had slept through most of an entire day.

Was that possible? Perhaps her head injury was worse than she thought. Maybe she had suffered a concussion, the effects of which were probably similar to the pain of a migraine. Perhaps her massive headache of earlier was a result of the injury. Certainly she felt groggy enough that the possibility of a concussion at least had to be considered.

Still, even granting the likelihood of a concussion, wouldn't she have roused herself at some point over the course of an entire day enough to take note of the passage of time?

And what about her captor? Was it reasonable to expect that he would have left her alone for that much time? Based on his actions up until the knife fight last night, Carli would have to say the answer was, no, he would not.

But maybe she had injured him worse last night than she realized. Maybe after he clubbed her on the head and dragged her back down to this makeshift basement dungeon he had staggered back upstairs and collapsed from loss of blood. Maybe he was, even now, stretched out on the filthy kitchen floor almost directly above her head, face down in a pool of his own blood, dying or already dead.

Carli felt a surge of that same savage, manic glee she had experienced a few minutes ago when she recalled slicing him open.

But then, just as quickly, the feeling faded, replaced by a truly terrifying thought. What if the perverted bastard really was dead? What then? Did he have any co-conspirators who might investigate when they didn't hear from him in the next day or so? Or would she simply lie here chained to a bed and slowly starve to death, to be found at some unknown future date by a cop investigating the ungodly smell emanating from the ramshackle home?

Horror washed over Carli like a rogue wave. It was a tsunami of fear, a tidal wave of terror, and it threatened to overwhelm all conscious thought. For the first time since the man forced her out of the school bus yesterday (was it really possible it was only yesterday?), Carli Ferguson considered the very real possibility that she might actually not survive this horrific scenario.

Up until now, the fear had been real enough, but it had never advanced to the point where she gave serious consideration to the thought she might die. Her father was coming for her; she was still convinced of that. But maybe he wouldn't find her in time. Maybe his best efforts would be wasted and she would die, tortured by a wrenching hunger and a tormenting thirst; lips cracked and bleeding and cramps blasting through her suffering body with the force of explosives.

Panic rippled through her and she yanked her hand against the bed frame, pulling hard, willing the cuffs to break free, barely noticing the pain shooting through her wrist and up her arm. She pulled and twisted her hand, over and over, sobbing and grunting and suddenly a tremendous *CRASH!* shook the entire house on its foundation.

Carli let out an involuntary cry of fear and surprise and realized that it was not dusk after all. She had not necessarily been unconscious for most of an entire day. It might be midday, or late afternoon, or heck it might even still be morning. The daylight struggling through the dirty basement window had been washed out because a thunderstorm was approaching, and from the sound of the suddenly frenzied activity outside, it was going to be a big one.

The wind had picked up as well. Carli could hear it roaring through the tree branches outside. It howled around the structure, working its way through cracks and holes in the walls and foundation, the sound angry and relentless. It was almost as frightening as the thunder had been. Gust after gust rocked the house.

Another *CRASH!* Incredibly, this one was even louder than the last. Carli wouldn't have imagined it possible and again she screamed in terror, all thoughts of her captor being dead and of herself starving to death forgotten.

Dazzling light from the lightning strike flashed through the windows, bathing the dusty basement in a brilliance that actually hurt Carli's eyes. It was as if a million cars had been positioned just outside the house and they had all flashed on their headlights—with the high beams on, of course—at the same time.

The flash disappeared and the after-image superimposed itself on the retina of her one good eye and for the third time in seconds, Carli screamed. This time her terror came from what she had seen outlined in the quarter-second flash of intense light.

Standing unmoving roughly six feet away, staring at her through eyes wide and unblinking, was her captor.

He wasn't upstairs lying dead in a pool of his own blood after all. How long he had been in the basement watching her she could not guess, but he looked much more menacing than before, if that was possible.

A dread formed of equal parts hopelessness and fear filled Carli Ferguson's gut. Instantly she knew: last night's incident with the steak knife had changed everything. All that had happened to her up to this point was merely the introduction. The preview to her own personal horror movie.

The main event was about to start.

And it was going to be bad.

It was going to be very bad.

48

Bill's van bounced and jolted over the rutted road leading—he hoped—to Martin Krall's home. He had taken the address directly off Ray Blanchard's bill of sale and punched it into the little GPS unit he kept in each of his delivery vans, being careful to transcribe the street name exactly letter for letter. The last thing he wanted was to carelessly type in the wrong address and end up miles from where he needed to be.

Miles from where *Carli* was.

He was positive he had entered it correctly but now began to doubt himself as the van creaked and groaned along the desolate road. The GPS instructions had taken him on a route directly through downtown Mason, although "downtown" was a misnomer if there ever was one. The "downtown" consisted of a drugstore, a movie theatre and a boarded-up hotel that looked as though it had been empty since Neil Armstrong walked on the moon. Where the police station was located, or if there even *was* a police station, Bill had no idea.

In spite of his growing doubts, Bill continued following the GPS directions. They were enunciated in a stuffy British voice that Carli had programmed into the machine months ago. She found the prissy dialect hilarious and Bill had never gotten around to changing it. Now every word it spoke to him broke his heart.

He wondered what he would find when he finally arrived at Martin Krall's house. Would she even still be alive?

He shook his head furiously and stomped on the accelerator,

angry with himself for even considering the possibility of his baby girl's death. Of course she was alive, goddammit, and of course he was going to save her. Goddamned right he was.

She's alive, he repeated in his head, over and over. *She's alive.*

After passing through the town of Mason, Bill followed Route 37, a two-lane county highway seemingly devoid of any other traffic. The road wound through rolling hills, bordered on all sides by massive evergreens and the occasional two hundred year old oak or maple. Every so often a small house would pass off in the distance, far back from the road, usually at the end of a long dirt or gravel driveway. For the most part, though, the area seemed deserted.

Finally the GPS squawked to life and ordered him to "Turn right ahead," an instruction Bill found odd because he couldn't see a road to turn onto. He slowed almost to a crawl and still nearly missed the exit. He would have missed it, in fact, were it not for the GPS's stuffy British insistence that he turn.

There! Branching off Route 37 at an exact ninety-degree angle was the road Bill assumed he had to take. There was no street sign. Nothing to identify it as a public thoroughfare. Great leafy maples towered over the narrow corner on both sides and if he hadn't been looking for it, he would have driven past the road for sure. The Brit might be stuffy, but he knew what he was talking about.

Bill made the turn. The new road featured a cracked and rutted surface that had to have been laid down during the Nixon Administration and showed no signs of having been maintained in any meaningful way since.

It was eerie, like being in a time machine, driving the road that time forgot through the town that time forgot.

He accelerated slowly and crept along the narrow path, hoping not to meet a car traveling in the other direction. If that happened, someone was going to have to back up, because there was no way two vehicles could pass each other, at least not on this portion of the road.

It seemed an unnecessary concern. This road was even more deserted than Route 37. No houses lined either side. No cars were parked along the edge of the road. No kids wandered aimlessly in the steamy afternoon. There was no evidence the road even led anywhere.

Bill moved on. The GPS insisted he was on the right track and he was determined to follow through to the end.

The lowering sky matched his black mood perfectly and it seemed as though the clouds would open up and drench the earth at any moment. They boiled overhead, black and ugly, building rapidly, ready to unleash nature's fury on the helpless world below. The wind whipped, catching the side of the van like a kite and pushing first to the right, then to the left, no rhyme or reason to it; the leaves on the trees flapping and upturned in a clear indication of the impending storm.

Bill moved on.

It was now so dark he considered flicking on the van's head-lights. If he encountered anyone traveling the opposite direction now, it might be the only thing that saved him, especially if that hypothetical traveler was moving too fast or not paying attention.

He decided to leave the lights off. He didn't know how much longer it would take to get to Krall's home—the GPS claimed he was nearly there, but Bill was becoming less and less confident in the stuffy British bastard the farther he went along this overgrown cow path—and he didn't want to advertise his presence to the man holding his daughter by shining a pair of headlights through his living room window.

He had now traveled nearly a full mile along the road that was no more than a rumor. Bill thought about a conversation he had once had with Sandra back in the days when they were happy and getting along and could actually do things like talk without one or both of them stomping off in frustration.

In this particular conversation—which he remembered vividly, as if it had occurred just yesterday and not years ago—Bill had expounded on his view of life: that it was like a marathon road race. Everyone had to slog through the equivalent of 26.2 miles to complete his or her race, struggling up the front side of hills and gliding down the back. The marathon route was different for everyone, of course, as each individual fought through his or her own personal obstacles en route to the finish line.

A few people, though, Bill had theorized, were special. Either by choice or by circumstance, those special few weren't finished with their races upon completion of the 26.2-mile marathon.

Those people were destined to continue past the finish line, past the cheering crowds and the water bottles and the towels and the satisfaction of a well-run race. They were destined to pass it all by, to continue slapping the pavement.

Those special few were destined to run another mile. A mile very few ever experienced, with no cheering crowds, no water bottles or towels, no one watching at all.

"The lonely mile," Bill had said, still speaking theoretically of course, and Sandra had listened somberly, nodding in understanding when he finished, although he had the feeling at the time, later confirmed, that she had thought he was full of shit and maybe even drunk.

That's what this is, Bill thought to himself. *This is the lonely mile, literally and figuratively. This mile I travel by myself, with no crowds cheering me on and no one to hand me a cup of water. This lonely mile will determine the success or failure of my life's race.*

And then he was there.

49

Angela Canfield swore in frustration when the call came in. Her team was busy scouring the home and property of the murdered bus driver, Leona Bengston, desperately searching for evidence without the slightest idea what that evidence might be. It was tedious work, repetitive and boring, literally like searching for a needle in a haystack when you didn't even know you were looking for a needle until you found it.

Without a single promising lead as to the Ferguson girl's whereabouts, however, it was the most obvious option. Go back to the beginning of the latest abduction and work the scene.

Keep busy.

Stay focused.

Try to make a break.

Given the years she'd been chasing the I-90 Killer she knew what she would find—nothing useful—but until a more promising lead came along it made the most sense and was therefore what she would do.

Then her cell phone rang.

It was the duty officer at the FBI Field Office in Albany, telling her some farmer's market proprietor had called with information regarding the search for the I-90 Killer and insisted on speaking to the Agent in Charge.

By name.

Special Agent Angela Canfield, he had asked for. He said it was important. It was about someone named Bill Ferguson. She frowned and took the call.

"This is Special Agent Canfield, to whom am I speaking, please?"

She listened for a moment and then said, "No, I haven't heard from Mr. Ferguson in hours, why?"

The man on the other end of the call spoke for a couple of minutes and the frown on Agent Canfield's face deepened into a scowl as she digested the information.

"How long ago did he leave your store, Mr. Blanchard?"

She looked at her watch. "That was more than forty-five minutes ago! Why did you wait so long to call me?

"Never mind," she continued. "I understand. You would have had no reason not to believe him when he said he was going to bring that information to me. But time is now absolutely critical. I need the name and address of the man to whom you sold your truck and I need it now."

She glanced around at her team as she dug a small notepad and ballpoint pen out of her pocket. Everyone was engrossed in their work and no one paid the slightest attention to her.

"Okay, go," Canfield said. She scribbled the name and address on the top of the page and thanked Ray Blanchard in a distracted voice before disconnecting the call.

Blanchard told her he had sat in his office for three quarters of an hour, picking up the phone and putting it down again, trying to decide whether to check up on Ferguson's story, before finally calling in what might be the biggest break ever in the I-90 Killer case.

He'd had no real reason not to believe Ferguson when the man told him he would deliver the bill of sale containing Martin Krall's name and address straight to the FBI, but the strangeness of the entire conversation and Ferguson's reluctance to speak to him in a straightforward manner had finally convinced him to make the call.

Canfield hurried to her second in command, a young agent named Mike Miller. He was movie star handsome, cool and collected. Thorough. The Hollywood vision of the ideal federal agent. When he got a little more experience under his belt he was going to turn into a damned fine one, too, Angela thought.

She pulled him aside. "I have a lead I need to follow up on. I won't be gone long but in the meantime I'm leaving you in charge here. Keep working the scene and let me know immediately if you find anything."

Miller nodded. "Sure, boss, what have we got?"

"Probably nothing," Canfield lied, shrugging and shaking her head, "but I can't just assume that."

"I understand. Who are you bringing with you?"

"Nobody. I don't want to pull another agent off this search. This is way more important."

Miller looked at her dubiously. She should have been teaming up with another agent but Canfield knew he wouldn't push the matter and he didn't.

"Okayyyy," he said with obvious reluctance.

She smiled reassuringly and clapped him on the shoulder before turning and hurrying away.

The moment she put her back to Miller the smile vanished. She swore under her breath for the second time in a matter of minutes. Things were already bad and had just gotten immeasurably worse. Ferguson had no idea the kind of shitstorm he was heading into. And he had nearly an hour's head start on her.

50

The ramshackle two-story colonial-style home appeared almost out of nowhere, looming out of the densely packed trees like a cancerous growth. It was the only structure Bill had encountered along the entire desolate stretch of roadway and he wondered idly how much farther the trail continued and where it terminated.

The wind had continued to freshen as he drove and the skies, incredibly, continued to darken until the house, although set back no more than a hundred feet from the road, was barely visible in the murky half-light of the approaching storm.

Bill stepped on the brake as soon as he spotted the building, then slammed the van into reverse and backed quickly out of sight. The GPS informed him he had reached his destination—a little late by Bill's way of thinking—and he hoped he hadn't been seen by anyone who might be looking out a window.

Once out of sight of the house, he pulled the van as far off the road as possible. It was no easy task considering the damned thing was barely wider than a cart path.

He considered his options for a moment—there weren't many—and then killed the engine. There was barely enough clearance for another vehicle to pass without leaving the road, but Bill supposed it didn't matter much. Based on the lack of traffic he'd observed while driving here, it might be a month before the next motorist came along.

Besides, he had more pressing issues to worry about.

He picked his backpack off the passenger side floor and

shrugged it on, then lifted his Browning Hi-Power off the seat next to him. He slapped a magazine home and racked the slide, then carefully checked to be sure the safety was engaged. Shooting himself wouldn't accomplish anything other than to provide Martin Krall with another victim and probably a good laugh besides.

Bill took a deep breath.

Blew it out forcefully.

Then he shrugged and stepped out of the van. No point waiting for help that was never going to come, nobody even knew he was here.

The wind whipped his hair and his shirtsleeves flapped against his arms as Bill followed the weed-choked road to the corner of Martin Krall's front yard. The grass was overgrown, badly in need of mowing. Faded brown paint covered the house, and from his vantage point at the edge of the woods Bill could see that one of the three wooden steps leading to the front door was broken and needed replacement.

The whole place looked like a personal injury attorney's wet dream.

The house appeared empty and forlorn. Between the thick growth of trees and the black clouds shifting and swirling in the sky overhead, the darkness was nearly complete, and Bill could not see a single lamp burning in a single window.

Did Martin Krall even still live here? Did *anyone* live here? This was definitely the address specified on Ray Blanchard's bill of sale, the GPS had confirmed that, but there was no way of knowing whether the man had moved away in the three years since purchasing the truck.

It felt right, though. If Krall was, in fact, the elusive and almost mythical I-90 Killer, this would be the perfect location from which to indulge his creepy and disgusting obsessions, in a house deep in the woods, far from prying eyes and ears.

But the fact that it *felt* right didn't mean it *was* right. There was no name on the mailbox because there was no mailbox. There was no lantern in the front yard with the name of the proud home-owner hanging from it. No street number adorned the front of the house. There was no identification of any kind to indicate the name of the person or people who lived here.

This made Bill's first task a simple one: He had to find out if he was wasting his time, or if Martin Krall—and by extension, Carli Ferguson—might be just a few dozen feet away inside that bleak-looking home.

Bill eased his way back into the reassuring cover of the forest and began making his way along the tree line toward the front of the house. He was careful to take his time, to do everything possible to avoid detection despite the fact that every fiber of his body was screaming at him to *go get Carli!*

If this really was the home of the I-90 Killer, he would have to proceed slowly and methodically or risk becoming another victim. And right now that meant staying out of sight, even though the big house across the yard appeared deserted.

It took nearly ten minutes to work his way through the trees. He climbed over downed branches and around deadfalls, finally arriving at a location roughly perpendicular to the front of the broken-down house. The wind howled and the trees shook and Bill considered the irony of getting this close to saving Carli only to be killed by a falling branch.

He tried to ignore the increasingly poor weather conditions and gazed at the house, hoping for a clear view inside at least one of the windows.

No luck. Without any lights burning inside the home, the window glass was as impenetrable as if shades had been drawn. He pondered his next move and decided it was critical he determine once and for all whether this was the right home.

Built next to the house at the end of the driveway was an attached one-car garage. It had clearly been added some time after the construction of the home and although its maintenance had lagged as badly as the rest of the property, it had suffered fewer years of neglect and therefore seemed in considerably better condition.

Relatively speaking.

A small foreign car sat in front of the big aluminum door—which was closed—and Bill wondered what, if any, vehicle might be parked inside. It stood to reason Krall wouldn't park the truck he used to kidnap girls outside in plain sight, even in an area as remote as this.

Therefore the garage was the perfect place to start his search.

Back into the woods he shrank, moving farther north, emerging from the reassuring cover of the trees approximately halfway along the length of the garage. Two windows on the side wall facing the woods provided some light for the interior of the structure.

He stood at the edge of the clearing and took a deep breath. From this vantage point he was shielded from view of virtually the entire main house, but once he stepped through the tree line and began crossing the side yard he would be totally exposed. If anyone walked out of the house or, even worse, if someone was currently inside the garage, he would have nowhere to hide and nowhere to run.

Wind roared through the trees and the loud crash of a branch falling somewhere in the forest behind him testified to the legitimacy of his concern about getting conked on the head. It occurred to Bill that he might not be a whole lot safer here than he would be crossing the yard, and he started toward the garage.

Fifteen seconds later he eased up to the siding, pressing his body between the two windows, only now realizing he had been holding his breath. He picked a window at random, the one to his left, and peered into the darkness of the garage. The lights were off and the stillness was undisturbed by movement.

Directly across the inside of the garage from Bill's position was a door. He assumed it must open into the kitchen or maybe a laundry room or mudroom. Gardening tools hung from pegs hammered into the rear wall and a set of rakes and shovels were clustered messily in one corner. They appeared to be cowering, as if shrinking in fear from the home's occupant.

Assorted detritus of rural American life littered the garage—a big bucket of salt to melt ice off the driveway in the winter, dusty plastic quarts of motor oil, a five gallon gasoline can—but Bill gave none of it more than a preoccupied passing glance.

Of far greater interest to him was the vehicle parked in the middle of the bay. It was Martin Krall's truck.

51

A quick inspection of the window frame through the dirty glass showed the thumb locks securely fastened on both windows. On the bright side, Bill could find no contacts or signs of wiring that would indicate the presence of an alarm system.

He set his backpack down on the ground and knelt next to it, unzipping the canvas bag and rummaging through the items he had taken from his store and packed away less than an hour ago. The moist wind whipped his hair and his sleeves flapped uncontrollably.

He found what he was looking for and lifted it out of the bag, then stood and faced the window to his left. He ran the razor-sharp diamond-tipped blade of the glass cutter in as wide a circle as possible over the pane directly above the lock's thumb latch, taking his time and applying a smooth, even pressure.

Then he returned the glasscutter to the backpack and withdrew a small hand towel. He wrapped the towel around the knuckles of his right hand and tapped sharply on the windowpane in the center of the circle he had just scored. A small piece of glass roughly the size of an Olympic medal popped out of the window and dropped to the cement floor on the inside of the garage.

Bill cringed, waiting for the glass to shatter and for Martin Krall to come running into the garage to investigate, undoubtedly carrying the Glock he had brandished last week at the traveler's plaza.

Neither event materialized. In fact, nothing materialized. The glass struck the floor on its side like a coin spinning on a table, made several wobbly revolutions, and came to rest directly under the window. Bill reached through the hole he had just made and thumbed the latch, then pushed up the entire bottom unit and clambered into the garage, crossing his fingers that he had been right about the lack of an alarm system.

His feet hit the floor and he pulled the bottom half of the window closed behind him. To his surprise it slid easily and noiselessly in its frame. Then he positioned himself between the two windows and stood silently, waiting for his eyes to adjust to the murkiness of the garage's interior. Although it was daytime, it had gotten so dark outside that precious little light penetrated the windows.

After a moment Bill walked to the box truck, Browning held in his right hand, backpack slung over his left shoulder like a high school kid. He didn't think the truck would be locked—what would be the point, parked out of sight inside a locked garage in one of the most remote locations Bill had ever seen?—and he was right. He pulled open the back door of the cargo box and his jaw dropped in amazement. Now he understood the significance of the box truck to Martin Krall.

Inside the cramped space, Krall had custom-built his own portable mini-torture chamber. On the right side of the cargo area a small metal-framed cot sat bolted to the floor. The cot had been outfitted with sturdy leather straps with adjustable buckles, presumably used to immobilize the arms and legs of his victims. A ball gag attached to an adjustable Velcro strap designed to fit around the backs of his victims' heads hung neatly on the side wall next to the cot. Traces of a stain, faded to a dull brownish color but still clearly recognizable as blood, covered the bed's thin, filthy mattress.

To Bill's left was a hard-backed chair, solid maple, also bolted securely to the truck's floor. More thick leather straps encircled the chair's arms and legs with more metal buckles, and an adjustable metal rod that look a little like a heavy-duty curtain rod was stowed neatly on the floor under the chair. Its purpose was obviously to hold the girls' legs apart.

Bill thought about Carli and his blood ran cold.

A tool chest similar to the ones used by contractors in the backs of their pickup trucks occupied the space at the front of the cargo box, bolted with angle irons to the floor and the cab's rear wall. The cover had been left open and Bill could see an assortment of knives, scissors, hammers, pliers and sex toys.

Rage and fear jockeyed for position inside Bill Ferguson's skull. The fear was sickening, paralyzing. It screamed at him that Carli was dead, that he had found her too late, that she had suffered degradation and humiliation and horrible debilitating pain at the hands of this sick bastard. He bent over, hands on his knees, and thought he might be sick right here on the floor of Martin Krall's rolling torture chamber.

That'll teach him, he thought crazily. *I'll puke all over his truck.*

Then he focused his mind on Carli, on the sweet, All-American-Girl exterior that belied the tough little fireplug within. If anyone could go up against this perverted motherfucker and come out alive it was Carli. He refused to accept that she was dead; would not acknowledge the possibility until he saw the evidence with his own two eyes.

Carli's alive, goddammit, and I'm damn well going to get her back. Right now.

Bill had seen more than enough. The objective had been to establish that this house belonged to the I-90 Killer, and he had certainly done that. His hands were shaking and his stomach rolled and churned like the storm clouds outside. He hoped he would be able to hit what he was aiming at with the Browning if it came to that.

When it came to that.

He eased the rear door of the cargo truck closed and moved toward the doorway on the far side of the garage.

On cue, as if signifying the portentousness of the moment, the storm outside broke with a vengeance. A crash of thunder shook the house on its foundation as lightning struck a tree that must have been just outside, maybe in the very spot Bill had occupied mere moments before. A half-second flash of brilliant white light shot through the two windows behind him and illuminated the interior of the garage, imprinting the scene on Bill's retinas like a snapshot.

He jumped in spite of himself, nerves jangling, thankful he had engaged the safety on the Browning. He wasn't certain he would have shot himself at the noise, but wouldn't have bet any significant amount of money against it, either.

He reached for the knob on the door that opened into Martin Krall's house, fearing it was locked, knowing it would not be.

It was time to find Carli.

52

"Our time together is limited," the kidnapper said, "and thanks to your little act of treachery last night we've already lost more than twenty-four hours." He glared at Carli like he expected an apology, like she was somehow in the wrong for trying to escape her fate.

She had been trying not to think about specifics, but that was an almost impossible chore. It seemed fairly obvious to Carli what her immediate future held in store for her: rape.

And the prospect was horrifying.

What were her options? Virtually none.

Pacifism seemed the best choice—the only choice, really—so she vowed to continue her strategy of delaying the inevitable as long as possible.

"Why is our time limited?" she asked, surprised at how calm and steady her voice sounded. She didn't feel calm OR steady.

She didn't really think he would answer but he surprised her.

"Because you don't belong to me," he said with a smile. He seemed, in his own twisted way, genuinely to want her to like him. Why else would he bother to explain himself?

"I'm just a middleman. I took you to deliver you to someone else and the agreement is that we get one week together before that delivery takes place."

Carli shivered. She couldn't help it. She didn't want to spook the guy, who was clearly more than a little disturbed, by showing her fear and demonstrating weakness, but the matter-of-fact lunacy in his voice was chilling.

"What happens after our week together? Where will I go? Who are you going to deliver me to?"

The man shrugged. He was still standing in the exact spot she had first seen him when the lightning flashed. Carli knew it was only a matter of time before he moved forward and began doing what she knew he was planning, but for now he seemed more interested in explaining himself than getting down to business.

She didn't want to do or say anything that might change the dynamic.

"Beats me," he said. "I think you're going to end up somewhere in the Middle East eventually, but all I'm really sure about is my end of the agreement. It's pretty standard every time I deliver a girl. I get her for a week and then the people who placed the order take possession after that. So when my seven days are up, I deliver you to a specific location and leave you there. Some time after that my colleagues—who I've never met, by the way—come by and retrieve you. Then I wait for the next order. That's all I know."

Hearing what the future held was terrifying, but even more so was the dispassionate way the man outlined it. Carli had learned about sociopathic behavior in a school psychology course last semester and this man was exhibiting the classic signs. A subject that had seemed theoretical and remote in a textbook, nothing more than words on a page and questions on a test, had become terrifyingly real.

In one way, though—oddly—she felt comforted by his words. If this lunatic was planning a weeklong love-fest, she had nearly six full days left before he carted her off to who knew where to face that unthinkable fate. One thing Carli Ferguson knew—of which she was absolutely one hundred percent certain—was that her dad would come and save her within a week.

He would never rest until he got her back. She didn't think it, she knew it.

The notion of being sold into slavery was as terrifying as it was hard to imagine, especially if it meant Carli would spend the rest of her life belonging to some Arab sheik in a dusty desert palace located halfway around the world, but she refused to dwell on that possibility.

If she were taken outside the United States, she knew she would disappear forever.

But it would not come to that. She refused to believe otherwise.

"You know," the man said thoughtfully, "I was planning on bringing you upstairs for a shower and some clean clothes before we consummate our special relationship, but I don't think I can wait that long, despite the fact that you've pissed your pants, you messy girl. You can clean up after we finish."

Another blast of thunder shook the house and the accompanying lightning flash illuminated the I-90 Killer as he strode forward, hands fumbling with his belt buckle. Carli shrank back against the headboard, acutely aware of the iron pressing into her back like the bars of a prison cell.

Rain pelted the lone window and she could hear the wind whistling and moaning, whipping around and through the shoddy construction of the house. She watched her attacker approach, her eyes wide and afraid. She was breathing heavily, almost panting and she told herself to settle down but could not. Her terror was complete and overwhelming.

She listened to the roar of the wind and it sounded like the approach of a freight train.

She wished she were out there in the storm.

Or anywhere else.

53

Special Agent Angela Canfield cursed the remoteness of the road leading to Martin Krall's home. Her Bureau Caprice leapt over a ridge, getting airborne for a moment before bottoming out as it landed, screeching and scraping over the cracked pavement.

Angela didn't know much about what parts were under a car but she doubted all of them would survive the trip. She sped grimly on, hoping none of what broke off would be necessary for the continued operation of the vehicle.

There were no speed limit signs posted along this God-forsaken cow path, probably because they were laughably unnecessary. Anything above maybe twenty miles per hour was nearly impossible to maintain, and right now Canfield was doing an admirable job of keeping hers near forty-five.

She risked a glance at her watch. It was stupid to take her eyes off the narrow road at these speeds in these weather conditions, suicidal even, but she just couldn't help herself.

Four-fifteen.

Three minutes after she had last looked.

Doing some quick figuring in her head, Angela decided she had probably made up thirty or so of the forty-five minutes she had been behind Bill Ferguson when she took the call from the farmer's market owner.

Would it be enough? She pondered the question and decided there was no way to know. It mostly depended upon whether Ferguson had jumped into his car and headed here immediately upon leaving Ray Blanchard's office. If he had done that she would likely be too late.

But what were the odds he would have come here immediately? Chances were he would go home and prepare. He would retrieve his gun—assuming he didn't already have it with him, of course—and then probably toss some supplies into a bag. It was what she would do under the circumstances.

If he had done that bit of prep work, then she figured she *might* have time to get there before everything finished going to shit, not that it wasn't already most of the way there.

She wondered if she was just being overly optimistic and decided she didn't know that either.

The right front tire of the Caprice sank into the sandy shoulder, slewing the vehicle to the right, toward the massive trees. Instinctively, without even realizing she was doing it, Canfield babied the wheel to the left and eased off the gas, waiting until all four tires had returned to solid ground—relatively speaking—before once again stomping on the accelerator and regaining much-needed speed.

A few drops of water struck the windshield, fat and loud, advance scouts for the army of rain that was undoubtedly about to fall.

Great. Angela cursed again, hoping she would not be forced to run through the rain but accepting that she probably would. It was just her luck.

She rounded a corner going much too fast and nearly plowed into the back of Bill Ferguson's van. She stood on the brakes, watching as the vehicle loomed in the windshield, certain she would not be able to stop in time. She envisioned herself stuck inside the wreckage of the Bu-car as the drama played out a couple of hundred feet away inside Martin Krall's home and cursed again.

Then the Caprice bounced to a stop, dust rising up around it, and her front bumper just kissed the rear of Ferguson's van, both vehicles lurching once before settling.

Special Agent Canfield leapt out of the car almost before it had stopped rocking. She drew her weapon and angled across the deserted road, breaking into an all-out sprint as she approached the dilapidated house.

54

Bill thanked God or karma or maybe just plain old shit luck—he was certainly due for some—for the noise of the storm. Between the crashing of the thunder, the keening of the wind in the trees, and the splattering of the gusty rain against the windows, the racket was deafening. It should mask the sound of his approach as he made his way through the house.

Of course, there was no way of knowing for sure whether Martin Krall was even here at the moment. Perhaps he was at work—assuming he had a job—or perhaps he was out shopping or maybe even haunting the lonely expanse of Interstate 90 in eastern New York State and western Massachusetts, searching for his next victim.

Bill didn't think any of those things were the case, though. The presence of that car parked in front of the garage suggested otherwise.

A more likely scenario was that he was right on the other side of the door, six feet away, sitting at his kitchen table sipping coffee, gloating about his successful kidnapping of Carli Ferguson and how he put one over on not just the FBI and the New York and Massachusetts State Police, but on Bill Ferguson himself.

It was impossible to know without opening the door and walking into the house. It was even possible the door would be locked, and then what would he do? Bill had no idea how to pick a lock. If he tried the doorknob and found that it wouldn't turn, he would be forced to break the door down and then—obviously—any hope of a stealthy approach would be lost.

But Bill didn't think the door would be locked.

Why would Krall bother to lock an entryway that was accessible through a locked garage? He didn't seem like the type to take extra precautions just because he kept kidnapped girls inside his house. He was careful in his methods but also not afraid to take risks, as his taunting letter prior to taking Carli indicated.

Bill was willing to bet the door would open when he tried it, and in a way he *was* betting on it.

He was betting his daughter's life on it.

Bill flicked the safety off the Browning and grasped the tarnished brass doorknob. He was sweating like he had just done fifty pushups. Another crash of thunder sounded outside and the resulting flash of lightning illuminated the garage like Fenway Park during a night game.

He turned the knob and walked through the door into an empty kitchen.

Dirty dishes littered the sink as well as the kitchen table, which was located next to the garage entrance. The dingy green and white tiles of the linoleum floor looked approximately three months overdue for a good mopping.

But the thing that drew Bill Ferguson's attention immediately upon entering the kitchen—as soon as he had determined no one was about to gut-shoot him—was the bloodstain.

It was large and terrifying, and the blood had splattered all over the floor and halfway up the wall. It looked horrific, as though someone had died a violent death here.

Recently.

Bill sidled across the kitchen, trying to look in every direction at once, concerned about leaving his back exposed but unable to stop himself from checking out the blood. He bent and studied it. It was brownish-red and sticky, clearly fresh, and just as clearly the result of a struggle. It would have been impossible for Krall or anyone else to inflict that much damage on himself accidentally.

A surge of crippling fear coursed through his body. A mental picture of Carli lying on the floor mortally wounded, leaking blood from a serious wound while the I-90 Killer watched in amusement, sprang unbidden into Bill's mind. He arose from the floor and set out to clear the rest of the house, moving much more quickly now.

The remainder of the home's first floor was just as deserted as the kitchen, although signs of habitation were everywhere. A dirty pair of white gym socks had been tossed haphazardly onto the living room floor next to a sagging green couch in front of the television. A newspaper, folded over to expose a half-finished crossword puzzle, awaited completion on top of a messy coffee table. Dirty drinking glasses were scattered around the room seemingly at random, some still half-filled with liquid.

But there were no people, injured or otherwise.

Bill repeated the exercise on the second floor, once again finding plenty of evidence that Krall lived here, but nothing whatsoever to indicate the presence of Carli Ferguson or any other kidnap victim.

By now Bill had reached the only logical conclusion: if she was here at all, Carli would be found in the basement.

It made sense. The I-90 Killer could have outfitted that area of the home with his own private dungeon, similar to the portable one in the back of his truck but more elaborate. Bill hurriedly retraced his steps down the carpeted stairway to the first floor and into the kitchen, back to where he had started his tour just a few minutes ago.

Adjacent to the entryway was a second wooden door, identical to the one from the garage, located to its right as he faced it. This had to be the doorway that would lead to the basement.

And to Carli.

Hopefully.

Bill allowed himself a pleasant momentary vision of Krall somewhere else. Anywhere else. In this scenario, Bill would waltz down the stairs, find his child safe and sound, untie her and bring her home. He would be more than happy to let Special Agent Angela Canfield handle the job of hunting down and arresting Martin Krall.

It was a nice dream. But Bill knew it was an unrealistic one as well.

He repeated his exercise of a few minutes ago, leaning up against the door and pressing his ear against it, straining to hear voices or footsteps or any other sound that would give him some indication of whether anyone was there, and if they were, what they might be up to.

The results were the same. It was disappointing but unsurprising. He could hear nothing but the relentless pounding of the wind and rain against the house and the occasional high-decibel crash of thunder.

Once more he grasped a brass doorknob with a sweaty hand and eased the door open, praying to a God he had most recently been castigating that his luck would hold.

Bill exerted a steady upward pressure on the knob, hoping the added tension would prevent the door's hinges from squeaking excessively and alerting Krall, if he was there, to his presence. The door eased open, revealing a wooden stairway disappearing into the gloomy semi-dark of the basement.

These stairs, like everything else in the home, appeared badly in need of renovation if not outright replacement. One tread, located roughly halfway down the stairs, had come loose and been thrown haphazardly onto the riser without even being nailed back into place. Bill would have to exercise extreme caution to avoid tripping on that or some other loose tread and falling to the basement floor.

He took one step, then two, then a third, and slowly descended into the stifling humidity of the cellar. Shadows moved below and Bill knew he had been right. Whatever was happening in this house was happening down here.

One more step and Bill's eye level was finally below the first floor joists, allowing him a view of the entire basement. He stopped in his tracks, horrified.

Chained to a bed, lying on a ratty, filthy mattress, was his little girl.

Dried blood crusted one side of her head, running from her scalp—which featured a mass of hopelessly clumped and knotted hair—down her face and under the collar of her Avril Lavigne T-shirt. Her jeans were a filthy mess, stained with dried blood and urine.

A man—undoubtedly Martin Krall, although his back was to Bill so he could not say for certain—approached Carli from the left of the stairs. His right arm was swathed in bandages and Bill flashed on all of the blood he had seen on the kitchen floor.

Was it possible Carli had inflicted that injury on Krall? He hoped so but couldn't imagine how that might have happened.

Krall knelt next to the cot as Carli cringed back against the grungy black iron bars of the headboard. Her eyes were screwed shut and her mouth drawn down in a grimace of fear and disgust. The man fumbled with her belt buckle and unsnapped her jeans, mumbling to her in a low voice. Bill could just make it out over the noise of the storm, although he could not hear what the man was saying.

Every fiber of his body was screaming at him to *Shoot! Shoot him! Do it now before he turns and sees you! Before he does any more damage to your baby!*

Bill raised the Browning Hi-Power. He sighted down the barrel and shook his head in mute frustration. Krall's body was positioned directly between Bill and Carli. If he took the shot and Krall moved at the last second, or if Bill missed—his hands were shaking badly, it was a definite possibility—or if he hit Krall but the round went through his body, it would strike Carli. There was no question about it.

Bill wanted to scream; would have screamed, in fact, if there were any way to do it without alerting Krall to his presence and giving up the advantage of surprise. He moved down another step and then another, somehow remembering in the tension and fear and frustration to avoid the faulty stair tread.

In a few seconds that felt like a lifetime he had reached the bottom of the stairway.

Krall still hadn't heard a sound.

He took two steps and put himself in position immediately behind Krall as the man was unzipping Carli's jeans. Bill could hear the sound of the zipper distinctly over the noise of the storm.

He lifted his gun to blow Martin Krall to Hell and—

55

—And he heard the distinctive sound of a slide being racked, the heavy metallic *KA-CHINK* that was at once menacing and unmistakable, and a split second later felt the deadly mass of a handgun barrel being pressed into his ear.

"Drop it," commanded a voice so softly that Bill could barely discern it over the shrieking noise of the storm.

For a moment nothing happened.

The wind howled and the thunder crashed and the rain pelted the casement window and Bill Ferguson knew if he surrendered his weapon he was condemning himself and his daughter to death. Confusion battled frustration in his head—fear was running a distant third—and Bill tried to imagine how someone had managed to sneak up behind him after he had just finished clearing the entire house.

"I said drop the gun," the voice repeated. "You have two seconds before I blow your fucking brains all over your little girl."

In front of him, Krall had finally realized something was happening and he turned slowly. His initial look of concern was replaced by a sly smile as he completed his turn and took in the scene.

Something was wrong here, something more than the fact that Bill had botched his rescue attempt. He couldn't put his finger on exactly what it was. Something about that disembodied voice behind him sounded chillingly familiar, but he couldn't place it. It was disorienting. He reluctantly held the Browning out to the side with two fingers on the butt of the pistol.

In his peripheral vision Bill watched as a hand snaked out and grabbed the gun. It was a slender hand, female, and attached to it was an arm covered with a soaking wet blue windbreaker.

An FBI windbreaker.

Immediately he placed the voice.

It was the same one he had heard gasping and moaning last night.

It was Special Agent Angela Canfield.

"This is the guy," Bill said, turning excitedly, wondering why she didn't get what the hell was going on here. How stupid could she be? "This is the I-90 Killer! Put the cuffs on him for Christ's sake before he has a chance to—"

"Shut up," Canfield said. She pistol-whipped Bill in the forehead, opening a gash and rocking him back on his heels. Blood spurted and rolled down his face in a thick wave. "Give me a minute to think."

As Bill stumbled from the force of the blow, Krall reached out and carefully plucked Bill's Browning from Agent Canfield's hand. He began examining it.

"What are you doing here?" he said to her. "I was supposed to have this chick for a whole week. Don't go cheating me, we had the usual agreement."

Both of them ignored Bill. He stood frozen in place, still more out of confusion than fear.

The I-90 Killer seemed utterly unruffled, unaffected by the fact he had come a half-second away from having his slimy head blown right off his perverted shoulders.

Carli moaned. It was the first sound Bill had heard her make. She looked at Bill with huge eyes filled with desperation and maybe even resignation.

And the truth began to dawn on him.

Martin Krall's abrupt change in expression from concern to relief.

Special Agent Angela Canfield's mystifying reluctance to train her weapon on the wanted kidnapper/murderer/slave trader.

Canfield's insistence instead on disarming *him* and allowing Krall to handle the weapon.

"Oh my God," he said, wishing he could comfort Carli but not having a clue how to do so. "You're involved in this, aren't you?"

He looked into Canfield's face and saw those ice blue eyes staring unblinkingly back at him, glittering and beautiful and suddenly also cold and calculating. He wondered how they could ever have seemed warm and inviting.

She continued to press her service weapon insistently into his forehead.

He refused to back off and more blood spilled, starting a second wave, running into his eyebrows. Soon it would begin to drip into his eyes.

"Duh," she said mockingly. "Great sleuthing, Sherlock. How the hell else do you think this moron could escape capture for so long?"

"What the fuck!" Krall protested, but Canfield ignored him.

"It's the perfect scam," she continued. "He takes the girls, enjoys them for a week in his own...unique way, and then we move them out of the country and along to their new owners."

Bill was stunned. "But...these girls are people! They're human beings and you're ripping them away from their families, sentencing them to a lifetime of servitude and torture!"

"There's money to be made."

"My God," he said in wonderment. "You are one cold bitch. What the hell is wrong with you? This guy here," Bill indicated Martin Krall with a nod, "has obviously got mental and psychological issues, but you..."

His voice trailed off and he shook his head in utter amazement.

"Oh, grow up, will you, Mr. Boy Scout?" Canfield said, her voice dripping with scorn. "I worked gangs for years when I first started in law enforcement and you want to know what I saw?"

Bill stared at her silently, in shock, and she continued. "I'll tell you what I saw. I saw people on the take everywhere. I saw money being made hand over fist, mountains of money, more money than you could ever count, all of it going to judges and politicians and high-level bureaucrats. I saw myself busting my ass, trying to make a difference, while all the fat cats got rich off my hard work.

"So when I got this gig and ran down the legendary Mr. Krall, here, I saw the chance, maybe a once in a lifetime opportunity, to make my big score. We teamed up and made the right connections and had a great thing going until *you* came along and fucked everything up."

She shoved the gun barrel into his forehead again and pain blossomed outward from the point of impact.

Bill barely noticed.

"I was within one or two more girls of having enough money to be able to chuck it all, to tell the FBI to fuck off and go live on a beach somewhere."

She sighed and shook her head ruefully. "This changes everything. Now I guess I'll have to work *longer*. On the bright side," she said, smiling coldly at Bill, "I believe I can make this all work out to my benefit. Or at least enough so I can live to fight another day. Yes, I'm pretty sure I can."

"But what about…" Bill began.

"Last night? What about it? You concerned me," she told him. "I had a feeling you knew more than you were telling me and I knew I needed to keep a close eye on you. You're no different than every other man on the face of this filthy fucking planet. I knew given the opportunity for a roll in the hay with me you wouldn't hesitate. And guess what? You didn't. You came through like a champ. So to speak."

Bill shook his head defiantly. "Tell yourself whatever you want," he said, "but I felt something for you. I saw pain and suffering and exhaustion in your eyes and it was like looking into my own in a mirror. I felt we could give each other a little support and comfort. That's why I slept with you last night, not because I'm some rutting animal, and I pity you if you believe otherwise."

Canfield barked out a laugh, short and cruel. "Sure, Bill, the only things missing last night were the rose petals scattered on the floor and maybe some sweet violin music playing in the background. There's no such thing as love in this world. There's pain and cruelty and nothing else.

"And that," she said, still smiling without a trace of warmth, "brings us neatly back to this moment in time. Here we are, all four of us, and the question is, how do we proceed?

"Mr. Krall, here, as useful as he is at procuring virginal young ladies for our little business venture, is nowhere near creative or clever enough to come up with anything resembling a workable solution to this problem. Fortunately for me, though, I am. And in fact, I believe I've already developed a plan that will satisfy my needs.

"It's not perfect, but what in this world is?" Agent Canfield no longer trained her eyes on Bill, but appeared to retreat back inside her mind. She seemed to be considering the feasibility of her "workable solution."

"Yes," she muttered, her voice now a near-whisper. "I think this will have to do."

She rotated her arm smoothly, shifting the barrel of her weapon just a couple of inches until it now pointed directly at a shocked Martin Krall.

"What the hell do you think you're—" he began.

Then she fired, blowing his head apart in a fine crimson stew of blood, brain tissue and pulverized bone.

56

The roar was deafening. It eclipsed the noise of the storm and drowned out Carli's scream. The spray of blood from the murdered I-90 Killer's head covered her face and her clothing. She thrashed on her bed in a panic, trying desperately to escape but unable, anchored to the spot by the unyielding handcuffs.

Before Krall's body had hit the floor Canfield rotated the gun and again brought it to bear on Bill Ferguson. The entire bloody incident had taken no more than a half-second's time and Bill now realized, too late, that he had missed what would likely be his only opportunity to take her by surprise and overpower her. In his shock and disbelief at the agent's actions, he had stood rooted to the spot.

The spot upon which he was now going to die.

He had brought his hands together in front of his face in a warding-off gesture, and Canfield screamed, "Get your hands above your head NOW!"

Bill obeyed and when he did, the knuckles of his right hand grazed something sharp directly over his head. He felt a stinging sensation and yelped, glancing upward and seeing that he had struck a pair of wooden crossbeams that had been added in an X pattern between the two-by-sixes supporting the first floor. Like everything else in the house, the support struts needed maintenance badly.

One of those supports had come loose. It hung off one side of the two-by-sixes and when Bill raised his hands he was rewarded with a set of splinters digging into the back of his hand.

"Dammit!" he cried, shaking his hand.

Canfield screamed, "Get your hands back in the air!"

Bill raised his hand again, ignoring the throbbing in his knuckles, well aware that a couple of splinters would soon be the least of his problems. Angela Canfield's entire body was shaking and sweat was pouring off her. It ran down her face. It stained the underarms of her white blouse. Her moment of relative calm had passed and she was clearly feeling the pressure of this life-and-death situation. Bill realized he was lucky she hadn't shot him already.

Carli lay panting and moaning on the bed a few feet to Bill's left, trying desperately to brush the blood off her face and succeeding only in smearing it around.

He tried to ignore her. The only way he could help her now was by slowing things down, by attempting to gain an extra couple of minutes for them. If he could manage that, he would then try for a couple more in hopes of figuring some way out of this mess.

At the moment it didn't seem likely.

Canfield glanced between Bill and Carli, back and forth, muttering to herself under her breath. It sounded to Bill like she was saying, "This could work."

She was still planning, strategizing, looking for a way out, and it quickly became clear she had decided upon one.

Bill glanced down at Martin Krall's dead body lying on the floor at the foot of Carli's bed/prison cell and nearly puked. The man's head had been blown apart. His ruined skull was unrecognizable as a human cranium except in the most basic way. Bill knew he needed to do something to avoid he and Carli suffering a similar fate, and he needed to do it fast.

But what?

"Agent Canfield," he said. "Angela." He kept his voice low and, he hoped, unthreatening, although the irony of trying to appear unthreatening when she was the one holding the gun was inescapable.

He was willing to try anything. "As a female yourself, how could you get involved in something like this? You're taking young women, barely older than girls, and dooming them to a life of sexual slavery, wrenching them away from their families, forcing them into a life of torture—"

"You'd be surprised at what you can survive if you don't have a choice," she said. She seemed marginally calmer, a little more under control, but still her glassy eyes glittered dangerously, a frightening testament to the strain she was operating under. "I'm a living, breathing example of that."

"What happened to you, Angela?" Bill could see she wanted to explain herself to him. He wasn't sure why, perhaps because of the emotional bond they had shared last night, but the reason didn't matter. Talking was good. If she was talking she wasn't shooting.

His arms were tiring from the strain of holding his hands near the rafters, but he concentrated on keeping them high. Lowering them would force another show of aggression from Canfield and that was exactly what he wanted to avoid.

"What happened to me?" She blinked and paused, either considering whether she wanted to answer the question or remembering. "My earliest memories are of my mother's boyfriend creeping into my bedroom at night, raising my nightgown to my neck and pulling down my underwear. 'Playing our secret games,' he called it. Hardly a night went by that we didn't 'play our secret games'.

"I was maybe four or five years old at the time the abuse started," she said. "He used toys and candy to buy my silence, and later, when I got older, he graduated to threats and intimidation. But what he didn't realize was I didn't *want* to tell anyone. I was ashamed and humiliated. All I wanted was for it to stop, for it all to go away. But it never did, until the day he finally went to prison—for something else, by the way—and got what was coming to him."

Agent Canfield's eyes were red-rimmed and teary but the hand holding the gun was steady as a rock. "He did things to me that you wouldn't believe if I told you, things so horrible and painful and damaging that I'm permanently sterile. He took a normal little girl and turned her into a shell of a human being. A dead husk. But I survived. I overcame it and I'm strong. So don't lecture me about taking girls away from the safety of their loving homes, because I know better. There is no such thing. If your precious little princess had been worth a damn she would have been able to overcome whatever fate had in store for her in her new home. She would have survived, too, just like I did."

Bill wanted to say "Like *you* did? I wouldn't wish what you've become on my worst enemy!" He wanted to scream at her and shake her and try to make her see beyond herself and her raging psychosis.

But Canfield's use of the past tense at the end of her sickening soliloquy stood out to him like a sore thumb. It was all he could focus on. *Your princess would have been able to overcome her fate. She would have survived.*

She had made her decision. She was about to act on her desperate plan, and allowing them to walk out of Martin Krall's house alive was not part of it.

He wasn't surprised. A dirty FBI agent knee-deep in international human sex trafficking couldn't afford to allow two eyewitnesses to survive.

Even if she had slept with one of them.

Hell, *especially* if she had slept with one of them.

Bill wanted desperately to keep her talking. Talking meant not shooting. But for the life of him he couldn't think of any way to prompt her to continue. What could she possibly add to the shocking history of abuse she had just related? What could he say to convince her to open up further, and did he really want to? Delving deeper into the horrors of her past didn't seem like the best way to keep her from killing them. If anything, it might just prompt her to finish them off that much sooner.

But it didn't matter. Agent Canfield had apparently decided the time for introspection was over. She bent over Krall's body, transferring her weapon to her left hand and continuing to hold it perfectly centered on Bill's chest. The she reached under the dead man's shirttail and lifted his pistol out of the waistband of his jeans. She flipped his body onto its back, meticulously avoiding the small but growing reservoir of blood pooled around his shattered skull.

Bill thought he knew what her plan was and it scared the hell out of him.

57

"Now," Canfield said, crouching next to the I-90 Killer's body. "This isn't ideal, not by a long shot. But under the circumstances it's going to have to do. I'm not going to be able to retire quite as early as I had hoped, what with Krall's revenue stream drying up, but with a little luck, this might still work out."

She placed Krall's weapon in his dead hand, wrapping her right hand around his. Then she placed her gun on the floor at her feet and used her left hand to steady her right. She angled Krall's weapon upward and toward Bill, who was no more than three feet away, hands still raised in the air.

"Here's what happened," she said, apparently deciding to run the story past her captive audience.

Bill didn't mind. Talking meant not shooting, although it had become crystal clear that the shooting would begin soon enough.

"You got Krall's address from Ray Blanchard and ran down here without telling anyone—bad idea, by the way, although even an idiot like you must have realized *that* by now—but the farmer's market owner didn't believe you when you told him you would bring the information to me. He called and advised me that you had been in his store and figured out Krall was the one who had your daughter. That much has the advantage of being true.

"As soon as I took the call I realized that you were in incredible danger. I jumped in my car, leaving Mike Miller in charge at the Leona Bengston crime scene, and rushed here to protect you. I'll probably get an official reprimand placed in my personnel file for coming here alone—it's against Bureau policy, and for good reason—but as you might have guessed by now, I don't much care about that."

Canfield smiled apologetically at Bill. He wondered how he could have missed seeing the utter lack of emotion in her shockingly blue eyes.

"Then, when I got here," she continued, "I came through the door just as the sound of gunshots erupted from the basement." The FBI agent now seemed to be talking to herself as much as to Bill, rehearsing her story and poking at it, checking for holes.

"I rushed down the stairs to find Krall, the infamous and extremely dangerous I-90 Killer, standing over the bodies of poor, unfortunate Bill Ferguson and his beautiful young daughter, Carli. I fired my service weapon, striking the murderer and killing him, but it was too late. You and poor Carli were already dead.

"I tried my damnedest to revive the two of you, performing artificial respiration on both of you all by myself, but it just wasn't to be. It's a tragedy, really."

She looked up at Bill, seemingly awaiting some kind of response. He stared back in shock and horror.

"Well," she said. "What do you think?"

"What do I think?" Bill shook his head. He tried to find words to express the revulsion he felt as he looked at her, the woman he had made love to less than twenty-four hours before, but none would come. Words seemed wholly insufficient.

Finally he gave it a try. "My God, you're a monster."

Canfield laughed. "And you're what? A hero? Maybe. But when this is all over I'll be a live monster and you'll still be a dead hero. For what it's worth, I will emphasize to my bosses and the media how agonizingly close you came to rescuing little Carli here. It's a great story and will go a long way toward shifting people's attention off any lingering questions they may have about *my* role in this whole thing. Not that the Bureau will want to dig too deeply, anyway."

Canfield's voice trailed off and she appeared wistful. It was the first hint of emotion Bill had seen in her otherwise blank eyes since she had snuck up behind him just as he was about to blast Martin Krall. In a way, seeing that tiny shadow of her former humanity was even worse than the almost robotic lack of emotion she had displayed to this point.

It looked like she had finally satisfied her inner need for explanation. That was bad. If she was talking, she wasn't shooting. If she was done talking, then that meant the shooting was about to begin. Time had run out, and Bill still had no idea what to do.

Some time in the last few minutes the storm outside had finally dissipated and he could hear the almost imperceptible sound of Carli sobbing on the filthy cot off to his left. It was as if she didn't dare make any more noise than she absolutely had to, but simply couldn't hold in the terror. His right hand throbbed from where he had scraped his knuckles on the splintered pine support strut hanging half off the ratty two-by-six beams that seemed to sum up this entire crumbling home perfectly.

FBI Special Agent Angela Canfield nodded to herself. "Yeah. This'll work."

She adjusted her two-handed grip around Martin Krall's dead hand, using the first two fingers of her own right hand to force Krall's lifeless pointer finger through the trigger guard on his Glock. She took dead aim on Bill Ferguson's chest.

"Look at the bright side," she told Bill. "At least you get to go first; you don't have to watch your little girl take one between the eyes," and she squeezed the trigger—

58

—And Bill Ferguson wrapped his throbbing right hand around the one-inch by one-inch pine support hanging uselessly off the two-by-six joist directly over his head. He yanked it hard, down and to his left, across his body, slashing at Canfield.

The two nails that had at one time secured the support piece to the main beam jutted out the front of the support at an oblique angle, and they pierced the skin of Canfield's delicate neck just as she squeezed Krall's trigger. For the second time in a matter of minutes, the ear-splitting BOOM of a handgun rocked the enclosed space.

Bill heard Carli's anguished scream and felt a burning sensation in his left arm above the elbow and he knew he'd been shot. There was no pain, though, not yet, although he knew it would arrive soon enough.

The bullet's impact spun him left but his momentum carried him forward and he continued driving the makeshift stake through Angela Canfield's neck. A spray of blood erupted, crimson and terrifying, as the stake ripped through her carotid artery.

Canfield fell backward, crashing into Carli's cot and tumbling onto her side, grabbing reflexively at the wound in her neck. Krall's gun flew from her live hand and his dead one, skittering across the floor through his pool of blood, coming to rest almost directly between the wounded FBI agent and the wounded father.

Bill stumbled to his knees as his makeshift sword dropped onto the cement floor and clattered away. He'd fallen away from the gun and he desperately tried to reverse direction before she recover and could reach the weapon first.

He watched in horror as Canfield rolled off her side and moved toward her gun. She slipped and slid in the spilled blood of the I-90 Killer as her own blood spurted between the fingers of her left hand, which was clamped firmly but ineffectively over the wound in her neck. She was injured grievously, maybe mortally, but like Bill, was operating for the time being under the anesthetic effects of adrenaline and self-preservation.

She was going to get there first.

He'd been marginally closer, the gun maybe a few inches nearer his body than hers, but his momentum had carried him away from the weapon while hers, after bouncing off Carli's cot, had propelled her toward it.

She dived through the blood, most of it Krall's but now a little of it her own, like a baseball player stealing second base. The gash in her neck began hemorrhaging blood the moment she removed her hand from it to heft her weapon.

Canfield rolled onto her back and lifted the pistol and once again took aim at Bill Ferguson's body. Again she aimed and again she pulled the trigger and—

59

—And Carli watched the whole thing develop with the dispassionate detachment of a shell-shocked war vet. She had lived through unspeakable horror in the last twenty-seven hours, and most especially in the last twenty minutes.

Her head throbbed from the gash Krall had opened in it with the dirty steak knife.

Her underwear was still damp after being pissed in several times and her pants smelled like a baby's diaper.

The pee stains on her jeans were covered with a new addition: blood stains, first from Krall's obliterated skull and now from the wound her dad had opened up on this crazy woman's neck.

And now she had to lie here on this disgusting mattress on top of this disgusting cot and witness her dad's murder, an act which would be followed undoubtedly by her own execution.

Her dad had somehow found her, just as she had known he would, and had nearly rescued her too, against all odds, turning the tables on the FBI woman, who he had mistakenly thought was one of the good guys but in reality was anything but. And he had apparently slept with her, somehow finding time to do that while searching for Carli.

Her father struggled for the I-90 Killer's gun, which lay on the floor of the basement like a priceless treasure. The idea that the fate of her dad and herself rested entirely on who would be the first to reach a lump of metal and plastic not much bigger than her hand was absurd, but of course it was no more absurd than everything else that had taken place over the last day-plus.

Carli could see that her dad was not going to make it. He turned his big body, struggling against the effects of momentum, which had been his ally when he was swinging the stick at the FBI woman but which was now most definitely his enemy.

And the woman was smaller and quicker, despite being so badly injured.

The agent reached the gun first as Carli had known she would, blood spurting wildly from her neck, geysering an impressive distance before splattering to the floor. She rolled onto her back and sighted down the barrel at Carli's dad and Carli knew he was going to die.

And then she was going to die.

And that was unacceptable.

This whole fucking nightmare was unacceptable.

Carli Ferguson bellowed, the sound rising from deep inside her chest where all the hurt and the fear and especially the anger were stored. She bellowed and yanked hard on the handcuffs, pulling them against the metal bed frame with all the strength she could muster from her one hundred five pound frame.

The pain exploded in her wrist and still she pulled.

The bracelet had been weakened by Carli's near-obsessive scraping of it against the cement wall behind her prison/bed and now, suddenly and without warning, it snapped.

A guttural shriek of pain and rage and fierce animal lust accompanied the snapping of the metal. Carli spun on her mattress—there was no time to get up—and swung her fist at Angela Canfield as the FBI agent pulled the trigger on Martin Krall's gun.

The razor-sharp edge on the broken silver handcuff glittered menacingly as it sliced into Canfield's throat, opening a matching gash to complement the one she had already suffered. Fresh blood splattered from the new wound, once again covering Carli, but this time she didn't gag.

She didn't even notice.

Instead she watched in transfixed horror as her dad dived to the right, over her cot and onto the floor, at the exact moment the gun roared. He looked like an Olympic swimmer flying gracefully into the water to begin a race.

Except there was no water on the other side, only concrete.

The bullet ripped into his leg and *his* blood began.

The Glock bucked in Agent Canfield's hand and fire ripped from the barrel and she fell back against the cement basement wall next to the metal bed frame that, until seconds ago, had been Carli Ferguson's prison. The agent's left hand waved in the air, reaching up to stanch the new wound on her neck.

She didn't make it. Her hand fell to the floor as she lurched sideways and lay still.

Bill hit the floor on the far side of Carli's cot and bounced once, his head striking the wall with a sickening thud. His limp body came to rest in the corner and he kicked his legs once and was still.

Blood oozed from the fresh bullet wound in his left leg.

And Carli screamed.

60

The FBI woman was alive. Carli checked for a pulse and it was there. It was weak and ragged, but for the moment at least she was hanging on.

Not that Carli gave a damn one way or the other. This woman, this supposed law enforcement professional, this Crazy Fucking Bitch, had tried to kill her dad, had shot him twice, and had planned on turning the gun on Carli next, so sympathy for The Crazy Bitch's predicament was in short supply.

She grabbed the I-90 Killer's gun, which had fallen on the floor next to the unconscious woman, and then picked up the agent's service weapon, holding it for the time being under her arm. Finally, she rolled Canfield onto her side and, grimacing with distaste, plucked her dad's Browning from under the waistband of The Crazy Bitch's slacks where she had shoved it after taking it away from her murdered co-conspirator. She was a one-woman armory.

Carli slid each of the weapons along the floor to the far side of the basement. She knew nothing about guns and hoped that one of them wouldn't somehow go off and blow her brains out—wouldn't *that* be ironic, surviving the I-90 Killer only to shoot yourself by accident—but she knew she wouldn't feel comfortable until she had gotten them away from The Crazy Bitch just in case she somehow came back to life like they always seemed to do in the movies.

For the first time since being kidnapped off the school bus

yesterday Carli was thinking clearly. She couldn't imagine being more frightened, but her dad needed her and after he had risked everything to save her, she was not going to let him down now. Her nerves thrummed and her stomach lurched and she felt as though she had drunk about seven cups of coffee and damned if she didn't have to pee *again,* but her mind was clear.

She crawled over the couch to her dad—*God, please let him be alive, please let him be alive*—and before kneeling next to him to check for his pulse, had a discomfiting thought. What if this Agent Canfield, The Crazy Fucking Bitch, snuck up on her while her back was turned tending to her dad and began strangling her or something?

Carli had seen enough horror movies to know that the bad guy was never truly out of the picture until the credits rolled, and even though The Crazy Bitch seemed barely alive, with blood oozing out of the two massive, gaping gashes in her throat, she didn't dare discount her entirely. So Carli reluctantly stood up next to her father's unmoving body—*remember, God, I'm still begging you not to let him die*—and walked past the fallen agent to a workbench in the far corner of the basement.

After spending hours on end trapped down here with nothing to do but saw those metal handcuffs back and forth against the cement wall, Carli had committed the entire basement and pretty much everything in it to memory.

She knew exactly what she wanted and where to find it.

She picked up a roll of electrical wire and a wire cutter and returned to The Crazy Fucking Bitch. Knelt and trussed the agent's wrists and ankles together with the stiff wiring, twisting the strands around and around to form her own set of impromptu handcuffs. Then she tossed the roll back onto the workbench, finally confident she could check on her dad without worrying about being taken by surprise from behind.

Her dad's pulse was much stronger than The Crazy Fucking Bitch's when she checked it. In fact, his eyelids blinked and he moaned and almost seemed to be trying to wake up as she knelt over him.

He had a pair of bullet wounds that were oozing blood—one in his right arm and one in his left thigh—and it was obvious he needed medical attention, but Carli guessed he wasn't in any immediate life-threatening danger. If either of the slugs had severed an artery she assumed the blood flow would be much more severe.

His unconsciousness was probably from being knocked out when his head hit the wall. He would have a massive headache when he woke up, and maybe even had even suffered a concussion, but that wouldn't kill him.

She realized she had been holding her breath and she let out a ragged chuckle. *Thanks, God,* she thought to herself. *I owe you one.*

Then she warily passed The Crazy Fucking Bitch's unmoving body and climbed the stairs to look for a telephone. The FBI agent probably had a cell phone somewhere on her body, but Carli couldn't bring herself to touch her. There had to be a phone in the house, probably in the kitchen, and that would be just fine with Carli.

As she climbed the stairs she wondered how she was managing to keep herself together and when she would start crying—she could tell it would be soon—and if she would ever stop once she started.

Then she spotted the telephone and got to work.

61

At first Special Agent Mike Miller thought the call was some kind of joke.

A really bad joke.

Some yokel claiming to be Sergeant Carter from the Town of Mason Police Department told Mike his partner, Special Agent Angela Canfield, was hanging on the brink of death in the basement of a crumbling home located out in the boonies at the westernmost edge of his town.

"It's a fucking bloodbath here," Carter told Miller, "and you're gonna want to see this. There are two witnesses to what went down, and they're both claiming your girl was involved in the I-90 Killer kidnappings."

Miller responded with one word: "Bullshit."

Then he hung up and pulled everyone off the search of Leona Bengston's property—they were getting nowhere anyway—and the team piled into their Bureau cars for the thirty minute drive to the address Carter had given him for the home in Mason. On the way, Miller called the SAC at the FBI's Albany Field Office, filling Special Agent in Charge Hamilton Granger in on the information he had, which was basically nothing.

"I'm told by this Mason Police officer that they suspect Canfield involved in the kidnappings," he told Granger as he navigated the lonely backcountry roads at high speed with three identical Chevrolet Caprices in tow.

A long silence greeted his statement as the Special Agent in Charge digested the news.

"Christ," came the terse reply. "Where is that coming from?"

"The Mason Police claim to have two eyewitnesses telling exactly the same story."

"Goddammit. Keep me informed. I want to know the minute you have any information. If it's bad, you can plan on seeing me on-scene ASAP."

"Roger that, boss." Miller terminated the call and shook his head. What in the holy hell had Canfield been up to?

The four-car caravan nearly missed the unmarked entrance to Turner Road. Miller screeched to a halt, cutting his wheel sharply to the right and then accelerating again onto the glorified cart path. The storm had finally departed the area, but branches hung low, heavy with accumulated moisture, and the road's sandy shoulder resembled a mud pit from the effects of the heavy rains.

It took the team nearly ten minutes of fighting their way through the mile of jungle-like terrain to arrive at the remote address they had been given. He rounded a turn, slipping and sliding in a more or less successful attempt to keep half his car's wheels on the paved portion of the road, and then nearly collided with a bulky red ambulance. The vehicle shot out of a weed-strewn gravel driveway, lights flashing and siren blaring, and turned toward civilization. It nearly sideswiped all four Bureau cars one after the other before continuing on the narrow road. It looked like a gigantic, rushing beetle.

A second ambulance blocked the driveway, its skillful driver somehow having managed a three-point turn without getting stuck in the mud. The vehicle sat empty, hazard lights flashing, engine idling, waiting for another victim.

Miller eyed the positioning of the big ambulance and wondered how the hell the driver had accomplished the turnaround. Smoke and mirrors, he decided.

With no room in front of the house and not wanting to block the ambulance's departure, the team parked their vehicles on the side of the road just beyond the driveway. They exited en masse and made their way toward the home.

Miller led the way, slipping under the yellow CRIME SCENE tape and descending Martin Krall's rickety basement stairs. He gasped as he got his first view of the scene. His initial thought was that Carter's description had been right on target. It *was* a fucking bloodbath.

A pair of paramedics worked feverishly over the body of Angela Canfield, who lay crumpled and unmoving on the basement's cold cement floor, just feet away from the body of a man—presumably the I-90 Killer—with half his head blown off. The man was clearly dead, an assumption confirmed by the medical team's complete lack of interest in him and their frantic efforts over Canfield.

Blood covered an area roughly six feet in diameter around the two prone bodies. It was an incredible amount of blood; the gruesome scene looked as though someone had attached a garden hose to a bucket of human blood and then sprayed it indiscriminately around the basement. The two bodies, one gravely injured and the other already dead, lay next to an old rickety bed with an iron headboard upon which lay a thin, filthy mattress.

Miller reached the bottom of the stairs and was approached by a tall, balding man who had been standing in a corner out of sight. The man wore a Mason PD uniform and held his hat in both hands, twirling it over and over before finally clutching it in his left hand and offering his right to Miller.

"You must be Special Agent Miller," he said. "I'm Greg Branson, chief of the Mason PD. We're a small department, ill-equipped to deal with this sort of situation, which is why we don't have investigators working the scene yet. I'm pretty sure, though, that your people will be all over this house in a matter of minutes, anyway, especially once you hear what our two witnesses are saying about your agent."

"It's a pleasure to meet you, chief, and I'd like to thank you for the expeditious notification. I'm sure it doesn't sit well with your officers that you will be ceding control of the investigation to the Bureau."

"Doesn't matter," Chief Branson answered. "Like I said, we're not equipped to deal with this sort of thing, anyway. If a Bureau agent hadn't been involved, we would be calling in the State Police for assistance."

"Still, I do appreciate it," he said. "Is Special Agent Canfield going to make it?"

"Good question," Branson answered and shrugged. "The two

EMT boys have been working their asses off for the last twenty minutes. They're way too busy to answer my questions. It looks like they're getting ready to transport her now, though."

As if on cue, the paramedics lifted Canfield's limp frame onto a body board and strapped her to it, immobilizing her arms and legs and securing her head. The one who seemed to be in charge had heard Miller's question to Chief Branson and he shook his head at them almost imperceptibly.

"It doesn't look good," he said in a near-whisper. "She's lost a lot of blood. If I was a betting man, I'd say she won't make the hospital alive."

Miller looked down and blinked in surprise as Angela Canfield returned his gaze. He had thought she was unconscious and now understood the paramedic's reluctance to speak at a volume she might hear. His partner's eyes were glazed with pain and shock but alive with understanding. Her skin color was bone-white and she shivered uncontrollably despite the heat and humidity the passing storm had left in its wake, and despite the fact she was covered with a heavy wool blanket.

"Angie," Mike Miller said as the paramedics trundled her past and started up the stairs. He tried—and failed—to keep the anguish out of his voice. "What the hell happened? Is it true what they're saying?"

To his astonishment she smiled. "A girl's gotta prepare for retirement, you know," she said weakly. Her voice was quavery and paper-thin. She sounded to Mike like a ninety-year-old lady rather than the sharp, lively, cat-quick young woman he had come to know over the past year.

"Oh, my God," he mumbled to himself.

He made a snap decision. There was no time to run this one by the SAC.

He hustled up the stairs behind the two paramedics, who were now carrying the board with the frighteningly wan body of Special Agent Angela Canfield down the hallway toward the front door. The men had apparently made the decision simply to carry Canfield rather than try to wheel her across the rough terrain to the ambulance.

"Hey, guys?" Miller said, falling into place behind them. "Would it be all right if I rode in the back of the ambulance with her? If she's up to it, I need to ask her a few questions."

The men shared a glance and Miller knew exactly what they were thinking. She was going to be dead soon so if he had questions, he had better hurry up and ask them.

"Sure," one of them said. Miller didn't notice which one answered him and didn't care.

62

"Why didn't you go to Agent Canfield with the name and address you got from Ray Blanchard like you told him you were going to? Did you suspect something was not quite right with Special Agent Canfield?"

Bill saw Agent Mike Miller eying him closely as he waited for an answer. They had been over this subject more times than Bill could remember in the twenty-four hours since he'd regained consciousness following surgery to remove one bullet from his arm and another from his leg.

In an adjacent room, Carli was undergoing similar questioning from another agent. Incredibly, besides the gash to the side of her head, which had required fourteen stitches to close, she had suffered only minor cuts and bruises.

Her mother and a lawyer were sitting in on the questioning, but the session was mostly a formality. Whatever Angela Canfield had told Agent Miller in the ambulance before dying en route to the hospital had apparently confirmed their story.

Bill shook his head. "No. It was nothing like that. I didn't suspect a thing. I certainly had no idea Angela...Agent Canfield...was involved with the I-90 Killer. I was just desperate to *do* something. I couldn't stand the thought of sitting around waiting to find out what might happen with a rescue attempt. And I suppose if I'm being honest I also felt like the FBI had screwed the pooch by allowing Carli to be kidnapped off the bus in the first place, so I guess I didn't entirely trust you guys. I thought I would just charge in there and get her myself. I know it was foolish to go into that house all alone against a guy like Krall, but I just wasn't thinking clearly."

Bill voice trailed off and stopped and then he abruptly changed the subject. He had been chewing on Canfield's actions obsessively, like a dog worrying a bone.

He shook his head in bewilderment. "How could she?"

He looked up at Miller, who had nothing to offer. The young agent looked equally perplexed. And hurt.

"I was her partner for over a year and I had no clue, either. She was a very private person, especially where her past was concerned, and now we're beginning to understand why."

"What was in her past that could have twisted her so badly?"

"We've only been digging for a little over a day, but what we've uncovered isn't pretty. Apparently she was molested by her mother's boyfriend for more than a decade as a young girl, starting when she was about five years old."

Bill nodded. "She made reference to years of abuse in the basement of Krall's home. But what about her mother? Why didn't she protect her child?"

"Her mother became aware of the abuse at some point, that much we know, but it's not clear exactly when. We're interviewing her now but we haven't gotten much so far. She's reluctant to talk about that part of her life, especially now. We do know, though, that even after she found out she did nothing to stop it.

"The guy was one scary dude—he's doing life in Cedar Junction for murder, which is the only reason Special Agent Canfield's mother is even talking to us—and she probably figured if she tried to stop the assaults he'd kill her and *then* where would Angela be?"

"But I don't get it," Bill said. "She told me she was a straight-A student, both in high school and in college."

"Lots of people who have suffered horrible abuse are very high achievers," Miller said. "It's a way for them to gain some form of control over their lives when they have very *little* control over what happens to them at home."

"So what happens now?"

"I'm sorry," Miller said, "But I really can't discuss an ongoing investigation."

Bill stared at him unblinkingly, the implication unspoken but clear.

"You're right," Miller said after an uncomfortable moment. "I suppose we owe you that much after what you and Carli went through. As you know, I hitched a ride in the ambulance with the paramedics while they worked on Canfield on the way to the hospital. I was able to convince her to reveal the location where the exchanges of the girls take place.

"As Krall alluded to in his remarks to Carli, the agreement was that he be permitted to enjoy the girls in any manner he chose, provided he did no permanent physical damage to them, for one week before turning them over to the broker for export out of the country.

"Initially, Angela—Agent Canfield—refused to provide any details that could be considered helpful, but as we got closer to the hospital, her condition worsened dramatically. She had continued hemorrhaging blood during the trip after losing so much inside the house. Finally the lead paramedic, who worked heroically trying to save her, came straight out and admitted to her that he didn't think she would survive the ambulance ride."

Bill listened, transfixed, to the final awful moments of the woman who had so successfully and completely fooled him.

As Miller spoke, it occurred to Bill that he wasn't the only one she had fooled. Miller was hurting, too.

He took a sip of lukewarm water from a plastic cup at his bedside and the agent continued. "Once she realized she really was going to die and had nothing to gain by keeping her mouth shut, Canfield spilled everything—in abbreviated form, of course. Since we still have a few days before Carli is supposed to be delivered to the broker, the plan is simple. We're keeping Angela's death under wraps, and will use the information she gave us to round up as many of these slimy bastards as possible."

"But you have no teenager to deliver now, how are you going to do that?"

"Special Agent Kim Adkins, stationed out of the Albany office, is going to become Carli Ferguson for a few hours. Agent Adkins is an experienced twenty-five year old professional who looks exactly like a seventeen-year-old high school girl. In most law enforcement scenarios, being that youthful-looking is a serious handicap, but for this situation it's perfect."

"I don't understand. How is something like this even possible? Human trafficking? Right here in the United States? In the twenty-first century?"

Miller frowned. "You might be surprised," he said. "According to statistics compiled by the U.S. State Department, between 600,000 and 800,000 people are trafficked against their will each year across international borders. Of that number, seventy percent are female and as many as half are children. And the majority of these victims are forced into the commercial sex trade."

Bill stared at the young FBI agent in horror. "That's unbelievable."

"Believe it," Miller said simply. "Worldwide, human trafficking is the third most profitable criminal activity, behind only the drug trade and arms trafficking, with an estimated seven *billion* dollars in profits earned annually."

"But right here? In the United States?"

"Oh, yes," Miller answered. "We're not unaffected. Much of the trafficking occurs in developing nations, where little if any barriers to the practice exist. But American girls are prized in certain parts of the world, particularly blonde, fair-skinned ones. Virgins are even more valuable. Spiriting them out of the country is the most difficult part of the process, but once they're outside our borders, it is almost impossible to get them back."

"Why is that?" Bill asked, sickened by what he was hearing but unable to let the subject go.

"Worldwide," Miller answered, "a three-tier system has been developed to determine what countries are doing the most—as well as the least—to put an end to this practice. In the most recent report issued by the U.S. Department of State, in 2009, seventeen nations have been identified as 'Third Tier' states, meaning they take virtually no action to combat the practice of human trafficking. Some of those include Saudi Arabia, where we theorize Carli was headed, as well as Kuwait, Cuba, Syria, North Korea and others."

"Hold on. Back up for just a second." Bill could feel his blood begin to boil. "Kuwait and Saudi Arabia? Those are countries American soldiers fought and died to protect. Are you telling me my child was headed to Saudi Arabia to be some sheik's sex slave?"

"We believe so," Miller answered quietly. "And you won't get any argument from me about it being against everything we stand for, or at least everything we *should* stand for. But the real risk for the traffickers in an operation such as this is in smuggling the girls out of this country. Once that happens, the issue becomes a diplomatic one rather than a law enforcement one, mostly due to the cultural barriers between societies."

Special Agent Mike Miller scuffed his shoe on the grey and white tiles of the hospital floor. "Canfield knew all these statistics as well as I do. Maybe better. So I can't explain to you how she could have been a part of any of this."

"She was obviously irreparably broken," Bill said. "And she alluded to what she called 'an early retirement from the FBI' when she was trying to justify her actions as she held a gun on me. Just how much money do you think she was making on these slave trades?"

Miller shrugged. "We have a team of specialists going over her banking records, so we should have specific numbers available shortly, but if I had to guess, I would say she alone was netting well over sixty thousand dollars for every girl she helped smuggle out of the country."

Bill whistled, doing the math quickly in his head. "She told me she found Krall and turned him after his first couple of kidnappings and murders. That means she was involved in at least ten successful cases. If she made anything close to what you think, that's well over a half-million dollars."

"And tax-free, too."

"Given the damage done to her as a child by her mother's boyfriend and the lure of all that cash, maybe it's not too surprising how she turned out. What about Krall? Do you think he was making the same kind of money per transaction as Canfield?"

"I doubt it," Miller answered. "His motivations weren't strictly, or even mostly, monetary. This is a guy who was sexually assaulting and murdering young women before he was co-opted by Angela... uh, excuse me, by Agent Canfield. We're combing his bank records and personal information, too, but my guess is he made just a small fraction of the money being paid to Canfield. The lure for him was the opportunity to get his rocks off with a different girl every couple of months, and then be rid of her in a way that virtually eliminated all risk, since the evidence was out of the country and on its way to the Middle East. And to top it off, his partner was the agent in charge of the investigation and the search for 'The I-90 Killer.'

"By the way," Miller continued, "I spoke to the doctors. I know they shouldn't have told me anything, but they did. Perk of the job, I guess. I understand Carli wasn't…"

"No," Bill said. "She wasn't raped. Somehow she managed to escape the fate the other victims suffered. I guess the sick bastard's libido was dampened a bit when she sliced his arm to the bone, but he was about to get down to business when I walked in on him."

"She's one helluva strong young lady," Miller said. "A hero. You must be proud of her."

"You have no idea," Bill agreed. "I always knew she was special, but even I didn't realize just how special."

A companionable silence descended on the hospital room. Outside, Bill could hear nurses and doctors and family members walking the halls. He wanted to see Carli but felt the pull of exhaustion and pain medication dragging him toward a deep sleep.

He forced his eyes open once more and focused on Agent Miller, whom he could see was taking the news about Canfield just as hard as he was. Creases lined the man's face from lack of sleep and worry.

Bill wondered if Miller had slept with Angela, too. He had no doubt now that she would have used her partner in the same way she used him if she thought she could benefit from it.

It didn't really matter, though. She was gone and she wasn't coming back and maybe that was a good thing, for Angela Canfield as well as for him.

"Do us all a favor," Bill told him, "and go get the rest of the people responsible for my daughter *having* to be a hero before even celebrating her eighteenth birthday."

"We'll do our best, that I can promise you."

Bill nodded. "I hope you nail every one of those suckers to a wall."

"Even if we do," Miller said reluctantly, "another organization will crawl out from under a rock to fill the void. It's a sad state of affairs but true. Human nature, I suppose."

"Maybe so, but I still want to see those assholes pay. That's human nature, too."

63

Steak sizzled on the grill, popping and hissing, broiling to juicy perfection. Bill leaned on one crutch and tossed a pass to Carli before dropping awkwardly into his outdoor lounge chair. The football made a lazy arc through the air, and then his daughter caught it and rifled it back like Tom Brady finding the open receiver.

To Bill and Sandra's amazement, Carli had shown virtually no lingering ill effects from the twenty-eight hour ordeal she suffered at the hands of the I-90 Killer. Bill guessed it was due to the fact that she'd been able to fight back rather than become a helpless victim. A psychologist who examined her informed them she might suffer nightmares for months or even years to come, but so far—if Carli was to be believed—that had not been the case.

Bill believed her.

He reached up to catch the football one-handed, wrenching his injured arm and nearly falling backward out of his chair as a plain blue Chevrolet Caprice turned into the apartment parking lot. The driver pulled the vehicle into an empty space and killed the engine.

Bill lofted the football toward the car and the driver leapt out and caught it on the fly. Instead of passing it back, though, Mike Miller tucked the ball into the crook of his arm and carried it toward Bill and Carli.

He stopped in front of them with a lopsided grin. "I was afraid to pass it to you. Don't wanna get sued for knocking you onto your ass and busting your stitches while I'm on duty," he explained.

"Don't flatter yourself," Bill shot back. "I took on two psychopaths with guns, remember? I can handle one Feeb."

"Remember? How could I forget? The entire Bureau will have to sit through lectures and training films about your little adventure for years."

"Hey, don't forget about me!" Carli chimed in. "I was there, too."

She bounded up behind Miller and wrenched the football out of his arms.

"Care to join us for dinner?" Bill asked. "I just happen to have an extra steak in the fridge upstairs. It might take me a while to get it with these crutches, but maybe my hero, the young lady who pulled my butt out of the fire, would be willing to handle that chore for me."

"That would be great!" Carli enthused. "Join us! It will only take a second to get the third steak, and we just started cooking, really!"

Bill laughed. His daughter's attraction to the agent was obvious to him, and he guessed to Miller as well. He waited a moment, enjoying the man's discomfort.

Finally he said, "You know, Carli, Agent Miller just told us he's still on duty. He probably only has a couple of minutes to spare."

"Yes!" Miller agreed instantly. "Just a couple of minutes. Maybe another time, though," he added quickly when he saw Carli's dejected expression.

"So, what can we do for you?" Bill asked, knowing what the answer would be.

"I thought you might like an update on the case."

"You're damn right we would. Shoot. No, wait, let me rephrase that. I don't think I like that expression any more. Let's try this one: go ahead."

Miller laughed. "Remember I told you we had a very young-looking agent from the Albany Field Office who was going to be our decoy during the exchange?"

"Of course," Bill and Carli answered in unison.

"Well, Agent Adkins played the part of the teenage damsel in distress perfectly." Carli playfully slapped at his arm and he ducked out of harm's way.

"She acted completely helpless. Nothing at all like Carli," he added as he dodged another body blow.

"That's more like it," she sniffed indignantly.

"Anyway," Miller continued, "Two men came to gather our fake Carli, arriving at the storage area about two hours after our fake Krall tied her up and left her inside. One of the men stayed in the car to cover the storage shed's entrance while the other went inside to collect their prize. We disabled the man in the car as soon as the other one disappeared from view and took the second man down without incident when he exited the shed.

"The whole operation went off without a hitch and took no more than three minutes from beginning to end once the traffickers showed. It was really pretty boring compared to what you two went through."

"Boring is good," Bill said simply.

"Absolutely. The best part, though, is that the two men we apprehended were just foot soldiers, hired muscle with absolutely no interest in taking the fall for their employers. The upshot is that they're singing like canaries. We believe we will be able to use the information they are giving us to take down a lot of very bad people."

Miller locked eyes with Bill, his expression intense. "Do you remember what I told you in the hospital? You know, about more cockroaches crawling out from under more rocks to take the place of the ones we capture?"

"I remember," Bill said. "And it pisses me off."

"Amen to that. And I'm still certain it will happen, eventually. But we're in the process of knocking a very big hole in this particular venture. It's going to be a long, long time before anyone can ramp up a similar operation. We owe you a debt of gratitude. You two saved innumerable young women from untold misery. You should be commended. Unofficially, of course.

"Officially," Miller said, grinning at Bill, "what you did—going after a serial rapist/murderer on your own—was foolish and irresponsible and cannot be condoned under any circumstances." He sounded like he was reading from a script.

Bill laughed. "'Foolish and irresponsible.' Now you sound like my ex-wife."

"Speaking of ex-wives…" Carli interrupted.

"Yes?" Bill said. "Do you have a deep, dark secret you need to confess? Perhaps an ex-wife of your own stashed away somewhere?"

Carli laughed. "No, silly, I was referring to *your* ex-wife specifically. You know, my mom."

Agent Miller began edging toward his car. "This sounds personal. I should probably be going."

"No, stay, just for another couple of minutes," Carli begged. "I want you to hear this, too."

Miller stopped, and he and Bill waited expectantly.

Carli took a deep breath. "I've decided what I want to do with my life."

"Awesome. But what does this have to do with your mom?"

"I need you to convince her I'm serious."

"Okay, fair enough. Serious about what, exactly?'

"I want to get into law enforcement."

Bill smiled as Miller whooped.

"Hey," the agent said, "Welcome to the team!" He gave her a high five. "How soon can you start?"

"Uh, I think I need to finish high school first. Unless…"

"There's no 'unless,'" Bill laughed. "Yes, you need to finish high school. Then, get a college degree. Then, after you graduate, if your goal is still to pursue a career in law enforcement, I guarantee we can convince your mom to go along."

"I wouldn't be so sure of that," Carli said. "She hasn't stopped hovering since I came home."

"That'll change," Bill said. "You were incredibly, unbelievably lucky to escape with your life, and it's going to take some time for everyone—your mom especially—to come to grips with the reality of what happened to you. But I know if you decide to dedicate your life to a career in law enforcement, your mom will be just like me: proud as hell.

"In the meantime," Bill said, "I believe these steaks are just about grilled to perfection. And in light of this big news," he winked at Miller, "I'd like to extend our offer of dinner one more time to Agent Miller. We've got ice-cold soda inside, not to mention coffee and baked potatoes and corn on the cob. What do you say?"

"You had me at 'steak.' Besides, I think I'd better start getting to know my future partner. I'm in!"

Carli beamed and Bill speared the steaks with a long grilling fork. He deposited them onto a serving tray. Then he handed the platter to his daughter and settled onto his crutches, ready to tackle the narrow stairs up to his tiny apartment. The place was small and cramped and hot and the scene of an encounter with Angela Canfield that he would just as soon forget.

But right now he loved that little piece of shit apartment.

Because Carli was alive and fine.

And that was all that mattered.

To be the first to learn about new releases, and for the opportunity to win free ebooks, signed copies of print books, and other swag, please take a moment to sign up for Allan Leverone's email newsletter at AllanLeverone.com.

Reader reviews are hugely important to authors looking to set their work apart from the competition. If you have a moment to spare, please consider taking a moment to leave a brief, honest review of *The Lonely Mile* at Amazon, Goodreads, or your favorite review site, and thank you!

Also from Allan Leverone

Thrillers

Parallax View: A Tracie Tanner Thriller
All Enemies: A Tracie Tanner Thriller
The Omega Connection: A Tracie Tanner Thriller
The Hitler Deception: A Tracie Tanner Thriller
The Kremlyov Infection: A Tracie Tanner Thriller
Final Vector
The Organization: A Jack Sheridan Pulp Thriller
Trigger Warning: A Jack Sheridan Pulp Thriller

Horror/Dark Thrillers

Mr. Midnight
After Midnight
Paskagankee
Revenant: A Paskagankee Novel Book Two
Wellspring: A Paskagankee Novel Book Three
Linger: Mark of the Beast (written with Edward Fallon)

Novellas

The Becoming
Flight 12: A Kristin Cunningham Thriller

Story Collections

Postcards from the Apocalypse
Uncle Brick and the Four Novelettes
Letters from the Asylum: Three Complete Novellas
The Tracie Tanner Collection: Three Complete Thriller Novels

Made in the USA
Middletown, DE
27 December 2017